Suffer Love

ASHLEY HERRING BLAKE

Houghton Mifflin Harcourt
Boston   New York

Copyright © 2016 by Ashley Herring Blake
All rights reserved. For information about permission to reproduce
selections from this book, write to trade.permissions@hmhco.com or
to Permissions, Houghton Mifflin Harcourt Publishing Company,
3 Park Avenue, 19th Floor, New York, New York 10016.

www.hmhco.com

The text was set in Photina MT Std.

Library of Congress Cataloging-in-Publication Data is available.
ISBN 978-0-544-59632-0

Manufactured in the United States of America
DOC 10 9 8 7 6 5 4 3 2
4500593677

For Mom.

And for my big brother,
Brandon, who dreamed
big and inspired me
to do the same.

Is love a tender thing? It is too rough,

Too rude, too boisterous, and it pricks like thorn.

—WILLIAM SHAKESPEARE,

ROMEO AND JULIET, ACT 1, SCENE 4

CHAPTER ONE

Hadley

His hand is warm on my bare back. Soothing. I bite the inside of my cheek to stop myself from leaning into it. Perched on the edge of the bed, I squint through the darkness and spot my shirt on the floor over the air vent, billowing up like a sheet drying in the wind. I slip it over my head and shiver, the cotton icy against my skin. His hand and the warmth vanish, along with any desire I had to remain in this room for longer than it'll take me to get from the bed to the door.

"Are you sure you don't want to stay a little longer?" Josh asks as I stand up. He props himself up on his elbows, his long body still sprawled across the bed. Party sounds filter upstairs and under the closed door, the steady *unst, unst* of the music pumping its way through beer-thick laughter.

In response, I toss him his shirt, straighten my still-buttoned jeans, smooth my hair.

"C'mon, Hadley." His words blend into a soft slur as he drapes his shirt over his lap.

I crack open the door. "So, um, this was fun . . ." My voice trails off as the hallway light blazes into my eyes, bringing me back to reality.

"Hello? Name's Josh. I'm in your English class."

I turn to face him, his close-cropped hair coated bronze in the dim light. He tilts his head at me, his full mouth open a little, like he really can't believe that I'm going to leave him here, half-naked and blue-balled. I force my lips into a smile. The one that pulled him toward me from across the room an hour earlier and had him whispering into my hair within ten minutes of hello.

"I know your name."

And then I leave.

Alone in the hallway, I press my back against the door, my fingers gripping the handle, and close my eyes. I take a deep breath and wait for all the pleasantly blurred lines to sharpen again. I can still feel his fingers on my face, caressing it like he actually cared. Like I actually cared. As always, it's a nice illusion. A break from the normal chaos going on in my head. I know it'll all come rushing back later, when I'm lying in my bed, staring through the dark at the ceiling in my perpetually silent house, but for now, it's nice to feel a hint of calm.

Down the hall, the bathroom door opens and Sloane Waters steps out in a denim skirt and a white top so sheer I can see the lace edging of her black bra. She freezes when she spots me, her top lip curling as if she smells something bad. Sloane had it in for me before I even officially met her. At her infamous back-to-school party a month ago, I made out with Isaac Jorgenson. Granted, Isaac was her ex and we might have ended up in her bedroom, but they broke up a year ago and she's dated half the football team since then.

Sloane's narrowed eyes roam over my rumpled hair and wrinkled shirt. I feel my cheeks warm, but I pull my expression into one of indifference and brush past her. She's mercifully and unusually silent. As I pass, I get a whiff of her grape bubblegum smell, so cloying I nearly gag.

Downstairs, I swim through the sea of writhing bodies and into the living room of some guy whose name I can't even remember. The music is so loud that I feel like it's coming from inside my skull. Despite the crowd, Kat manages to find me seconds after I surface.

"So?" she asks. Her breath smells like orange Tic-Tacs. She slips a blue plastic cup into my hands.

"No, thanks." I push the cup away, but she shoves it back with an eye roll.

"Lighten up. I'm not trying to get you drunk so I can have my way with you. It's just water."

I pinch her arm and she swats at me. The water is cool and clean and washes away Josh's lingering taste of beer and spearmint gum. We make our way to the edge of the huge living room where it opens up into the kitchen. I lean against the wall and drain my cup, my heart rate finally slowing after having Josh's lips on my neck.

"So?" Kat asks again. She tucks her short blond hair behind her ears and takes a sip from her beer. A couple squeezes past us, the guy's hands on the girl's curvy hips. Kat presses into me as if she's afraid she might catch something.

"So what?" I look at her arched eyebrows. Kat was born and raised in Woodmont. We've been best friends since we were twelve and met in the swim class my dad taught. We've always lived a town apart until a few months ago, when my parents convinced themselves that a change of scene would help untie the massive tangle that is our family. They truly believed the move from Nashville to suburban Woodmont for my senior year would *make the whole thing easier* and bring my father's little girl back from whatever pit I had banished her to. Four months later, Kat is still the only flower on the crap pile that is my new life.

"You're not going to tell me anything? Come on, Josh Ellison? He's cute. He's supposed to be the best third baseman the school has had in, like, a decade."

"Really."

"Yes. God, Hadley. Don't you know anything about him?"

"I know he plays baseball." I move my eyes around the room, tucking its inhabitants into neat little boxes. Seventeen girls, eleven boys. Sweaty, scruffy, clean-cut. Bored, nervous, horny, drunk. My gaze lands on Matt Pavers, Josh's best friend. He lifts an eyebrow at me and I look away, tugging my shirt lower over my hips.

"Do you like him?" She sticks out her forefinger, counting. "Henry was too cocky, Isaac was too Ivy League–obsessed and wore argyle socks and was, well, pretty much still Sloane's. And Jeremy was . . . what? Didn't he smell like soup or something?"

"Pot roast." My correction slams into her granite stare. I cross my arms over my chest, my empty cup dangling from my forefinger, and shrug. "What? It was like kissing him right after he downed Grandma's Sunday dinner."

"So do you like Josh?"

I release a breath. "No, Kitty Kat. I don't like him."

"What's wrong with him? He's nice."

"And a total player."

"Well, yeah, I guess so, but—"

"Liking him isn't the point."

5

"Here we go." She snorts and then coughs and I bite back a laugh. She's never been good at disdain, no matter how heartfelt. "Well, what if he likes you?"

"I doubt it. Josh Ellison stores his brain in his pants. He isn't the dating type." At least, I don't think he is.

Since everything in my life went to crap, I haven't exactly been on the prowl for heart-fluttering romance. I would have sworn off guys altogether, but there's something about the way they look at me right before they lean in to kiss me. Head tilted, eyes fixed on mine, thumb swiping across my cheek. It reels me in every time. I would hate myself if it weren't so damn therapeutic.

Plus, it's not like I've ever let anyone beyond second base. In the past six months, there have only been a few guys, but whenever Kat talks about it, she turns into her mother and starts blah-blah-blahing about control issues and daddy issues and vulnerability issues and trust issues. Her mouth forms a neat little knot, her tongue running over her teeth the way she does when she's trying to figure something out. After all, she was friends with the old Hadley. The old Hadley believed in romance and lasting love. Craved it, would wait a lifetime for it, same as Kat.

The new Hadley knows better.

"Have you seen Rob?" I ask, to change the subject.

She tries to resist. The battle between her quest for my rehabilitation and shameless drooling over her five-year-long crush wages in her face. Eventually a grin presses dimples into her cheeks. "I saw him while you were upstairs. He smiled at me. Can you believe it?"

"And?"

She puts her cup to her lips but doesn't drink. Even in the dim light, I can see the crimson spilling into her face. "And what?"

"Kat, just go talk to him."

"I can't. He was playing pool with his swim buddies, and besides, what would I say? 'I think you're gorgeous and I've loved you since the first day of seventh grade when you walked me to the cafeteria because I got lost'?"

I shrug. "Might be a bit too subtle. I'd go for 'I think you're a god and I want to bear your children.'"

She smacks my arm and laughs.

"Or better yet," I say. "How about 'Hi. Great party. Nice job on the four hundred IM last week. Wanna dance?'"

"Oh, God, I can't ask him to dance."

"You can and you should." I try to nudge her forward a little, but she angles out of my reach. "You can't just wait around for some grand gesture, Kat."

She shakes her head. "I'm not like you, Hadley. I want more than five minutes of feeling special."

My jaw nearly hits the floor. Kat focuses on her cup, picking at a snarled piece of plastic on the rim. Before I can question her, tense voices, sharp and high-pitched, rise up behind us. Kat and I turn and see Sloane and Josh arguing in the kitchen. Josh's brows bunch together and Sloane gestures wildly. Jenny Kalinski stands between them, biting her bottom lip, her dark pixie hair framing her petite features. I watch Josh shake his head and try to pull Jenny toward him. Sloane pushes his chest, her face contorted.

My breath catches when I hear my own name wedged in between some foul words. Josh flinches and rakes his hand down his face. He grabs a beer from a nearby cooler before stumbling out the back door onto the porch.

A sick feeling settles into my stomach. I run the pad of my thumb over each of my fingertips, one by one. I watch Jenny try to follow Josh. *Index finger.* Sloane grabs Jenny's arm and stops her. *Middle finger.* Sloane's red glare takes flight and lands on me. *Ring finger.*

"Uh-oh," Kat says, her eyes wide on the scene. "Hadley?"

I don't respond, but stiffen my spine as Sloane crosses the room, Jenny in tow. *Pinkie finger.*

I gulp down my surprise as Sloane gets in my face. She's so

close, her features blur together into one snarling mess. I step away, my back hitting the wall.

"God, Sloane. What the hell?"

"Running out of single guys, Hadley?" she asks. "What do you think you're doing with Jenny's boyfriend?"

Jenny and I lock eyes. Hers are red and watery and huge, like an ingénue in an old silent film. The effect is so familiar, something knots up in my chest.

I force a dry heave down my throat and push myself off the wall, straightening my shirt. "Her boyfriend? Since when?"

"Since whenever we say, bitch."

We've attracted the attention of half the room, all the conversation replaced with laughs and wide-open stares. Sloane either doesn't notice or doesn't care. Her green eyes are unflinching on mine, and I struggle to school my expression.

"Oh, let me guess," she says. "You had no idea they were together."

"No. I didn't," I say, battling to keep my voice even. I try to focus on steadying my heart rate, the hardness of the floor beneath my feet, the feel of my nails digging into my palms. It's no good. All I can think about are dozens of tiny papers fluttering in the wind, my mother's silence and her mouth an open circle of shock, my father dragging his hands through his hair.

"Yeah, right." Sloane shoves my shoulders. Jenny winces

when I smack the wall, but still says nothing. My chest constricts, ready for her to yell at me, say anything to me, but she just stares at her feet.

Kat slips her hand into mine. "Sloane, calm down. Hadley really didn't know."

"Stay out of this, Pussy." I feel my best friend shrink next to me as Sloane spits out Kat's horrible nickname from middle school.

"Why don't *you* stay out of it, Sloane?" I say. "How is this even about you?"

She leans in close, her fruity smell twisting my stomach. "It's about me because *I'm* about Jenny. No one effs with—"

"Whatever," I snap, turning away from her. Jenny watches me, her expression a mix of sadness and curiosity and simmering anger. "Jenny, I didn't . . ." But my voice trails off into the music, into the blood roaring through my ears.

Do you have a girlfriend?

A beat. Heavily lidded eyes on mine. *No.*

I let him kiss me. His mouth was warm, gentle. A relief.

Are you sure?

I think I'd remember.

"Look," I say, letting my anger take over. It's fiery cold and numbing, like snow blanketing a volcano. "Your problem is with Josh. He told me he didn't have a girlfriend, so he's the ass-hole here, not me."

Jenny's mouth falls open, but Sloane gets in my face again. "You're done, *St. Clair*." Then she grabs Jenny's hand and stalks off through the gawking crowd.

"Oh. My. God," Kat says, pressing her hand to her chest. Everyone resumes dancing and talking and sucking up all the oxygen in the room. "Jenny and Josh? I had no idea they were together. Must be super recent."

I swallow hard, but it gets stuck. "I need some air."

She frowns and squeezes my shoulder. "Hey, I bet no one will remember this by Monday. Josh is a jerk, so what? Jenny didn't even look mad."

"I just need some air." I push through the crowd and make my way out the back door, ignoring the whispers that follow me. I walk quickly through the expansive yard, littered with blue and red plastic cups. When I hit the woods at the back of the property, I break into a run. I run until I'm out of breath and my head aches and the sounds from the party have faded behind a fortress of trees.

I stop at a huge oak tree and press my palms against the cool, rough bark. My eyes spill over as I turn, sliding down the trunk until I hit the ground. The October night air is cool and thick. Leaning my head against the bark, I look up into the dense leaves and try to breathe normally. Something red and diamond-shaped is caught in the gnarly branches. A kite maybe.

Minutes pass and with each one some guy's face blooms in my memory. Guys I barely knew except through Kat or from my old neighborhood swim team. Guys who really meant nothing to me.

I wrap my arms around knees, pulling myself in further and further. I drop my head onto my arms, breathing in the earthy, damp smell of the ground below me. I shiver, but it has nothing to do with the cold. Instead, my own anger and embarrassment pull goose bumps from my skin, exposing them to the wind. I always ask the guy if he has a girlfriend. *Always.* And I've trusted myself to be able to sniff out a lie. I've had enough experience with lying assholes, that's for sure.

Jaw clenching, I push myself to my feet and make my way back to the house. I run again, nerves and anger coursing through my veins, surging me forward. The back deck is packed when I jog up the steps. Music blasts out of the open door, and bodies move in its rhythm. I elbow my way through the crowd, my eyes searching for Josh.

"Hadley!" Kat calls, edging through a clump of dancing girls.

"Have you seen him?"

"Who?"

"Josh-I'm-a-lying-jackhole-Ellison."

She frowns. "I saw him leave with some guys from the team."

"Dammit!" I shove my hands through my hair and slump down onto the rough wooden bench that encircles the deck.

A lip-locked couple bumps into Kat, propelling her forward. She shoots them a halfhearted dirty look and sits next to me. "Why do you want to talk to Josh?"

"I just do."

Kat shakes her head and sighs heavily. "Just let it go, Had. He's a jerk, but it's done. Let it go."

I dig my nails into my jeans, but say nothing. *Let it go, Hadley.* Those words are in every look my dad gives me, every irritated sigh issued from my mother's lips. Every wary glance from Kat.

Kat says something about making her curfew. We weave through the crowd and into the house, making our way toward the front door. In the living room, I see Jenny balled into one corner of the love seat, knees tucked to her chest. Our gazes lock and she shakes her head slightly before looking away.

Just get over it, Hadley.

CHAPTER TWO

Sam

If I've learned anything in the past six months, it's that life is a fickle little bitch and there's not one damn thing I can do to tame her. It's almost laughable, really. That after everything, I'm back in Tennessee about to waste away in one of Nashville's suburbs.

"Have you talked to your dad since you got back?" Ajay asks. He's laid out in a ratty hammock strung between two reddening maples in the backyard of our new rental house. Livy and I are sprawled on the prickly grass nearby, taking a break from the sea of boxes that seem to multiply every time I manage to empty one.

"Nah," I say.

"He knows you moved again, right?"

"I think my mom told him."

"You think?"

I sigh. "Does it really matter, Age? He's like a thousand miles away. And he has my number too."

"Ah. I almost forgot about this whole *Whatever, man* with a side of *I don't give a shit* dish you've been serving up lately."

I grin. "Refreshing, isn't it?"

"Not even remotely."

"Sam's not like that," Livy says, twirling a dandelion between her fingers. "He gives a shit about a lot of stuff."

"Whoa." Ajay grabs the hooks in the hammock, pulling himself up. He tosses me a bewildered glance that I don't return. "When did this start? What's up with the foul mouth, little elf?"

"You started it."

"Yes, but I'm an uncouth, ill-mannered seventeen-year-old boy."

Livy shrugs as she ties the stem of the browning weed into a knot.

Ajay's dark eyes squint at my sister through the dwindling evening light, and he frowns. He hasn't seen us since June, when my dad moved to Boston and my mom bolted out of Nashville like a fugitive, reluctant kids in tow, to live with my grandmother in Atlanta. A lot can change in four months. Livy used to look like a freaking descendant of Legolas, with her white-blond hair and pale blue eyes. Now, barely fourteen and clad in black from eyelids down, she looks more like some undead character from a vampire show. Her occasional brush with expletives is the least of my worries.

After his careful study, Ajay sighs and scrubs a hand through his black hair. It sticks up from all the junk he uses to make it look effortlessly messy. "My little elf is all grown up." He lies back down, avoiding my eyes. He knows "growing up" has crap to do with Livy's whole goth-girl persona.

"Can I borrow your drill?" he asks. He rocks his body from side to side and the hammock pitches sharply. I'm just waiting for it to dump his ass on the ground.

"What for?"

"Let's just say mine's insufficient for my current project."

I laugh and shake my head. I don't even want to know. "Sure. It's in a box somewhere."

"Excellent." Ajay slows the hammock and beams at me, that freaky I'm-the-next-Doctor-Frankenstein glint in his eyes. He's my age, but started taking AP classes in ninth grade. He's technically got enough credits to start college as a sophomore, but his mom thinks he needs a "developmentally appropriate social environment" and refuses to let him take courses at Vanderbilt or Belmont. So he's a senior with about two minutes of actual classes during the day who spends his abundant free time reading Gogol and welding crap together in his garage. If I hadn't known the guy since I was six, I'd probably report him as a terrorist threat.

The back door creaks open and Mom sticks her head out. Livy stiffens next to me and I give her arm a gentle nudge. She reaches into her pocket and takes out her inhaler, tossing back a few lungfuls of the medicine.

"Hey, guys." Mom walks down the steps and into the yard. "I'm back. Why are you just lying around? We have a ton of unpacking to do."

I nearly snort in response. Mom hasn't unpacked crap. We'd barely gotten home from registering Livy and me at Woodmont High School this morning before she was back in the car, a glowing smile on her usually wan face as she hightailed it to the sticks-up-their-asses private school where she got a job teaching creative writing because the regular teacher's out having a baby or something. The school she didn't want us attending with her. Well, didn't want *me* attending with her.

"We're taking a break," I say. "And Livy's room is completely done."

"Fine." She pulls her blond hair out of its tight bun and runs her fingers through it. "I know we have nothing in the house, so I thought I'd order Indian for dinner."

Before I can respond, Ajay pops up in the hammock. "From where?" he chirps.

Mom startles. "Oh. Ajay. I didn't see you there. How are you?"

"I'm excellent. How are you, Mrs. Bennett?"

Mom flinches and tries to cover it up by scratching her nose. "I'm well. And *please*, Ajay, call me Cora."

"Oh, I don't think I could do that, Mrs. B," he says in his best parents-love-me voice. Although right now, his syrupy tone is having the exact opposite effect on my mother, which Ajay knows perfectly well. "And you should try Sitar in downtown Woodmont. It has the most authentic Indian food around here. Excellent naan."

"I'll do that." She smiles tightly. "Sam, may I have a word?"

Jesus, here we go. I groan and roll myself off the ground. Grass sticks to my legs and a few blades from my hair inch their way down my shirt collar. I shake them out, keeping my head down as I reach Mom.

"Maybe you could ask Ajay if he wouldn't mind giving us a little space to settle in," she says. "We've had a long day and I think we could use some family time tonight."

Family time? "He hasn't seen us in months. He just stopped by for a while. I don't think he's planning on moving in."

She presses her fingers to her temples and takes a deep breath. "Sam. Please. We just got into town last night and I'm exhausted. I want a quiet evening."

"Every evening is a quiet evening, Mom."

She lifts her eyes to mine and they harden, two blue lakes in the dead of winter.

"Samuel, your sister has to start high school all over again in a couple days. I need you to help make this transition as smooth as possible. For her." Her eyes soften a little as she looks over my shoulder toward Livy, who's still lying in the grass, ankles crossed and hands folded on her chest like a corpse in a coffin. "Is that something you think you can do?"

My fingers curl into my palms. I want to tell her to piss off, that watching out for Livy is all I've done for the past six months and I'll keep doing it despite Mom's passive-aggressive request. But I don't tell her that. My mother is the people-believe-whatever-the-hell-they-want theory personified. So I just walk away and go tell my best friend of eleven years to get out of my house.

Hours later, after a virtually silent dinner on paper plates and virtually silent unpacking and virtually silent shuffles to our own rooms, I lie in my bed and blink at the plastered ceiling. Since last April, sleep hasn't come easily, and it sure as hell won't come easily in this unfamiliar house stuffed full of a bunch of familiar shit I'd just as soon toss in a dumpster than bother unpacking.

Dishes my parents got when they married.

Framed pictures starring a family of four, plastic smiles glued to their faces.

Old baseball trophies, both mine and Dad's, dating back to his days playing at Auburn.

Literary magazines featuring Mom's short stories and essays.

Just trash it all.

I flick the switch to my bedside lamp and leave it on for a couple minutes. Flick it off again. The stars on the ceiling, left by the previous tenants, glow a sickly green. There are a ton of them, arranged in chaotic patterns and swirls, covering nearly every inch of space. I stare at them until they fade and then disappear altogether.

A soft knock on my door brings the room back into focus. I sit up and glance at the clock. Past midnight. I flop back on the bed and rub at my eyes. I was wondering if this would start up again.

"Come on, then," I say.

Livy slips inside and clicks the door closed behind her. Orange from the streetlight pours in through the window, lighting up her purple and black flannel PJs. She doesn't say a word. She just drags her puffy green sleeping bag next to my bed and crawls inside, curling her body in the fabric so that she looks like an inchworm.

"My pillow smells like Grammy's house," she says after several minutes of silence.

"Baked beans and gardenias?"

"Yep."

"Yum."

"It's disgusting." She flips the pillow over and inhales. "Ugh." Then she rips the sunshine yellow pillowcase off and tosses it into a box-covered corner.

"I don't know." I sniff dramatically. "Better than this place." Earlier today, when I first swung open the front door, the stale, unbreathed air snaked out and smacked me in the forehead. "This house reeks like an open grave."

Livy laughs. "I do miss Grammy, though. It was nice . . . having someone else around."

Grammy, Mom's mom, was the rubber around the Bennett bumper cars this summer. Good ol' Grammy lacks any kind of internal filter. Her constant chatter, which used to grate on my nerves, saved Livy and me from having to interact with Mom too much. When Mom wasn't snapping at Grammy to give her a moment of peace or casting worried glances in Livy's direction, she was scouring the Internet for jobs or locked in her room or out doing who the hell cared what.

Whatever she was doing, she spent all summer perfecting

the art of ignoring her only son as much as humanly possible, which, as it turns out, is a lot.

"Check this out," I say to Livy, clicking on my lamp.

"What?" She squints against the sudden brightness.

"Just wait a minute."

She huffs out a breath. I throw my leg off the bed and find her head, ruffling her hair with my foot. She yanks my leg hair.

"Ow! Jeez."

"*Sooorry*," she croons, a smile in her voice.

"All right, here we go." I turn off the light and the ceiling ignites.

"Whoa! That's a ton of stars. Wish my room had some."

"We'll get you some tomorrow. They're . . . *luminous.*"

A beat. "Shiny."

I grin in the dark and tuck my arms under my head, settling in for our game. "Bright."

"Glittering."

"Radiant."

"Shimmering."

I scrunch up my nose, trying to think of another synonym. Mom started this game around the time Livy entered kindergarten. "It's a great way to increase vocabulary," she said when I'd asked why she kept chirping out words like "Pretty" and "Beautiful" and "Cute" to my confused-looking five-year-old sister.

Once Livy caught on, though, she loved it. Sometimes she'd just play by herself, happily spitting out synonyms in the back seat of the car or while practicing her handwriting. Dad and I would join in every now and then, but it was really Mom and Livy's thing.

Until last April.

I find myself pulling Livy into the game more and more lately. She always plays along, usually with a little pucker between her eyebrows. I'm pretty sure she knows why I want her to play all the time, as if this stupid word game can somehow keep her connected to the wide-eyed, curious girl she used to be before life shit all over her.

"Do you surrender?" she asks.

"Never!" I shake my head and concentrate. "Oh! Sparkling."

"Incandescent."

"Damn, that's a good one. I got nothing after that."

She giggles and I smile. It's worth getting my ass kicked at this game over and over just to hear her laugh.

She says good night and rolls over. I do the same and my eyelids just start to grow heavy when her voice startles me awake again.

"Sam?"

"Mm?"

"You think Dad'll come visit us here?"

I shift to my back and release a sigh to the fading stars.

"I don't know, Livy."

"Yeah."

Her breathing eventually grows soft and even, but mine stays hitched in my chest. It's stuck on what I didn't tell my sister, what I really think about Dad and the possibility of him coming back to Nashville.

Not a chance in hell.

CHAPTER THREE

Sam

Mom pulls the car up behind five or six school buses at Woodmont High School and says something. I yank out my earbuds. "What?"

She exhales through her nose, but doesn't look away from the visor mirror as she slicks on bright red lipstick. "I said, is it okay if I drop you two off right here. You'll have your car back tomorrow and I don't want to be late this morning."

"Fine." I grab my messenger bag from the floorboard, stuffing in rogue papers before slinging it over my shoulder.

When I reach for the door handle, Mom stops me with one finger on my arm. She looks at my sister in the back seat. "Guys, listen. I know things have been hard and that moving back here was sudden, but I really think things will be better for all of us now. Please make an effort."

Better. I look at my reflection in the window—hair way

longer than I'm used to, dark circles under my eyes, a thin layer of stubble over my jaw because I couldn't even drum up the energy to shave. In the back seat, Livy's tight clothes are strategically placed to give Mom a coronary. We're starting school more than a month later than everyone else here. No friends. No dad. Just a mom who's pissed off half the time and lost in her own world the other. Oh, I'm sure this year will be a huge improvement.

"Olivia, you have your inhaler, right?" Mom asks as we climb out of the car.

"Mm."

"The nurse has one on hand as well, if you need it. Don't hesitate to go there at the first sign of tightness or wheezing. The last thing we need right now is a bad asthma attack, and you know how stress—"

"I've got it, Mom. Jeez." Livy stomps across the lawn. I can't hide my smirk as I follow her.

Livy tugs at her ass-tight black skinny jeans (the ones that make me want to wrap her in a tablecloth), while other pairs of ass-tight skinny jeans and hipster glasses swarm around us on the school's front lawn. We make it through the front doors and I pull Livy to a stop alongside the rows of puke green lockers. From my bag, I take out the schedules Mom picked up on Friday before she dragged me to the gym to talk to the baseball coach and dropped off Livy's inhalers. I scan them and find where Livy's homeroom is located. We head down the hallway in silence.

"So you'll be okay?" I hand her the schedule in front of her classroom.

"Yeah." She starts walking through the door.

"Hey." I tug on her backpack and stop her. "Text me if you need anything. I mean it."

"I won't need anything." She lifts her lined eyes to mine and gives me a smile before she takes a pull on her inhaler. "But thanks."

I watch her meander through the rows of desks and find a spot in the back. Plenty of eyes follow her. Plenty of guys blatantly stare at her ass as she walks by. I force myself toward my own class before I embarrass her by knocking their teeth down their throats.

Homeroom is predictable. First period Calculus, mystifying. American Government, one big snore. I get more than enough curious glances, which I don't return. This whole thing would be a hell of a lot easier if Ajay were here, but I'll manage. I'm not here for new friends. I'm not here to avoid them either. As far as I'm concerned, that kind of shit just sort of happens whether you want it to or not.

"Hey. You Bennett?"

Case in point.

"That's me." I slip my new books into my locker before third period English. I close the squeaky metal door to find a guy with light brown hair and a tight purple shirt leaning against the lockers. I recognize him from homeroom. Or rather, I recognize his shirt.

"I saw you coming out of Coach Torrenti's office last week," he says. "You play ball, right? Pitcher?"

"That's what they tell me."

A smile tugs at one corner of his mouth and he jerks his chin at me. "Josh Ellison. Third base."

"Sam."

He nods. "So, listen, I know the season doesn't start until January, but a bunch of us usually get together at the field to play and get in some batting practice if you're interested."

"Maybe. When?"

"Every Wednesday."

I pucker my lips, considering, when really there's a little girl squealing inside my head. With my dad licking his wounds in Boston, I haven't played decent ball since last spring. I got in a little play with the team from the school I went to in Atlanta for the past month, but they sucked ass.

"I'll be there." I hitch my bag higher up on my shoulder.

"Awesome." Josh claps me on the back. He opens his mouth

to say something else, but quickly snaps it shut and turns his body toward the lockers, hugging them so close, it's almost indecent. "Shit."

"Uh, something wrong?"

"Nah. I'm fine. It's just . . ." He cuts his eyes toward the hallway again. "Ah, fuck."

I look around for the source of his turmoil and spot a girl walking down the hall. Sure, there are a lot of girls walking down the hall, but this one has dark eyes leveled at Josh like she wants to deep-fry his balls and shove them down his throat.

She's also holy-shit gorgeous.

When she gets closer, she hesitates, and I think she's going to lay into him right there in the middle of the hallway. Josh stays pressed against the locker, pretending to fiddle with the lock. Finally, her face slackens and everything softens. It's like watching an entire story—a history of some unknown world —shift and unfold right in her eyes. I just stare at her until she moves on down the hall. Then I keep staring at her, because, God, how can you not? All eyes and mouth and curves and tangly dark hair down her back.

"She's gone," I tell Josh as the warning bell rings.

"Oh. Thanks, man." He turns around and rakes a hand through his hair. "Only for the moment, though. She's in my next class."

We start down the hall. "Who is she?"

"Hadley. And don't even think about it, dude."

"Think about what?"

He just smirks at me. "Yeah, she's hot."

Hot? Hot is not the word I would've used. *Unsurpassed. Magical. Wistful.* But you can't say that kind of shit to guys without being called a pussy, so I keep my mouth shut.

"But she also gets her kicks out of rendering your junk completely useless for half an hour, if you know what I mean." Josh clicks his tongue as he pops into a classroom, which, as it turns out, is also mine.

And hers.

I hover in the doorway like a dumbass for about ten years before the teacher, Ms. Artigas, finally calls me in to sit down. Josh grins as I slide into an empty desk behind him near the door. The room separates us from Hadley, who sits near the windows with her arms folded. All her previous softness is gone and she's staring machetes at Josh again.

"What did you do?" I whisper as Ms. Artigas calls roll.

"Nothing you wouldn't do."

"I seriously doubt that."

"Mr. Bennett?" Ms. Artigas's voice cuts through the room. Hadley flicks her eyes to mine before I can look away.

"Ma'am?" I ask in my best compliant-southern-boy voice.

She tosses her clipboard onto her desk and sits on its edge. She's sort of plump and pretty, with that kind of relaxed, satisfied look of teachers who know they've got you by the balls.

"All right, everyone, this is Sam Bennett," she says, gesturing toward me. "He'll be joining our merry band of fools for the rest of the year, so try not to embarrass yourselves."

"Don't you mean try not to embarrass you, Ms. A?" A huge guy, who I can only assume is some sort of wall on the football team, winks at Ms. Artigas.

"That too, Mr. Cone." She picks up a stack of papers from a file box on her desk. "Before we continue with act two of *As You Like It*, let's go over the unit projects. You and your partner will rewrite an act of your choosing from the Shakespeare play you are assigned." She starts walking up and down the aisles and I breathe a sigh of relief that she didn't make me stand up and tell three truths and a lie about myself or some crap like that.

A girl in the back with glasses and two pencils stuck through her hair raises her hand.

"No, Miss Kendall," Ms. Artigas says, "you may not choose your own partner."

The girl puts her hand down and a few other kids grumble, but I'm relieved. Not knowing anyone, I'd have probably been left picking my nose for five minutes while everyone paired up with their friends.

"Your partner's name is listed next to yours at the top of your packet." Ms. Artigas heads down my row. "Pick up a copy of your play from my desk, get with your partner, introduce yourself if need be, and set a time to meet. Remember, this assignment is about interpretation, theme, setting, characterization, and creativity, not about how many times you can refer to various body parts in one monologue."

Josh snaps his fingers like he's disappointed as Ms. Artigas drops a packet on my desk. I pick it up and read my fate.

Sam B./Hadley S.

I stare at our names for a minute, not sure if I feel excited about the prospect of getting a closer look at this girl or a little nervous about her clear disdain for the male species. Then again, maybe it's just Josh.

"Aw, dude. Good luck with that." Josh smacks me on the back of the head and walks down the aisle to join Pencil Girl. "You might want to bring your strap and cup next class," he whisper-yells over his shoulder.

"Get moving, Mr. Bennett," Ms. Artigas says from behind her computer.

I grab my stuff, a copy of the right play, and find Hadley across the room, scribbling furiously into a neatly divided notebook. I slide into the desk next to her and wait while she writes. And then I wait some more while I try not to look at her lips, which proves to be more challenging when she pauses in her writing and slicks on some shiny stuff, the palest shade of pink. Now I'm trying not to think about all the ways I could find out if her mouth tastes like a strawberry Starburst.

Finally, she caps her pen and meets my eyes. Hers are large and the lashes are thick. And her skin is really smooth. But her *eyes* . . . Jesus, they're like —

"Hello?"

Oh, God. "What?" I ask, shaking my head to clear my brain.

She twists her mouth. "I said, Are you Sam?"

"Oh. Yeah. You're Hadley, right?"

She nods and looks over her paper. "We have *Much Ado About Nothing*. Ever read it?"

"Yeah, I read it last —"

"Are you friends with Josh?"

"Huh?"

"Josh Ellison. Are you friends with him?"

"Um. I just met him about twenty minutes ago."

"Because he's an ass."

"Okay."

"I realize you're new here and everything, but just so you know, Josh Ellison is a dick."

"Uh-huh."

"He lies."

33

"Did you guys just break up?"

She recoils back into her chair like I called her mother a whore. "What? No. I never dated him, I just . . ." She shifts her gaze away and her shoulders droop a little as she tries again. "He . . . I didn't mean . . . he just—"

She flinches and looks down, because my fingertips are resting on her hand. I'm not sure how the hell they got there, but I'm definitely touching her skin and she's staring at me, her mouth parted and eyebrows lifted.

I force myself to stare right back, pretty damn sure she doesn't really want to talk about how Josh broke her heart or didn't say hi to her at lunch or whatever. "So, Shakespeare?"

She pulls her hand back and scratches the place where my fingers rested, like I made her itch or something. "Right. Sorry."

"No problem." I flip through my copy of *Much Ado.* "I like this one. It's really funny and has all these crazy misunderstandings."

She looks at me for a moment longer before sliding her eyes down to her own book. "Yeah, I've read it. Benedick is kind of a jackass for most of it, right?"

"Hence his name. Love gets him in the end, though. Sucker."

She laughs. It sounds like that wind chime that used to hang from my grandmother's front porch. God, I am a pussy.

"He and Beatrice both," she says.

We scan the play in silence for a while. I try to keep my eyes on the page, but my brain's not registering a word. Hadley keeps crossing her legs and letting out these sighs and twirling her long hair around her slim fingers. This is so not going to work.

I snap my book shut. "Okay, what act do you want to—"

"Do you think that's true?" Hadley blurts, her head tilted, mouth pursed.

I stare at her for a few charged seconds, trying to get my brain to catch up with whatever the hell she's talking about now. "Do I think what's true?"

She points at my T-shirt.

I look down. I don't even remember putting this one on. My room is a cardboard landscape right now. I'm lucky I found something that didn't smell like the inside of my cleats. I pick at the gray cotton and the black block letters etched across my chest. APRIL IS THE CRUELEST MONTH.

I bought this shirt to piss off my mother. It's the first line from her favorite poem, "The Wasteland" by T. S. Eliot. She did her graduate thesis on it, which is so ironic, it's almost amusing. Or maybe it's just incredibly depressing. April is the month she defended her thesis at Vanderbilt. It's also the month that everything came out, everything fell apart. Dad didn't leave until the summer, but I'll never forget the afternoon of April fifth.

"Yeah, actually, I do think it's true."

"Why?"

I open my mouth to give her a lame answer, maybe even some deep spiel about Eliot's meaning that will impress her, but the way her chocolate eyes narrow softly on the text of my shirt like it's a living thing makes me not want to lie. I've lied enough this past year.

"Because sometimes life shits all over you when you're expecting sunshine."

She lifts her eyebrows. I know she's about to ask for a more coherent explanation, and I don't really have one to give her. Luckily, Ms. Artigas raps on her desk with a ruler.

"Five minutes, people," she calls.

"Oh." Hadley shuffles through her notebook. "I guess we should meet sometime this week to get organized. Are you busy after school?"

I exhale slowly. "I have to pick up my car today, but I'm free tomorrow."

"The library?"

"Sure."

I try not to breathe as she leans over and writes her number in my notebook, but then I give up and just inhale her clean, gingery scent.

"In case there's a change of plans," she says as she draws back.

I give her my number as well and she treats me to a genuine, death-ray-free smile. The bell rings and she slips into the hall. I'm putting Hadley's number in my phone when Josh joins me.

"How'd it go with Maneater?"

"Maneater?"

"Yeah. Hadley. Chews 'em up, spits 'em out. Maneater."

I can't help but laugh. "As you can see, I'm still in one piece." I sling my bag over my shoulder and fall in step with Josh toward the door. "Hey, what's her last name?" I type her first name into my phone.

Before he can answer, the hallway explodes into an uproar of "Oooh!" and "Damn!"

Josh and I reach the doorway at the same time to see a small crowd standing around Hadley, who's staring at her locker with a shocked expression on her face.

"That's her last name, dude." Josh points toward her locker. He shoves a hand through his hair. "Damn, Sloane is pissed."

Scrawled over the dingy metal in thick red marker are the words *St. Clair — Patron Saint of Sluts.*

Hadley clenches her jaw and throws her shoulders back. She pulls her locker open, slides her books in, slides a book out.

A short blond girl joins her, eyes huge as she reads the writing. Wordlessly, they link arms and walk robotically down the hall, disappearing into a thick throng of goggling eyes and snickers.

I should probably be wondering about the whole slut thing or who Sloane is or how it's not even a good insult. It's basically saying Hadley takes cares of sluts, which seems pretty charitable, if you ask me. But one thought crowds out all the others as I stare at that red writing.

"St. Clair?" I turn around to face Josh. "St. Clair is Hadley's last name?"

My voice must sound tight or squeaky, because Josh frowns at me and backs up. "Yeah."

I rub my forehead. That can't be right. I know it's a pretty rare last name, but there's no way she's *that* St. Clair. Maybe it's just a coincidence. A twisted, evidence-that-God-is-one-sick-son-of-a-bitch coincidence.

"You're sure?" I ask. "Has she gone here since her freshman year?"

Josh twirls a pencil over his knuckles. "Nope. She moved here before this year. Sometime in the summer."

"From where?"

"I don't know, man. Damn. Nashville, I think."

I feel my mouth fall open.

"Hey." Josh shakes my shoulder. "You look like you're about to hurl. You see a ghost or something?"

I blink, forcing myself out the door. I'm not sure if I'm about to crack up laughing or find a padded room and curl into a ball.

"Yeah, man," I say. "Something like that."

CHAPTER FOUR

Hadley

The minute I walk through the door, I wish I could turn around and leave. I used to love coming home. My house in Nashville always smelled like cinnamon and clean cotton and paper from the books in my dad's study. As soon as Dad saw me he would bellow, "Daughter, what cheer?" or "How now, sweet Hadley?" Even if I was just coming home from swimming laps or a trip to the grocery store with my mother, he always treated my return with poetic fanfare. It became a sort of game to see how he could twist his greeting into something creative and theatrical, and we kept a running list of all the phrases on a magnetic pad on the refrigerator. But ever since that day I came home to a front door peppered with fluttering strips of paper screaming at me in thick black marker, I get nauseated just thinking about being in the same room with my parents.

In this house, there's no cinnamon or Elizabethan welcome. Just a whole lot of quiet and averted gazes.

This afternoon, I taught three swim lessons at the Y's aquatic center and then swam laps until my fingertips turned pruney and my limbs felt like jelly and my mind cleared of those ugly red words on my locker. I would've stayed in the pool until I dissolved, but my parents expect me for dinner every night, and not even six months' worth of strained conversation will persuade them to let me out of it. These dinners are part of the "homework" their therapist assigns every week. It's supposed to increase a sense of interfamilial community and empathy, but the only thing it really increases is my mother's acerbic tone of voice and the frown lines around Dad's mouth.

I walk into the dark kitchen. The only one to greet me is Jinx, the mottled calico cat my dad got me last month as a painfully obvious peace offering. She slinks between my legs. I sit down on the tile floor against the dishwasher, pulling Jinx into my lap and nuzzling her fuzzy head. Her purring mingles with the old clock in the living room tick-tocking toward six-thirty.

The side door connected to the garage creaks open. The light flicks on and Dad walks in, clad in slim gray dress pants, skinny tie dangling. He slaps an armful of papers and notebooks onto the granite island. Then he disappears, returning with a couple of paper bags, grease stains leaking up the sides.

"Oh. Hadley."

I blink into the now bright kitchen.

"Why are you sitting on the floor, sweetheart?"

"I don't know."

He starts unpacking Chinese food. "Okay. Where's your mother?"

"Again, I don't know. I just got home too."

"She's not here?" He frowns and checks the clock on the microwave. "Huh."

Yes. *Huh.* Mom works at Sony Music in Nashville. It's her job to bring in new songwriting talent and then connect the songwriters with recording artists and producers. In the past, she operated on a strict nine-to-five schedule with a little traveling dropped in here and there throughout the year. She loved her job, but she loved my swim meets and cooking with Dad and trading funny stories about their day even more. But for the past few months, her own boundaries are blurring on both ends of the clock. Half the time, Dad and I start dinner without her.

Dad sighs heavily and pulls down three plates. Jinx wanders off and I get up to set the table while he rifles through the stack of notebooks. One is red, like the journal he used to write in every Sunday morning. He started it when I was born, and one of my first memories is of him tucked into a big leather chair, pen scratching over the creamy paper as he wrote down things he thought I needed to know about life. About myself.

I couldn't wait to read that journal. Now the very thought of it makes me want to scream. I haven't seen that thing in six months. Squinting at Dad's collection of junk, I see now that the red notebook is bigger and newer than the journal about me. Breathing out, I force my eyes to my task. Fork on the left. Knife on the right. Napkin folded into a triangle.

A few silent minutes later, Mom glides through the door. Even at the end of the day, she's pristine in sleek black pants and heels, tailored blouse and blazer, her dark hair in a flawless ponytail low on her neck.

"Hello," she says. She flicks her eyes to me and gives me a tired smile before setting her bag on the corner desk and flipping through the mail.

"Hi, honey," Dad says, pressing a dry kiss to her cheek. She barely moves, keeping her eyes on the bills and her latest *Real Simple* magazine.

From there, all our movements fall into a well-practiced routine. Glasses are filled with ice and water. A wine bottle is uncorked. A family gathers around a table. "How was your day?" is thrown around without any expectation of a real answer.

"Nothing too out of the ordinary about my day," Dad says. He doesn't elaborate, and neither Mom nor I ask him to. We don't want to hear about his classes and graduate students at Vanderbilt any more than he wants to tell us about them. "How about you, Hadley?"

I feel Mom's eyes on me, but I don't remove mine from my cashew chicken. I'm almost positive Kat's mom, Jocelyn, called her and told her about my locker, expressing her concern. Jocelyn, as luck would have it, is the guidance counselor at Woodmont High, which means she's constantly trying to get me into her office to talk about my feelings while I squeeze all my stress into one of those squishy balls. Jocelyn is also the only person Mom still talks to at any length or depth.

"Fine." Standard answer. Mom moves her steamed broccoli around her plate, drawing lines in the brown sauce. She actually looks bored.

"How's your English class going?" Dad asks. "Your teacher —what's her name?"

I sigh. There was a time when small talk was a four-letter word in our house. Dinner used to look like a game of Trivial Pursuit, filled with questions that actually mattered and bizarre facts my parents had picked up from their respective jobs. Now small talk is the bread and butter of St. Clair repasts, full of empty calories that leave a sour aftertaste on the back of my tongue and a cavern in my stomach.

"Ms. Artigas."

"Right. She went to Vanderbilt for her bachelor's. I hear she's excellent. A real Shakespeare aficionado."

Mom exhales so loudly, Dad flinches.

"She has a graduate degree," I say. "Did she get it at Vanderbilt? Your department, maybe?" Ms. Artigas *did* get her master's at Vanderbilt, which I know full well, but in education rather than literature.

Dad twists his mouth to one side. "As much as I love the Bard, you know Shakespeare's not my department."

Oh, I know. "It's all literature."

"I hadn't heard either way, Hadley. You'll have to ask her."

"I'll do that."

Mom releases a tiny cough and I shift my eyes to her. She's not looking at me, but she's smiling slightly, like the two of us are in on some secret joke. I wait for a smile to lift my own mouth, but it never happens. Dad presses two fingers to his temple and rubs, chewing robotically.

I stuff some rice in my mouth to keep from screaming.

Mom scoots her chair out and grabs the wooden pepper mill from the island. Leaning over Dad, she grinds a small black mountain of pepper all over his chow mein. He blinks down at his plate, his nose already twitching.

"Hadley?" Mom says sweetly, holding up the mill.

"Uh . . . no, thanks."

She places it back on the counter before sitting down. Dad sneezes, but digs into his food with a wordless sigh.

"So," he says after a few more sneezes. He clears his throat. Twice. "The Spring Kite Festival is in May."

My fork clangs against the plate. "And?"

He takes a sip of water. "And I hoped we could enter this year. Make a kite from scratch like we used to. Remember our sled kite? I would really love to finish it."

"Oh, for God's sake," Mom mumbles, bring her glass of wine to her lips. Dad frowns, but says nothing.

"I remember," I say. Last spring, we had planned to do this beautiful and ambitious sled kite, with silky blue and green inflatable spars. We never made it to that festival. The kite's packed in a box somewhere in the garage, half made.

"Had, I understand why you didn't want to do it this past year. But this festival . . . we've participated in it since you were three. It's part of our family. Can't we at least try to get back to normal?"

Normal? Dad's been clawing his way back to normal for months and still hasn't figured out that it no longer exists.

"I don't know, Dad, you tell me." I'm so tired of this whole scene. "What level of *normal* is normal enough for you? Me back on a swim team? Me proofreading your papers and sharing a laugh over how you always confuse *y-o-u-r* with *y-o-u-apostrophe-r-e* when you type too fast, just like old times? If that's normal, then . . ."

My throat rebels against me, tightening, and I scoot my chair back. It scrapes against the tile and Mom winces. "May I be excused?"

"No." Dad sniffs and rubs at his red nose. "No, you may not. We need to talk about this."

"About what? There's nothing to talk about!"

"Hadley, I can't keep—"

"Jason." Mom's voice is all jagged edges, and it silences him. "Let her go." She nods in my general direction as her thin fingers wrap around her wineglass, lifting it over her untouched food to her pale lips.

Dad's face darkens. "Annie, we need to—"

"*We* don't need to do anything. Hadley, go on."

I don't waste any time. Bolting upstairs, I barely close my bedroom door behind me before falling onto my bed and unleashing a scream into my pillow. Once my throat is loose and raw, I roll over, my eyes grazing over my bookshelves packed with neglected favorites. I pluck a small rectangular strip of paper from the drawer in my nightstand. I've handled it so much, stared at it so many nights, it's wrinkled and as soft as cotton.

There used to be a lot more of them, maybe fifty or so, but my dad fed them through the shredder. I sat on the porch steps, open eyes seeing nothing, while he raked his hands down the front door to dislodge the accusations. One got loose and floated toward me. I pocketed it. A reminder that nothing is ever as it seems.

I had come home early one day this past April from my private swim session with Coach Lyons. My shoulder was sore from an exhibition meet the week before, and she sent me home with instructions to ice it and rest up. I knew my mom would still be at work, and Dad rarely got home before seven because of a big paper on T. S. Eliot he was preparing for some academic journal. I parked in my usual spot at the end of the driveway, but had barely clicked off the ignition before I noticed the papers blanketing the front door. They danced lightly in the afternoon breeze, graceful and deceptively beautiful.

When my feet hit the sidewalk, I could see the handwritten words, but I couldn't really read them until I was standing on the steps. Even then, the writing blurred and I barely recognized the name on the paper. I remember releasing a single laugh. When the sound first split the warm air, I thought it was all a joke. By the time my voice died, a thousand little puzzle pieces had snapped together. All the late nights. All the Saturdays spent in his office.

I plucked one of the papers from the red painted wood. A piece of clear tape came with it and stuck to my finger. I could still smell the strong, pungent scent of permanent marker.

I read the messy scrawl.

JASON ST. CLAIR IS FUCKING MY MOTHER

That's all it said. Every single piece of paper said the same thing, though some were barely legible. No signature. No *Hi there, just thought you should know* on the back. Nothing but my father's name and an ugly verb and the whole heavy reality when you put all the words together.

Mom came home first. I was sitting on the porch steps, my bag in the grass, my hair still wet and laced with chlorine. A few neighbors had passed by, curious about the weird door decorations, but I didn't acknowledge them. I had thought about taking all the notes down. Going to my dad privately and asking him what was going on. But I didn't do that. And honestly, I have yet to regret that little act of revenge.

Mom usually entered the house through the garage, but she saw me and called out with her usual broad, straight-toothed smile, arms full of contracts that needed revising. When she approached the door, her face went so white, it was nearly translucent. After she read every little note, barely blinking, she went inside without a word.

Dad came home soon after that and stared at the door with shaking hands, shaking mouth, shaking head. Even his tie was shaking. We locked eyes and that's when I knew for sure it wasn't a joke or a mistake. His eyes said everything. They always did.

He went to work on the door. It was clear in under a minute, a pile of accusations on the porch. I followed him inside and everything got really weird. I expected yelling, crying, gnashing of teeth, and the mournful tearing of clothing. My mother was famous for her frankness. Underneath her cool exterior lurked a fireball who never had any problem calling you on your crap. She didn't do soft or subtle.

I hovered in the doorway of the kitchen while my parents faced each other. I braced myself for the rumblings, the eruptions, and the groveling. Or the leaving.

But she didn't say a word.

Not one damn word.

She just stood in the kitchen and stared at my dad over the island.

"Annie, let me explain."

She put up a hand.

"I'm sorry. I don't know what to . . . I'm sorry."

She closed her eyes.

"I'll end it. It's over. Right now, I'll end it."

She left the room. I watched her go, my jaw on the ground.

"Hadley," Dad said. "Honey, I don't . . . I'm so sorry." He reached out, trying to soothe me with a hand down my hair the way he always did when I was upset or sick. Part of me wanted him to because I suddenly felt unmoored, like a kite with severed strings, and I needed something — anything — to hold me down.

But his touch only rolled my simmering anger into a boil. I yanked away from him, disgusted at everything he had done, everything the verb on those notes implied. "Don't ever touch me again," I said through my sudden sobs.

That's at least one request he's honored for the past six months.

He heaved a trembling breath and raked both hands through his hair. A silent minute passed, but my heart's hammering didn't soften as he dug his phone out of his pocket. After he scrolled through it, supposedly landing on *her* number, he went out onto the back porch and closed the door behind him.

We never found out her name. He said she was a graduate student and he had been seeing her for a year.

An. Entire. Year.

365 days. 8,760 hours. 525,600 minutes.

All lies.

Mom said she didn't want to know any other details. She asked Dad to delete all emails and texts and the woman's contact information from his phone and computers. She asked Jocelyn to go through all of his devices afterward to make sure it was done. Jocelyn did it, leveling him with a terse "Who's this?" every time she came across a name she didn't recognize. I've never seen my father look so small as he did that day, standing in his study while my mother's best friend sifted through his electronic life.

There was a part of me that didn't understand my mother's need for ignorance. The Annie St. Clair I knew would want to know more about the woman her husband chose over her. But I never asked for an explanation for his affair either, and he never offered one.

My parents started counseling, which I refused to attend, even when the therapist requested it. If they've ever discussed anything outside of therapy, I've never heard a word. In my opinion, they're just throwing away three hundred dollars an hour. A sort of cold war broke out in our house, and divorce started sounding as enticing as a Hawaiian vacation. No one spoke beyond the logistics of running a household. No one touched. Dad seemed to know that I didn't want to talk to him, could barely look at him, and the space he gave me in the beginning morphed into habit. I kept waiting for Mom to talk to me about it all and help me understand, for some sort of alliance to form between us. I figured we were in this together, on the same team wading through enemy territory, but instead, she filled up whatever void Dad's affair created with work. With tasks. With black pepper on her allergic-to-pepper husband's dinner. Other than a few shared glances that only made me feel uncomfortable as opposed to comforted, I'm pretty sure she forgot I was in the house half the time.

I think what really kept me up at night—what still keeps me up—were those notes. I'm not sorry my dad was outed. I'm not even sorry he was humiliated. But I'll never forget how I felt when I first saw those words, when their meaning first penetrated through my unbelief. It felt like part of my life was dying right before my eyes.

We moved from Nashville to Woodmont in June. Life was supposed to change. Dad tried to make things right, texting me all the time and asking me about Sunday-afternoon swims and movie marathons. But the only thing that really changed was that I started looking for a distraction. I started looking for something to make me forget that I was lonely even when I was with Kat. What changed was that I started craving some kind of validation, some comfort that I never got—or wanted—from my parents anymore. Even Kat seemed afraid to touch me, like I was a grenade and one hard tug would set me off.

That's the nice thing about guys. They're never afraid to touch you.

CHAPTER FIVE

Hadley

Kat knocks on my door a little past eight. I'm over my memory-fest, the note tucked safely away, and my dad finally stopped tapping on my door after a record-low four attempts. Jinx is sprawled across my feet on the bed while I flip through an SAT vocabulary book. Last May, when a lot of juniors were preparing to retake the SATs, I was watching life as I knew it disintegrate. So I'm taking the test again in December. It's my last chance before most college application deadlines.

"Meow!" I call, knowing it's Kat by her coded one long, two short knock.

"I wish you'd stop mewing your greetings." She flops next to me on the bed.

"What? It was Jinx."

"She didn't say anything, did she?" Kat reaches over and scratches Jinx behind the ears.

"Well, she does tend to purr when people pet her like that."

Kat pinches my thigh and I yelp. Jinx's ears go flat.

"Your mom, genius. About the locker."

I smirk. "What do you think?"

Kat releases a frustrated grunt and Jinx flinches again. When I started messing around with purportedly single guys behind closed doors, Kat nearly had a stroke. As a result, she doesn't stop Jocelyn from reporting any disturbing details of my life she gets wind of to my mother. And therein lies Kat and Jocelyn's naiveté—thinking that information of my declining reputation will enliven my mother into action.

"Look, it'll be old news by tomorrow," I say, waving a hand. Then I stuff it under my butt because I realize it's shaking a little. "I just messed up with Josh."

"Jenny dumped him. I talked to her in Trig. Apparently they'd just gotten together near the end of the summer, but he told her he really liked her and then something happened with meeting her parents and he totally freaked. She seemed okay, though." She runs her hand over my comforter. "I don't think she had anything to do with the whole locker thing."

I scratch my head with my pencil, squeeze my eyes closed. "Can we not talk about this right now? It's been a crappy day."

Kat puffs out her cheeks. "Right. Sorry."

"It's fine." I flip through vocabulary, tracing over the words with my capped pen. *Absolution. Blighted. Credulous.*

"So get this," Kat says, crossing her legs. "You would've been proud of me at practice today."

"Oh?" *Defunct. Exculpate. Fractious.*

"Like, buy-me-a-pint-of-Peanut-Butter-World-ice-cream proud."

"That's serious." I lay down my vocab. "Peanut Butter World is not intended for the average accomplishment."

She nods, a half smile on her face. "I talked to Rob."

I let my eyebrows speak for themselves.

"Yep. For warm-ups, I was anchor on a freestyle relay and my team won. He complimented me on my *form.*" Predictably, her cheeks pink up. "Can you believe it?"

"Yes, I can." Kat is one of those girls who has no idea that she's beautiful or funny or talented. Her dad's been out of the picture since she was ten, but until Jocelyn finally kicked him out, he enjoyed whittling his daughter down like a piece of wood about everything from her nonexistent weight problem to an A-minus on a spelling test. When Kat met my dad in the swim class and his gentle voice actually encouraged her through the water, I'm pretty sure it took her a week to realize he was talking to her. Several years later, Rick, who would become her stepdad, wooed her mother with such swoon-inducing tenacity that he restored Kat's confidence in romance, but not so much in herself.

"And what did you say back?" I ask.

"I said thanks."

Again, I let my eyebrows do the talking.

"What?" she says. "That's a lot for me. Plus, I got flustered. He was just standing there, smiling down at me, and his chest and stomach were all wet and slippery-looking and there were little drops of water on his lower lip, just hanging there, and— oh my God, what is so funny?"

"Nothing, nothing!" I laugh into my hands. "You're just so hilarious when you get all hot and bothered about Rob. It's as if you've spent your pubescent years underground and have just now been set loose. Hide your teenage sons, Woodmont! Rawr!"

She crosses her arms, hands hooked on her elbows. "No. No 'Rawr'! I'm not hot and bothered. I'm . . . appreciative of his . . . his . . . *form.*"

"You're horny."

"Hadley!"

"Concupiscent. Libidinous."

"Hadley Jane!"

"Prurient."

"I don't even know what those words mean."

"They mean 'horny.'"

"God help me."

I grin and lean my hands on her knees. "Come on, Kitty Kat. Admit it. Rob is so hot that whenever you see him, your panties get a little—"

"Okay, okay!" She slaps her hands over her ears. Kat hates the word *panties.* "Just stop. I want him, all right? I want him so bad, I accidentally moaned a little during Government today when I imagined his Speedo slipping off when he dives into the pool."

I laugh so hard I snort. "You *moaned?*"

"I was quiet. At least, I think." Her face is full-on scarlet now, and she picks at her bottom lip, trying to glare at me. "I actually like Rob, you know."

I nod slowly. Yes, I know. Romance, true love, yadda yadda.

I'm still laughing when my phone rings. I grab it from my pillow and nearly fall off the bed when I see the name flashing on the screen.

"Oh. It's Sam."

"Sam? The new guy? You know him?"

"Yeah. I'm paired with him for that Shakespeare project in English."

She jumps onto her knees. "You didn't tell me that! He's in my Government class. He's sort of hot."

"Did he hear you moan too?"

She smacks my leg. "Answer it!"

I stick my tongue out at her and slide my finger over the surface of the phone. "Hello?"

Silence.

"Hello?" I say again.

"Hadley?"

"Yeah."

"It's Sam Bennett."

"Hey."

"Hey. So, listen, I need to change our plans for tomorrow."

"Oh."

"I was wondering if you could come here."

"To your house?" Kat's mouth drops open. "Wouldn't the library be easier?"

"Not for me. Is that a problem?" His voice sounds weird. Not that I know his voice really well or anything. It just sounds . . . strained and sharp. In class, he sounded so relaxed, so amiable.

"Is everything all right?" I ask, my heart suddenly hammering.

"Yeah. Why wouldn't it be?"

"I'm not sure. You just sound . . . funny." Kat raises her eyebrows at me and Sam clears his throat.

"I'm fine. Can you come here tomorrow after school or not?"

"Um. Sure, that's fine."

"Great. I'll text you the address."

"Okay, see you—"

Click.

I flinch and stare at my phone. *Sam B. Call Ended.*

"What just happened?" Kat asks.

I manage a weak laugh. "I'm not sure, but apparently I'm going over to his house tomorrow to work on this project."

Kat frowns and then releases a colossal "*Ohhh.*"

I look at her. "What do you mean, '*Ohhh*'?"

"Um. Nothing."

"Uh-uh. That '*Ohhh*' was not a nothing kind of '*Ohhh.*' It was a very loaded '*Ohhh.*'"

She blows some air into her bangs. "It's just—You were supposed to meet in the library?"

"Yeah."

"You set that up before the whole locker thing?"

Nod.

"Well, I mean . . . He's new and doesn't really know anyone, but then he saw the locker. So what if he thinks . . ."

"*Ohhh.* You think he wants to hook up with me?"

She shrugs. "I don't know. You said he was acting weird on the phone."

"He was, but it's not like I'm acquainted with his normal MO." My stomach somersaults as I think back to English.

60

"Crap, he was talking to Josh before class. And after class."

"I heard he's a baseball player."

"Ugh." I drop my head into my hands. Did Sam really change the place so we could hook up? Not that I consider myself particularly alluring, but it is suspicious considering the whole locker debacle. I run my fingers over the top of my hand and feel suddenly nauseous. He just seemed so different. Like when I looked at him, I saw something I recognized and could understand. I'm not even sure what it was. Something about him was just . . . familiar.

"Hadley, I hate to tell you this, but this is kind of your own—"

"Don't. Don't say it."

She sighs. "Are you still going to go?"

I pause, thinking. I hear my dad's study door close downstairs, hear the clink of a glass against a bottle in the kitchen. I ball a hand into my comforter. I roll my shoulders back. "Yes. I am."

Kat groans. "Please don't tell me you're actually going to—"

"There's no way I'm going to let some asshole assume crap about me after reading what a bitter bitch wrote on my locker." I snap open my vocab book and flip.

Kat's eyes widen, but she shuts up.

Galvanize. Hubris. Inexpedient.

CHAPTER SIX

Sam

I click my phone off and throw it on my bed. My breath is going in and out way too fast. I can't believe I invited Hadley to my house just to piss off my mother. What the hell is wrong with me? I rub my eyes and walk myself back through the last ten minutes. I scrolled through my iPod. I tapped on Sea Wolf. I opened my calculus book, picked up a tooth-gnawed pencil, and scanned number 11, where I'd left off an hour earlier. Then my fingers were flying over my phone and I was talking to *her.* Inviting *her* to my house.

The entire day was one shitstorm after another. After English, the rest of school went by in a blur. I honestly can't even remember what class I had for seventh period. Mom picked Livy and me up after school and sped like a bat out of hell to the shop to pick up my car, yammering about her *amazing* new job and how *amazing* her students are and what an *amazing* commitment the school has to the arts.

After she paid for my two new tires that had finally rubbed bald on the trip from Atlanta, she went back to her job. Seriously. It's our first day of school, our house looks like a warehouse, and the woman goes back to work—again—to finish tacking posters that say shit like *Imagine* and *Believe to Achieve* on the walls in her classroom. Livy nearly bit a hole through her lip, but neither of us said anything. As usual.

When Livy and I got home, I started dinner. After digging the pots and pans out of a box, I put on some music and took out stuff to make pasta primavera. Easy. Livy set up at the kitchen table and started her homework. As I cut up vegetables and set the water to boil, I kept flicking my eyes to her. I wondered if she had heard the name *St. Clair* drifting through the hallways. She didn't look angsty or anything, but I should probably warn her, just in case. It's been nearly six months since everything happened, but Livy's a little unpredictable these days. The morning we left Atlanta, she came downstairs in a neon blue wig—this sleek bob that actually looked pretty freaking cool, but still. It was a wig. It was blue. Mom spluttered her coffee back into her mug and I'm positive Livy cracked a grin.

"So, Livy," I said, adding oil to a skillet. "How was your day?"

She shrugged. "Fine, I guess." Her pencil scritched across her paper, her geometry book open in front of her. Her voice sounded like an automated recording.

"Do you like your teachers?"

"I guess."

"Did you meet any cool people?"

"Sure."

"Who?"

"I don't know." *Scritch, scritch.*

I added the pasta to the boiling water, set the timer, and went over to my sister. "Livy."

She lifted her vacant eyes.

"Mom's not here." I tugged on the ends of her blond hair. No wig today, but there is a light purple streak in the front. "It's me, remember? Thammy."

Her mouth twitched at my use of her kid name for me, back when she had a lisp. And then her eyes cleared and her shoulders let go of her neck.

"Now tell me about your day," I said. "I really want to know. No more vague crap, okay?"

She smiled and nodded. I went back to the stove. For the next hour, she told me everything about school. She and a girl named Annalise bonded over Evanescence (I made a mental note to step up Livy's education on good music), a kid named

Jared kept making obscene gestures at her during Biology (I made a mental note to find this asshat and break his legs), and her photography class, which she had been put into accidentally, was the only part of the day that kept her from chewing off her own tongue. Her words, not mine.

"I think I might go to the Photography Club meeting tomorrow after school," she said.

"Wow. That's serious. You're getting *involved?*"

She laughed and threw a balled-up paper at me. "I don't know, I just really liked it. I was lucky I could get the lens cap off the camera today, but I love the whole idea of capturing these little moments and making them, like, last forever. Mr. Grayson showed us this one photo of a little girl chasing a plastic bag down an alley. I mean, that doesn't sound very interesting, right? But it was. The way the light hit the bag and made it seem like it was alive, the way the girl reached out for it like it was . . . I don't know. More than a bag." She shrugged and glanced up at me. "Um. It was cool."

"That's does sound cool, Liv." I smiled. I hadn't seen her excited about anything in a long time. "When's the meeting over?"

"I think around six-thirty? It's sort of a kick-off-the-year party thing. Annalise will be there too, and she said her mom could give me a ride home."

I slid the peppers into the hot oil. "Sounds good."

Then I told her about baseball and Josh, but I had no desire to mention Hadley yet, even if her last name were Jones. Back in Atlanta, Livy was constantly on my case about why I didn't have a girlfriend and whether or not I still talked to Nicole. I expected our time in Woodmont, or wherever the hell we were, to be no different. Livy wasn't exactly a little girl anymore, but seriously, she's my little sister. I wasn't even thinking about telling her that I'd met a girl — a girl I had deemed *magical*, for Christ's sake — but she'd turned out to be a blast from the past of our own personal hell.

As soon as dinner was ready, Mom blew in the door.

"Oh, wonderful. You made dinner," she said in greeting.

Hello. You're welcome.

She dropped her work bag by the fridge while I piled pasta onto three plates. Livy slammed her books closed and cleared the space so we could all sit down at the table.

We started eating in silence. Mom refused to let us eat in front of the TV. She said dinners were family time. What a joke. I wouldn't mind just me and Livy, so we could talk, but you add Mom to the mix and it's like a few feet of chains have been wrapped around both of our throats.

"How was school, Olivia?" Mom asked.

"Fine."

"Make any friends?"

"Sure."

"And your asthma? Any —"

"Fine."

Mom pressed her lips flat. "What about photography? Will you be all right in there or do you need a schedule change?"

Livy shrugged. "It's fine, I guess."

Mom nodded and I wiped my mouth with my napkin to cover my grin.

"Did you know we're only about a mile from the Y, Olivia? I signed us up for a family membership," Mom said while popping a pepper into her mouth. "You can ride your bike there — slowly — and swim a little. What do you think about that?"

"Maybe," Livy said, and I tapped her foot under the table. She smiled without looking at me. Dad always said Livy had some mermaid blood in her. There was rarely a time from April to October that she wasn't in the pool we had at our old house in Nashville. Not that she was going to smack a kiss on Mom's cheek for the suggestion, but I knew my sister. She'd find her way to the Y sooner or later. It's the only exercise she could do that didn't aggravate her asthma. Something about the warm air and humidity wasn't as hard on the breathing tubes as the conditions of other cardio workouts.

"What about you, Sam?" Mom asked.

"What about me?"

"School?"

"School is school, Mom. Same here as it is everywhere else."

"I wouldn't say that. Hunter Academy is so different from anything I've ever experienced. I wish I'd gone there as a teenager. The staff really believes in fostering individual talents. It's amazing."

"Well, we don't go to Hunter, do we?"

Mom dropped her fork and leveled me with a glare. "You wouldn't like it."

"Sure. Whatever you say, Mom."

"Why do you have to make everything so difficult?"

I sat back, almost flabbergasted. Almost. "I'm not making anything difficult. I'm here, aren't I? I moved. Again. I made your dinner. I helped Livy unpack her room. What do you want from me?"

"A little less attitude."

"Sorry, I'm having a hard time knocking that back a notch. Something about being dragged away from my few friends for the second time in less than six months, with Dad up in Boston, just leaves a sour taste in my mouth."

She tugged on her earlobe, something she always does

when she's nervous. Or when we're nervous. When I had bad dreams as a kid, I used to cower on her lap while she sang and ran her thumb over my ear.

"Your father chose to go to Boston," she said, dropping her hand. "And he chose to go alone. That's not my fault."

Livy chewed on her lip, moving her food around her plate. Mom sighed and pressed her eyes closed. For a second, I really thought she was going to apologize. But she forged ahead, her hands white on the edges of the table.

"We wouldn't be in this situation, Samuel, if you had been a little less rash and a little less selfish."

My jaw tightened. Out of the corner of my eye, I saw Livy's head snap up. Mom and I stared at each other, and right there, in that moment, I almost told her about Hadley. I wasn't positive this was the right girl, but something in my gut said I knew exactly who she was and I wanted to see Mom's face when she found out.

But Livy was in the room.

So I shut up.

But I couldn't shake this overwhelming urge to pour all of my shit on Mom the way she'd done to me for the past six months. To change the tide, if that was even possible.

So two hours later, I got a better idea. No big deal. Hadley and I needed to work on the project anyway. This was just a way to get under Mom's skin a little.

Now, standing in my room, Hadley's voice still echoing in my ear, the prospect of her gingery smell filling up my house, that "better idea" makes me feel like a complete douche.

CHAPTER SEVEN

Hadley

My legs, which I had locked into place right before I rang the doorbell, turn to water as soon as he opens the door.

Because he looks good.

Not in a Josh Ellison I-can-get-any-girl-I-want kind of way, but in this boyish, relaxed sort of way that makes my resolve turn to mush. His hair is sticking up like he's been pulling on it and his light blue T-shirt hugs his trim torso. His blue eyes are wide on mine, as though he's a little surprised I showed up.

"Hey," he says without smiling, but his gaze slides up my body in a flash. "Come on in."

"Thanks." I give him a smile and let my shoulder brush against his chest as I pass. He smells like some cool, clean soap and . . . Is that cinnamon?

"Sorry about the mess." He weaves through a maze of cardboard boxes. "We just moved in last week."

Like this isn't obvious. "Where did you move from?"

"Atlanta. We lived with my grandma for the summer." He pushes a box labeled LINENS away from the stairs and turns to face me. "Lived in Nashville before that."

"Really? Me too. We moved this past summer."

"Yeah, I know." He rubs the back of his neck and looks away as my phone pings in my bag.

"Sorry." I dig it out and find a text from my dad.

Hope your day went well, sweetie. Love you!

I stuff my phone in my bag without replying.

"How do you know?" I ask Sam, who's rummaging through a box filled with paperback novels and shampoo bottles.

"How do I know what?" he asks, standing up with a few books. The top one is a tattered copy of *Romeo and Juliet*.

"That I used to live in Nashville."

"Oh. From Josh."

I fight to keep my lip from curling. "Ah. I see." I'm sure Josh has been a wealth of information.

He runs his hand along the tawny wood of the banister, starting up the steps. His fingers are long and slender, almost elegant. "All my books and stuff are in my room."

Sure they are. I follow him, glad his back is to me so he can't see the smirk that's taking over my face right now. I managed to go all day without talking to him. Ms. Artigas drowned us in her lecture on the power of disguise in *As You Like It*, and I made sure I sat in the back of the room. Luckily, my locker had been scrubbed clean and Sloane had yet to strike again, so I flew under the radar most of the day. I'm almost positive Sam is in my lunch block, so I ate in the library with an *Us Weekly* while the Sci-Fi Club sketched pictures of balloon-chested intergalactic spacecraft captains onto posters advertising for new members. This is my riveting social life. The only person I said more than three words to was Kat, who leveled me with plaintive are-you-sure-about-this looks every thirty seconds.

"I mean, you're basically going to manipulate him into thinking you want to hook up," she whispered while we changed for gym. "You really want to be that kind of girl?"

"What kind of girl?"

Kat pressed her mouth flat and she busied herself with her shoelaces.

"Besides, I'm not manipulating," I said, pulling on a royal blue Woodmont High T-shirt. "I'm just . . . proving a point."

"Are you sure that point doesn't have something to do with making the whole of the male population suffer needlessly?"

"I'm sure."

By the time I got to Sam's, I wasn't sure about anything. I've never played around with guys like this, and honestly, I'm not sure I know what I'm doing. Usually I get with a guy because *I* want to, and then I stop things before they go too far. Even though I pick guys who aren't assholes—Josh Ellison represents a grave lapse in judgment—I'm fully aware that I've developed a reputation as a tease in a few short months. But it's not a game to me. It's not a power trip. It's comfort without too much risk. No one gets too close. No one gets hurt. At least, not until Jenny Kalinski.

Sam's room is pretty much what I expected. A mess that makes my palms itch. Boxes everywhere, clothes draped over the unmade bed and desk chair. Stacks of books and magazines. Some guitar-driven music pumps out of an iPod dock.

From his desk, he grabs his laptop and trades the paperbacks for a copy of *Much Ado* before settling on the floor against the bed.

"So what act do you think we should do?" he asks, flipping through the play.

I sit down next to him and take out my own stuff. "I'm not sure. It's been a while since I've read it."

He flips through his notebook, a few wrinkled papers sticking out from every direction. "Do you have the packet explaining the project? I can't find mine."

I open my binder and find it immediately. "It says we need a multimedia component."

"Can I see it?"

"Oh . . . um . . ."

"Thanks." Before I can stop him, he slides the paper from between my fingers. I inhale deeply and watch him while he reads.

A grin ambles across his mouth. "Am I seeing things, or did you correct this teacher handout?" He holds up the paper, his finger on a paragraph where several red marks bleed across the page.

I snatch the paper back from him. "You'd be surprised how many teachers make spelling and grammatical errors."

He nods, pressing his tongue to his top lip, probably to keep from busting up laughing at my neurosis.

"Oh, shut up," I say, cracking a smile and brandishing my red pen at him. "What act are we doing?"

He blocks my pen with his book and finally laughs, a resonant boom from deep inside his chest. "Why don't we skim the play really quick and see what we think?"

"Okay."

So we do. In silence. I watch him for a minute, waiting for a sidelong glance or a subtle brush against my arm. Nothing. He just reads and keeps checking his phone, like he's waiting for something better to pull him from my presence.

Finally, he slaps his book shut. "I think we should do act three. It's long, but it's when everything starts really heating up. Beatrice thinks she might love Benedick, Claudio thinks he sees Hero in bed with what's-his-name. It's a good tension-building act."

"I like act five." Actually, act three sounds good to me too, but I don't feel like acquiescing so easily.

"Why?"

"It's the resolution. The happy ending."

He makes a sound in the back of his throat, something between a laugh and a snort.

"Everyone wants a happy ending, Sam, even if you don't believe it's possible."

He glances at me and puts his book down. "*Is* it so impossible?"

"Have you ever seen one? A real, honest-to-God happy ending?"

He frowns and opens his mouth. Nothing comes out, but he keeps looking at me. With our eyes locked like this, I know this is the moment. I need to lean in, let him get within a millimeter of my mouth, whisper what an asshole I think he is for assuming words on a locker somehow mean I'm going to sleep with him, and then leave.

I angle my body toward him and press lightly against his arm, holding his gaze. I hear him suck in a breath and I look at him from beneath my lashes. All those little tricks I used to abhor. But something stops me from going any further. For one thing, he doesn't move closer. He doesn't even blink. Just maintains this baffling intensity that chews at my stomach. It's not the same type of look I got from Josh or Henry Murphy or Isaac Jorgensen, like I was their favorite flavor of ice cream. It's a different kind altogether.

His gaze flicks down to my lips once, but he remains a fortress. Unreadable. I shift away from him and fiddle with the neckline of my shirt.

"All right," he says hoarsely before he clears his throat. "Let's give your happy ending a shot."

I nod and write *Act V* in my notebook, tracing over the letters again and again while I wait for my heart to stop hammering. I feel unsettled, like I'm face-to-face with a mirror, only I don't quite recognize my own reflection. I look around Sam's room, but it's all unfamiliar, making my head even lighter.

A strident beep sounds from somewhere downstairs, and I startle.

"Oh, just a sec." Sam gets up and heads for the door. "I need to get this out of the oven."

"Did you just say *the oven?*" He doesn't answer and I follow him downstairs, entering the kitchen in time to see him pull a casserole dish out of the top of a double oven.

"What's that?" I ask, taking a seat on a stool at the island.

He places the dish on a trivet on the counter. "Chicken Georgia. Or maybe it's Tennessee." He waves a gloved hand. "Whatever. It's dinner."

"You cook?"

He smiles while he moves aside some mushrooms and melted cheese, cutting into a piece of chicken to inspect it. "Surprised?"

"A little."

"I started when my dad left. My mom's not very domestic."

"Oh. I'm sorry. About your dad I mean."

He shrugs and lays down the knife. "He had a good reason." I'm not sure what to say to that, but he saves me by continuing. "Anyway, it was either cook or let my sister live on frozen pizzas. After a few rubbery chickens and a couple of kitchen fires, I actually got pretty good. It's fun."

"Kitchen fires?"

"No one was hurt except an oven mitt or two."

I laugh, breathing in the savory smell of the casserole before he covers it with foil. Another timer dings and he slides a coffeecake out of the bottom oven. Cinnamon.

"Wow. And you bake?" I lean over the counter and inhale again. "That smells incredible."

"Thanks. My grandma taught me how to make this while we lived in Atlanta. Took me a while to get it right."

My mouth spreads into a smile as he sprinkles some raw sugar over the top of the cake.

"What?" he asks, one corner of his mouth ticked up.

"Nothing. It's just . . . well, you're a baseball player, right?"

"Yeah."

"And a guy."

"Astute observation."

"You have to admit, it's a little unusual to meet a teenage-boy-slash-baker-slash-athlete."

He purses his lips and opens a door next to the refrigerator, disappearing into what I assume is the pantry. I hear him rummaging around, and when he emerges, he's smocked in an extremely ruffly green and white striped apron. He spreads his arms wide. "Well, now you've met one."

I cover my mouth and laugh. "I guess I have. What would Josh say?"

"He'd say 'Dude, this cake kicks ass.'"

"Oh my God, you sound just like him."

"He's not a tough one to imitate." He takes out two plates from the cabinet. "Want to try some?"

"Yeah?"

"Sure. You can be my taste-tester."

"Okay, but only if you take off that apron."

"Not my color?"

79

"I don't think the color is the problem."

He removes the apron as he rounds the island. Before I have a chance to protest, he loops it over my head and pulls my hair out of the strap's grasp. His fingers graze my neck a little and I bite the inside of my cheek to keep from shivering.

"You're right. Looks much better on you."

I laugh nervously and look down at the starchy, cottony stripes. He grins and returns to the cake, slicing two large pieces onto the plates. He slides one over to me with a fork. I quickly take a bite, my mouth already watering.

"Holy crap," I manage through a sugary mouthful. There must be a pound of butter in this thing. "That's amazing. I'm officially impressed."

His smile is huge, spilling into his eyes and crinkling the corners. "It's Livy's favorite."

"Your sister?"

"Yep. She just turned fourteen in July."

"Are you close?"

He nods and digs around in a cardboard box near the sink, coming up with two glasses. "She's a pain in my ass half the time, but I love her. She's all I have, really."

I want to ask what he means by this, but any question I form in my mind sounds intrusive. I finish off my cake as he pours Coke into the glasses and hands one to me. "I'm an only child. I've always sort of liked that, but . . ." I take a sip of Coke, my throat suddenly dry.

He tilts his head at me. "But what?"

I take a deep breath. "I don't know. I used to be super close with my dad, but now . . . it's just . . . my parents are going through a hard time. I guess it would be nice to have someone else there with me. Someone who's not them, you know?"

I slide my gaze to him, but he's focused on his plate, blinking rapidly and rubbing at his forehead. "Why aren't you close with your dad anymore?"

I swallow hard. My lower lip feels unsteady, so I press my teeth over it until it stills. "He just . . . isn't who I thought he was. And I can't seem to get over it."

God. My voice sounds so small and pathetic. Weak.

"I'm sorry," I say a little too loudly, sitting up on my stool. "I don't know why I'm talking about this." I barely know this guy. I hardly talk about my parents to Kat, much less a ballplayer who's probably only interested in whether my bra's clasp is in the front or the back.

But from the way he keeps moving the salt shaker in front of the pepper shaker and back again, his eyes a little glazed on the black and white ceramic, it doesn't look like my bra is what's on his mind at all.

"No, it's fine." He finally knocks over the salt, and white

granules skitter over the counter. "I get it. When things get too heavy, Livy and I always head out to the movies. We spend all day theater hopping and making ourselves sick on popcorn and candy."

"That sounds like a good distraction."

"Yeah." He sweeps up the salt and tosses it in the sink. "The best is when we get a slasher movie back-to-back with some Disney flick or cheesy romantic comedy."

"Sort of like a visual yin and yang?"

"Exactly. And Livy is hilarious to watch rom-coms with. She eviscerates them. The acting, the plot, the saccharine endings. It's classic."

I laugh. "I think Livy and I might have a lot in common."

His smiles fades a little, but he finally looks at me. "Maybe you could come with us next time. Get your mind off things." He blinks and steps back a little. I feel the unmistakable warmth of blood seeping into my cheeks. To cool them, I take a too-large gulp of Coke and half of it slides down the wrong tube, bubbles searing my nose.

Sam raises his brows in concern as I proceed to cough up a lung. He hands me a bottle of water and I take a few sips while he moves around the kitchen, unpacking only half a box before moving on to another. Outside the window over the sink, a female robin lands and pecks at the sill.

"Oh, shit." Sam's voice pulls my eyes from the window. Off the kitchen, an automatic garage door rattles and creaks. Sam's face is completely white.

"What's wrong?" I slip off the barstool, a pinch in my stomach. "Is that your mom?"

He hangs a hand on the back of his neck and shakes his head at the ceiling. "Yeah, and you need to go now."

CHAPTER EIGHT

Sam

I circle the island and grab her arm, all but dragging her from the kitchen toward the front door.

Shit, shit, shit.

It wasn't supposed to happen like this. She wasn't supposed to look at me like that and feel like that, all smushed up against my arm, and talk about her dad like he broke her heart into a million bloody pieces. I sure as hell wasn't supposed to invite her to the goddamn movies.

I spent the day avoiding her and distracting myself with Josh and couple other guys from the baseball team, Matt Pavers and Noah Harrington. Even though Josh spent the entire lunch block staring at a cheerleader with a pixie cut, my new friends kept me occupied, reliably steering clear of topics other than boobs, asses, and PlayStation. During English, I slouched down in my desk and texted with Ajay the entire period just to keep myself from looking at Hadley. So beyond double-checking that Livy wouldn't be home until after six, I didn't have much time to think about what a sick son of a bitch I am.

Until she rang the doorbell.

And then her hair fell on my shoulder and the sweet smell of her skin attacked me, addling my damn brain. Then she laughed and ate my cake wearing that stupid apron Livy bought me for my birthday as a joke. Then she got all haunted and hopeful at once.

"You need to go," I say, opening the front door. I hear Mom's key in the side door between the kitchen and the garage.

"Why? What's wrong?" Hadley asks, pulling out of my grip.

"I'm an idiot, that's what's wrong."

"What?"

"Nothing. My mom's just . . . she's . . . going to be tired and bitchy and I don't want you to have to deal with it."

"Sam, it's fine."

The door hangs open, a cool breeze blowing her hair into her face. I clench my hands at my sides so they won't betray me, but she brushes the strands aside and my hands release.

"Hadley, I need you to leave."

She frowns. "All right. If that's really what you need."

"Yes. Thank you." I nudge her shoulder toward the door, but she walls up against my hand.

"My stuff is upstairs."

"I'll bring it to you tomorrow."

"How very gentlemanly of you, but I have homework tonight."

She's getting pissed, but I don't really care at this point. I wave her upstairs and peek around the corner into the kitchen as she heads to my room.

"Sam?" Mom calls. "Are you home? This smells wonderful!"

I meet her in the kitchen. "Yeah, hey. I'm here."

"Hi. How was your day?" she asks while she unpacks her bag.

"Great. Um, I'll be right back."

I go to rush Hadley out of the house, but she's already stepping through the front door without a word. I feel bad that I'm pretty much kicking her ass out, but there's not much else I can do. This was a bad idea to begin with, and at this point, I'd sell my nads to the devil himself to keep my mom from meeting her.

Unfortunately, the devil's not interested in a trade. As Hadley steps onto the front stoop, Mom click-clacks down the front hall toward the stairs.

"Oh," she says as she spots Hadley. "Sam, who's this?"

Hadley freezes and turns around. "Hi," she says, flicking her eyes to me.

"Um, yeah. Mom, this is a friend from school. We were working on a project. She's just leaving."

"Hi there." Mom's voice is as bright as a 150-watt bulb. "I'm Cora." She holds out her hand.

Hadley hesitates in the doorway and then I start cracking up. I mean, I'm laughing like a crazy person, because that's really all you can do when you've willingly jumped into a pile of your own shit.

"Sam, you're being very rude," Mom says, folding her arms.

I manage to get it together and clear my throat. "Sorry." Clenching my jaw into place, I take Hadley's arm and draw her back inside while she looks at me like I could benefit from some psychopharmacological intervention.

"As I was saying, I'm Cora. Sam's mom."

I watch Mom hold out her hand again.

"Hi, I'm Hadley."

Mom's color vanishes. My heart thump-thump-stops in my chest. She holds it together enough to shake Hadley's hand, never taking her eyes off the dark-haired girl in front of her.

"That's an unusual name," Mom says, her voice more of a 15-watt now.

Hadley's perfect mouth slips into a mirthless smile. "My dad's a modern literature professor at Vanderbilt. Hadley was the name of Hemingway's first wife, which, if you knew my dad, is really ironic—" She stops and lowers her lashes, her face flushing red. "Um. He's a Hemingway fan."

"Right," Mom says slowly. "Well. I need to take care of some things upstairs." She cuts her eyes to me, slicing deep. "Nice meeting you." And she's up the stairs, two at a time in her heels.

"You too," Hadley says, a little divot digging between her brows. "Is she okay?"

"Yeah. She's just tired, like I said." I stuff my hands in my pockets. I feel like a complete asshole. But what did I expect? I set out to use this girl as a human cannonball and fire her at my mother.

And that's exactly what I did.

"Look, I'll see you tomorrow, all right?"

"Yeah."

She doesn't move, and when I glance up, her eyes are on me, all darkness and questions.

"Are *you* okay?" she asks.

I blow out a long breath. Inhale again. It's still not enough. I need a sky's worth of air. And then another and another.

"I'm good." I smile. She smiles back, but it's closed-mouthed and sideways. I don't think I've convinced her. "It's been a long week, with the move and all."

"Sure. I guess we can talk soon about when to meet again?

And we should probably watch the movie, too, just to see the play performed."

"Great."

"Thanks for the cake."

I nod and watch her walk to her car. Watch her climb in and drive away until she's just a little speck of silver among all the reddening maples. She's long gone before I remember she left still wearing the apron.

When I finally close the door and turn around, Mom's already at the bottom of the stairs. Her eyes are rimmed red, but her expression is ten degrees of pissed off.

"What is that girl's last name?" she asks before I can side-step her.

I look down at my Vans. My favorite pair. Too small for me now, really. The toes are ragged from when Dad and I used to work on my changeup at the park. That was almost a year ago, before everything went to crap.

"Samuel. What is her last name?"

I look up at her and shrug. "Why do you want to know?"

"I think you know the answer to that."

I smirk at her. I can't help it. I know I'm the asshole here, but I wouldn't even be in this position if it weren't for her. None of us would. "Then I think you know what her last name is."

She sinks down on the step, deflated. "Oh my God. Oh my God, they live here?"

"Apparently."

"I didn't know . . . I swear I didn't know." Her eyes widen. "Does Olivia know?"

"Not yet. But I'm going to tell her because she'll find out eventually. Hadley goes to our school and she's . . . pretty well known." Her locker flashes in my mind. I still haven't asked her or Josh about that whole mess. I'm not sure I want to know.

"She doesn't know who you are?"

"I don't think so." I have no idea which St. Clair found the papers on their front door. All I know is what happened before, in our house in Nashville on a rainy afternoon. All I know is that afterward, my mother took a phone call and fell apart to the point that she stopped eating for a few days, Dad moved into the spare room, and Livy slept on the floor of my room for the next three weeks.

"Are you going to tell her?" Mom asks.

"No, I'm not." I wasn't sure about this until the words were already out of my mouth, but it feels like the right decision. What would be the point? She clearly has no idea who we are and I don't need a Ph.D. in psychology to figure out that she's still dealing with the repercussions of all this crap. I guess we are too. I can be civil with her, finish this project, and then pretend she doesn't exist. Easy. "But for her sake, and Livy's, not yours."

Mom frowns and opens her mouth, but snaps it shut without speaking. Then, after the awkwardness has taken up most of the oxygen in the room, she says, "Why did you bring her here?"

"We're in the same English class. We have a project."

She shakes her head, balls her hands in her skirt. "That's not why you brought her here, Sam. And you know it."

"Look . . ." I know I should apologize. The words are right there, waiting to come out of my mouth, but I stuff them back in. "I need to get the bread in the oven for dinner. Livy'll be home soon."

I walk into the kitchen, leaving my mother alone. As I adjust the temperature on the oven and listen to Mom as she finally trudges up the stairs, I think about what Hadley said about wanting something you don't even believe is possible. I wonder now whether she was really talking about a happy ending or whether she was just talking about the kind of life where you don't have to fight so hard to feel at home with your own family.

CHAPTER NINE

Hadley

"I'm telling you, it was just weird," I tell Kat after we slide into a booth at Wasabi's and order Diet Cokes.

"Weird how? Creepy weird? Uncomfortable weird?"

"I don't know. Just weird. Like she was scared of me or something. And Sam . . . God. He's . . . I don't know." I huff in frustration, tapping the floppy plastic menu on my forehead. I haven't really talked to Sam since leaving his house two days ago. During English, we've locked eyes about a jillion times, tossed each other little smiles that held the promise of a future conversation, but when the bell rang at the end of class, he bolted out of the classroom.

Kat grins a little. "I've never heard you call an encounter with a guy *weird* before. And you didn't even kiss this one."

I roll my eyes at her. I told her about what happened at Sam's—the intense looks and the cooking and his mom—and all Kat can focus on is that I didn't make out with him. I can't decide if I'm insulted or amused.

"I don't think he even wanted to hook up. I was pretty much sitting in his lap and he barely blinked." I can feel my face turn crimson just thinking about it.

"Well, only the truly brave can resist the charms of Hadley St. Clair."

"Then he's William Wallace."

Kat's eyes widen. "Did you actually climb into his lap?"

"No! God, Kat. Seriously?"

"Well, I don't know. Seems like something you might do."

My mouth drops open and she has the decency to look at least moderately embarrassed. I sip on my soda, chewing on the straw until it's nearly shredded.

"So, when is your dad getting here?" Kat asks.

I sigh, relieved to move on from talking about boys. "With any luck, late enough that the kitchen says, 'Oops. Sorry. We're closed.'"

She throws me a weak smile. Dad and I go out for sushi together on Thursday nights. Alone. Kat knows how much I dread it every week. This little tradition was not my idea. It's yet another part of his therapy homework that's infringing on my life. Tonight he called from work to tell me he'd be a few minutes late and would meet me at the restaurant. I immediately finagled

Kat into coming with me. She loves my dad and was nearly as heartbroken as I was when she found out about his affair, but since she breaks out in hives at the thought of even frowning at an adult, she can chat him up over miso soup a whole lot easier than I can.

"Hadley, be nice. The last time I came here with you two, it was so awkward, I hid in the bathroom for half the meal."

"It's not my fault the man can't stop talking about how *amazing* it will be if I go to Vanderbilt and become a renowned *woman of words.*"

Before Kat can say anything else, the man himself shows up. I get out and let him into the booth so I can sit on the outside. I can't stand to be wedged between him and a soy sauce–stained wall.

"How fare my two favorite girls?" Dad asks as he sits down. His aftershave and that warm car smell waft up my nose. "I'm glad you're joining us, Katherine."

"Thanks for letting me come, Mr. St. Clair," Kat says, and I stick out my tongue. She kicks me under the table.

"You're always welcome." Dad turns to me and smiles. "Hi, sweetheart."

"Hi."

After a few minutes of silent menu perusing, the server—a guy named Niko with indecipherable tattoos running laps up his arms—comes over to take our order. I list the maki rolls I want while Dad orders nigiri, the kind of sushi that's just a big blob of raw fish over rice. Ugh. I prefer my barely dead seafood hidden in avocado and cream cheese. Kat, true to her two-year-old commitment to fleshless eating, orders vegetable rolls and a salad with that yummy ginger dressing.

Kat and Dad chat about school while I grunt acknowledgments and add "Uh-huh" and "It's a hard class" every now and then.

When our food comes, Dad launches into a new topic. "So, Kat, how would you like to help us with a kite for the festival this coming spring?"

My stomach balls up like a piece of discarded paper. "Dad. Let's not do this here. Please?"

"Do what?"

"I already told you I don't want to do the festival. Kat doesn't want to either."

"Sure I do," Kat the Betrayer says. "I loved it when you guys used to make those things." She pops a huge piece of rice and avocado into her mouth. "You'd really let me help?"

"Of course," Dad says. I know he's only offering because he thinks if he can rope Kat into it, I'll follow suit.

"Kat, you don't have to," I say, desperately trying to communicate with my eyebrows.

"I know that. I want to. I've always wanted to make a kite and learn how to fly it. It sounds fun."

"It is." Dad's eyes are alight. "It's beautiful. When she was little, Hadley didn't even care about trying to fly our kite. She'd just lie in the grass, watching all those colors dancing in the sky." He nudges me with an elbow. "It'll be fun, Had."

"No, it won't. It'll be pointless and depressing and I don't want to do it."

Dad leans away from me and sighs. He sets his chopsticks on his plate and wipes his mouth with his napkin. "If you ladies will excuse me for a moment."

I get up and let him out, careful not meet his eyes. I sit back down and start lining up my remaining rolls by size.

Once Dad disappears into the bathroom, Kat leans forward, whisper-yelling. "God, Hadley. Will you ease up?"

"What?"

"You're doing it again. I'd rather be getting a cavity filled right now."

"What am I doing?"

"You seriously don't realize how bitchy you're being? It's just a stupid kite festival."

"I'm not trying to be a bitch," I say, and it's the truth. When it comes to my dad trying to bond with me, there's a lot I can put up with. It's not hard to fake my way through a meal or a movie or a poetry reading. But the Kite Festival is different. It's my childhood. It's his strong hand over mine on the tail of a kite. It's Dad and me hunkered over a kite in the making, night after night, agonizing over every little detail. I can't just go back to that place. Once something breaks, you can never put it back together like it was. There will always be cracks and glue stains and uneven surfaces.

"Could've fooled me," Kat says, pulling soda through her straw.

"I'm not. I just don't like pretending to feel something I don't."

She nods, but her expression remains hard. "I get it. Just don't invite me to dinner next time, all right?"

I rub my eyes, confused about how this whole meal suddenly turned into an issue between me and Kat. She's supposed to be here supporting me, making it easier, not ganging up on me and pointing out everything I'm doing wrong.

"Hadley," Kat whispers. Her eyes are wide on something over my shoulder as the door's bell dings, signaling a new patron. "Isn't that Sam Bennett?"

I turn and see him. He's wearing a worn black sweater, jeans, and flip-flops, even though it's cool out. A girl is with him. She has his same wavy blond hair, but is sporting a streak of purple in the front. She's pretty, her delicate features contrasting sharply with her tight black jeans and gauzy black shirt and black boots. They lean on the front counter and look over a menu while the redheaded, lip-glossed hostess looks over Sam.

"Yeah, it is. I think that's his sister."

Dad comes back and slides in next to Kat. "You girls about ready?"

"Sure," Kat says, but I can't get my eyes off Sam. He turns around and our gazes touch. Sam starts to smile, but looks around our table and stops himself. His eyes darken and narrow on Kat or my dad or maybe me. I can't tell. Then he barely nods his chin at me and turns back around.

Dad gets the check and slaps his credit card down while Kat tries to give him money. They argue back and forth while Sam props his arm on the girl's shoulder and says something to her. She eyes our table and nods. Then they leave the restaurant without another glance in our direction.

"I'll be right back." Before I know what I'm doing, I'm following them out the door, my heart knocking against my ribs. "Sam!" I call when I see them next to a navy Honda Civic. He turns and holds a hand to his forehead, blocking a sliver of the setting sun breaking through the thick gray clouds.

I cross the lot and meet him at his car. "Hey," he says, stuffing his hand in his pockets.

"Hey." I fold my hands and run my thumb along my palm. "Why did you leave? It's a really great sushi place."

"Um. Yeah, we just decided we wanted something else." He looks to his sister for confirmation and she nods. "Sorry I didn't say hey. You were with your family."

I wave a hand. "It's fine. It's just my dad and my friend Kat."

He nods and scratches his forehead. "Oh. This is my sister, Livy." He puts a hand on her back. "Livy, this is Hadley, the girl I was telling you about."

He told her about me? He seems to realize how this sounds, because he quickly amends his statement. "The girl I have that project with."

Livy nods and smiles, but it's all wrong on her face.

"Hi," I say. "Nice to meet you."

"You too." She looks down at the pavement, scuffing her boots over the concrete.

Sam squeezes her shoulder. The movement is light and easy, like it's a reflex. "Well, we need to get dinner. My mom's waiting."

"Oh. Yeah, I need to get back. I just wanted to say hi, I guess."

"I'll see you tomorrow."

I nod and head back to the restaurant before he can see how red my face is.

"Hadley," he calls, and I turn around. He looks at me for a minute, the fading sun spilling gold into his hair. "Thanks for saying hey."

"Sure." The clouds glaze over the sky again as he gets into his car and drives away.

I'm still watching his car, wondering why I felt so compelled to chase him into the parking lot just to say hello, when I feel my dad next to me.

"Who was that?" he asks. He stares after Sam's car, his brows cinched in the middle.

I blow out a breath. "You know, I'm not really sure."

"Huh." He digs his car keys out of his pocket, still watching Sam's car stopped at a red light. "Well, I'll see you at home, sweetheart."

"Okay. Thanks for dinner," I say without looking at him, relieved he didn't ask for more details. I head toward Kat's car.

"Did you talk to him?" she asks as we climb in.

"If you'd even call it that."

"What does that mean?"

"I don't know. He acted weird. And his sister acted weird."

"There's that word again." She starts the car and adjusts her rearview mirror. I slide her huge CD case out of her glove box.

"Would you prefer *strange*? How about *odd*? *Abnormal*? *Eldritch*?"

"*Eldritch*? That can't be a real word."

"It means weird. Actually it means an eerie kind of weird, but it could still work."

"When is the SAT again?"

"December seventeenth."

"Not soon enough." She slides her hand down through the air in front of me. "I'm ready to trade in this dictionary for a real best friend."

I laugh and she slaps my hand away from the CDs. "Would you stop?" she says.

"What? I'm looking for that new Florence and the Machine."

"And alphabetizing."

"If you'd get an iPod or put music on your phone, we wouldn't have this issue."

"I like the liner notes."

"You know you can download most of those, right?"

She rolls her eyes as she stops at a red light. "So if Sam's weird and keeps acting weird and his mom's weird and his sister's weird, why did you run after him?"

Rain starts to plink onto the windshield. I slide the CD in the

101

player and watch the stoplight turn green, a drippy neon glow through the shower. I don't really have an answer to Kat's question. Because no matter how weird Sam Bennett might seem, there's something about him that I don't want to stay away from. I don't even know *what* that something is. And that scares me more than any kite festival.

CHAPTER TEN

Sam

I slide into the car with a bag full of tacos from a place called Cactus Caliente. Livy stares out the window as the greasy, cheesy smell stinks up the space between us. She's pale and slack-jawed, just like she was when I told her about Hadley two days ago. She had sat on her bed and blinked at me so many times, I thought her eyelashes were going to fall off. Then she pulled her chemistry book into her lap and started balancing equations, her knuckles white on her pencil, and that's the last time we talked about it. If you'd even call that talking.

My own hands are still shaking a little from seeing the back of Jason St. Clair's dark head, just sitting there in a restaurant. Like the man actually breathes and eats and shits like a normal human. And Hadley across from him, her eyes on me, waiting for me to do something, anything but leave like I did. Before that moment, a little part of me still hoped I was wrong. Hadley St.

Clair wasn't *his* daughter. But seeing them both together like that, sucking up the same air, felt like a punch in the gut from my best friend or something.

Livy wipes her cheek. Black smears over her face. "She's pretty."

I laugh through my nose. Hadley *would* be the one Livy's worried about. "Yeah. I guess she is."

"She seems nice."

I put my hand on top of Livy's head. "She is nice. It's not her fault, you know."

She pushes my hand away. "I know. That just makes the whole thing that much more horrible."

"Livy—"

"I don't ever want her to know, Sam." She angles toward me, her blue eyes huge and shiny. "Ever. Please . . . not . . ."

I feel a jolt as her words fall away and her breath stutters and wheezes. Her face drains to white and she clutches at her chest.

"Shit. Livy. Where's your inhaler?"

She points to her huge black canvas bag on the floorboard at her feet. I dig through a sea of crap, heart in my fingertips, and finally get a lock on the inhaler. She grips my wrist while I hold it up to her lips and she gulps the medicine. After three more draws and a few minutes that feel like hours, the wheezing fades into empty-space breathing — clear air.

"Jesus," I mutter, sliding a hand down my face.

"*Please, Sam.*"

"She won't know, I promise. All right? Just breathe."

"I'm sorry," she says, still raspy.

"Hey, don't do that, come on. We promised each other we wouldn't do that anymore, remember?"

She nods, and swipes at her eyes again.

"Good. Now buckle up and tell me about this photography project you have to do."

She heaves some air and gives me a small smile. My chest loosens a little. "Well," she says slowly, still getting her breath back as I start the car. "Mr. Grayson says we can choose any subject we want, but the theme has to be about hope."

"So you have to take pictures of candles burning in chapels or something cheesy like that?"

She laughs weakly. "Not necessarily. It might be a series of shots of a Coke can. I just have to be able to capture how my subject might communicate hope. To me. You know, like, interpretation."

"Sounds cool."

"Yeah. Except I have no idea what to choose . . ." She turns toward the window again. In her reflection, I see her eyes are vacant again, staring. "What gives me hope? I mean, real hope, not just some bubbly, temporary fix?"

It starts raining as I turn onto our street. I think of Mom and Livy. I think of that rainy afternoon and the notes and Dad's face the morning he left for Boston. I think of Hadley and the way she looked sitting in my kitchen, wearing my apron, talking about being lonely.

"I wish I knew, Livy."

The next morning, Ajay's voice clips in my ear like gunshots. "Wow. That's. Sam. Just. Wow."

"Thanks for that analysis," I say into my phone as I wave goodbye to Livy at her locker. I hurry down the main hallway, which is clearing rapidly. Before we left for school, Mom freaked out about the length of Livy's skirt and told her that her eye makeup made her look like a raccoon with a hangover. Unsurprisingly, this led to a volcanic argument. Then Ajay called while we were driving. By the time we fought through the morning traffic and I'd filled Ajay in on the soap opera that is my life, I'm almost late.

The final bell rings as Ajay fires off another stuttering round, and I slow my walk. I'm already late, might as well enjoy Ajay's rare inability to form coherent sentences.

"And she has no idea who you are?" Ajay asks. I hear the buzz of an electric saw in the background. I'm not even going to ask.

"Nope."

"Is she beautiful?" I laugh as I round the corner toward my locker. Ajay's always saying stuff like this. He sees a girl he likes and it's never "Damn!" or "She's hot." It's "She's beautiful." But I can't really give him shit about it. I'm the guy who thought a glowing halo surrounded Hadley's head the first time I saw her.

"Yeah, Age. She is."

"Is she smart?"

I make a frustrated sound through my nose. "Can we talk about something else? What's up with you?" I get to my locker and throw my stuff in.

"Sara and I finally copulated."

"Jesus. Do you have to call it that?" I get out my calc book, swallowing my laugh. "How old are you, forty-five?"

"What? You know I don't like saying 'We had sex' or 'We screwed.' I feel like a Neanderthal and it sounds dirty. 'Making love' sounds like I'm a character in one of those abysmal Hallmark movies that my mom loves."

"Well, 'copulated' sounds like a science experiment."

"How about 'had intercourse'?"

"Maybe. If your name is Dolores and you're teaching Sex Ed."

Ajay laughs. "Anyway, *it* happened and now she's acting strange."

"Strange as in clingy or strange as in you're an asshole?"

"The latter, but I have no idea why. She's the one who planned out the whole night."

Sara, Ajay's girlfriend of a year, suffers from a perpetually bad mood. She's usually pretty cool with me, but she's one of those girls who always seem to have their claws out for one reason or another. One time she laid into Ajay for fifteen minutes about how loudly he swallowed water, for Christ's sake.

"Maybe it's because you use words like 'copulated,'" I say.

"Okay, okay. Point taken." The sawing sound cuts off, followed by an electric drill, probably mine. "By the way, Sara said Nicole's been asking about you. Why haven't you called her?"

My stomach twists and I start down the hall again toward class. A teacher passes me and motions for me to get off my phone. I shoot her a thumbs-up and keep walking.

Nicole Gilbert. My non-girlfriend from right before all the shit hit the proverbial fan. We were never officially together, but I learned how to utilize a condom with her. Several times. All through this past spring of yelling followed by days of silence and my dad finally leaving. Ajay would call her my copulate-buddy. When we found out I was moving to Atlanta, she didn't seem all that upset about it. We texted for a while, but it eventually faded out.

"I don't know, Age. I haven't seen her in months. It's not like we had a deep, meaningful relationship." Okay, we did, but just with our bodies. Her body got me through a very shitty time. And that makes me an asshole, I know. "She can call me if she wants."

He sighs loudly, crackling the phone line. "Whatever you say."

"Listen, I need to get to class." I stop outside my homeroom and look around. "Maybe we can hang out this weekend or . . ." My mind goes blank as my eyes land on a collection of . . . What the hell is that? There's a pile of stuff on the ground in front of a locker down the hall. Hadley's locker. And she's standing in front of it, hugging her books to her chest.

"Sure," Ajay says. "You should come here and we can—"

"Oh, hell." I step closer and see one of those tall glass candles with Jesus Christ or some saint on the front on the tile floor. It's actually lit, the colors illuminated like a stained-glass window. Surrounding the candle are unwrapped condoms and several pairs of pink and purple thongs, a pair of handcuffs, a black whip, a freaking dildo, and five or six phallically shaped drinking straws. It's like an X-rated version of one of those memorials you see on the side of the road at the site of some fatal crash.

"Sam? What's wrong?"

"I gotta go," I whisper into the phone, and end the call.

Hadley lifts her head and turns, her gaze meeting mine. Her mouth drops open and a flush floods into her cheeks. She squeezes her eyes shut and looks away.

I turn abruptly and head in the opposite direction.

I find a janitor's closet and wade through mop buckets and bottles of Windex and Drano until I find a garbage bag. I walk back to her locker. She's still there, glued in place, eyes blurry on the flickering flame. I kneel down, blow out the candle, and start shoving stuff into the garbage bag.

"Oh, God. Sam. No, please." Hadley's voice cracks a little, but I keep cleaning up the mess. "Sam, stop." She kneels down and pulls at my arm. "Don't."

I stop and meet her eyes. They're so dark, I can't tell where the color ends and the pupil begins. They're also red and wet. "You want to leave all this crap here?"

She flinches and removes her hand. "No. But . . . you don't have to do this. Please . . . it's fine. I'll do it."

I shake my head at her and keep stuffing. The candle is the last thing in and I throw it inside, spilling red wax onto a thong.

She stands up and turns away from me, wiping at her eyes with the back of her hand.

I tie off the bag and get up. "Come on."

She turns and frowns. "Where?"

"Just come on." I take her elbow and she walks with me down the hall toward the nearest exit. She digs in her heels when we get to the doors.

"I can't leave."

"Why?"

She juts a thumb behind her. "I have class. I have work to do."

"Do you really want to go to class right now?" I heft the bag up on my shoulder. "If you do, fine. I'll throw this stuff away and we'll both go on with our day. But it looks like you could use a break."

"If I leave, she'll know this bothers me."

"Not necessarily. But if you walk around the halls looking like your kitten just got run over by a truck, then yeah, whoever 'she' is will know you're a little bit bothered."

She swipes under her puffy eyes. "Is that what I look like?"

"Yeah." I pinch the air between my thumb and forefinger. "Just a tad."

Her hands whiten over her books and she presses her teeth over her lower lip. I can almost see her mind running through her calendar, all the assignments she has due, all the makeup work she'll be responsible for. I should just toss the junk in the garbage and walk with her to her class, go to my own, forget this whole thing. But I don't want to do that. I want to know why some bitch is terrorizing her locker. I want her to come with me and I want her eyes on mine and her words to fill up the space in my car. There are a million voices in my head right now, screaming about what a delusional idiot I am, but with her standing in front of me, her lashes fanning her pink cheeks, they're easy to ignore.

I watch her square her shoulders and take a deep breath. I gulp down my own shaky little-boy breath, because I know I'm about to get exactly what I want.

"Let's go," she says, and walks past me out the door.

CHAPTER ELEVEN

Even before the sex-toy locker incident, the morning sucked. I woke up to the sound of vacuuming downstairs. Loud, clumsy vacuuming. I sat up and winced as the appliance banged and whacked into walls and doorways. Mom's usually an early riser, but cleaning before the sun came up seemed like a little much. I hauled myself out of bed, showered, and dressed. By the time I got downstairs, the vacuum was still running, but it was lying on its side in the family room, *vroom-vroom*ing while it attempted to suck up any errant dust particles from the air. Through the kitchen archway, I could see my parents sitting at the table, sipping coffee and buttering toast like this was completely normal.

"What's going on?" I yelled over the noise.

"What?" Dad yelled back.

I pointed to the vacuum. He shook his head and brought his cup and bowl to the sink. "She won't let me turn it off."

"Mom?"

"Of course your mother."

I glanced at Mom, already dressed in a gray pencil skirt and a light pink silk blouse for work. She was perfectly postured and coiffed, her mouth a tight knot.

"Why not?" I ask Dad, even though I was pretty sure I knew the answer. Dad's weekday mornings bordered on sacred and consisted of a steady diet of strong coffee and a bowl of granola, a newspaper, and *quiet.* In fact, both of my parents usually started their mornings this way, easing into the day the way one would start a long-distance run.

"Hell if I know, Had." He scratched his chin and stared out the window for a few seconds, eyes glazing on the coloring leaves outside. He looked so lost, I almost reached out to squeeze his hand the way I would've done just a few months ago. A left-over reflex from a different life.

"I'm going to work a little early," he said while I cemented myself in place. "Have a good day, honey. Maybe we can watch a movie tonight?"

I said nothing and he seemed to settle for my one-shouldered shrug. Without another glance at Mom, he picked up his work bag and left through the garage. As soon as Dad was gone, Mom stood and glided over to the vacuum. She flicked the power switch, filling the room with a ringing silence. I watched her slide a piece of bread into the toaster, presumably for me, and then go about cleaning up crumbs and drops of spilled almond milk.

"Mom?"

"Mm?"

"What was that about?"

"What?"

"The vacuum? Dad?"

"Oh." She waved a dismissive hand. "Nothing." She wiped up a sprinkle of coffee grounds from the counter. "I might be late tonight."

"Again?"

"A new client needs some coddling." Buttering my toast, she flicked her gaze up to mine and back down. "Why? Do you need me at home?"

Her question sounded benign enough, but impatience edged her voice, like my potential *need* was an inconvenience. Over the past few months, she felt more and more like a house-mate than a mom. Just someone who occasionally joined us for meals and helped out around the house from time to time, but who had very little interest in my comings and goings. It bothered me how much I wanted her to *want* to be at home, even though I could barely stand to be here myself.

"No," I said. "No, it's fine."

"Hadley..." We stared at each other, and her mouth twitched, as if it was full of words that wanted out but were trapped somehow. Finally, she settled for a weak smile and a "Have a good day" before gathering her things and heading off to work.

By the time I choked down my breakfast and got my stuff together, I was still so flustered by the whole morning that I was running late. At school, the late bell rang right as I walked inside, and I picked up my pace. I passed Sam Bennett laughing into his phone, but he didn't see me and I didn't slow down. I hated being late, and now the knot in my stomach that started with the vacuum had turned into a colossal tangle of worry and anger and irritation.

When I rounded the corner into the hall where my locker was located, I stopped abruptly. My boots squeaked on the shiny floor and I heard myself gasp. In front of my locker, Sloane Waters sparked a lighter and dipped it into a tall, glassed-in candle. I looked around for a teacher, anyone, but the hall was empty. She fiddled with some things on the ground that I couldn't make out, a satisfied grin on her face. Then she rose and took off down the hall, red hair flapping behind her.

As I walked to my locker, all I could do was stare at that candle's little orange flame. Tears welled up and spilled over on my cheeks before I could stop them.

Then Sam was there, looking at me with this horrified expression on his face, and all I wanted to do was dissolve into the floor and disappear.

Now, as I slide into Sam's car, embarrassment still warms my cheeks. I flip down the sun visor and inspect myself in the tiny mirror. I clean off the smeared mascara while Sam throws the trash bag into his back seat. His car is a mess. Empty soda bottles and books and balled-up papers cover the floor, mixed in with at least five baseballs, two gloves, and a mesh bag full of cleats and jerseys.

"So, I didn't have breakfast this morning," Sam says as soon he gets in and starts the car. "Are you up for some food?"

I buckle my seat belt slowly and look at him. He scans his iPod lazily, seemingly unbothered that he could open up a sex shop out of the back of his car right now. "Yeah, I guess."

"Any good local places?" He presses play on his iPod and a moody song blasts out of the speakers, all guitars and violins.

"Um. There's a coffee shop called the Green-Eyed Girl that has really good scones."

"Sounds great. Where is it?"

"On Church."

He smiles and pulls out of the lot. I take a deep breath as the school fades behind us. It's just one day. And Sam's right. I'm in no mood to sit through classes and try to pull myself together enough to act like nothing is wrong. Plus, Kat would see right through it and flutter around me like a mother bird.

We don't talk again until we're settled at a corner table, lattes and pumpkin scones steaming on thick glazed plates in front of us. The Green-Eyed Girl is one of my favorite places in downtown Woodmont. It's small and cozy, with rugged wooden tables, mismatched chairs, and local art on the light green walls. And it always smells like cinnamon and butter and coffee.

"Those are really cool," Sam says. He points to the space behind us. Six or seven photos of the human eye hang on the wall. They're all black and white except for a little splash of green. On one it's the iris, on another the pupil, another the lashes, and on one green is slicked under the eye like a bruise.

"Yeah, I think the owner did those." I watch Sam as he chews and soaks in the photos. "Suzanne. She used to be a photographer and named the shop after that series."

"I need to bring my sister here."

"Does she like coffee?"

He shrugs. "She's more a tea girl, but she's getting into photography lately."

"Kat loves the chai tea latte here."

"She's your best friend, right? I think I have a class with her."

I nod. "Government." I immediately blush—again—and

take a too-large bite of my scone. Sam just grins and sips his coffee, graciously saying nothing about how I seem to know his class schedule.

We talk about stupid stuff — schoolwork and our project and his compulsory need to always have music playing, my job teaching swimming at the Y. He tells me that his sister loves swimming and how he used to be terrified of water because he fell off the dock at Radnor Lake when he was four. I keep waiting for him to bring up the locker, but he remains infuriatingly quiet on the subject. I just want it over with. It feels like a giant elephant is standing on the table and I have to look around it to see him clearly. Finally, I snap.

"Aren't you going to ask me about this morning?"

He cocks his head to one side and lays his fingers on the rim of his mug. "I figured that if you wanted to talk about it, you would."

"Aren't you curious?"

"Curiosity doesn't mean it's any of my business."

"You made it your business when you rode over on your white horse and threw everything away."

He frowns and leans forward, his blue eyes narrowed. A shimmery ring of gold encircles his pupils. "Okay. I'm sorry. You're right, I shouldn't have taken charge like that, but I could tell you were upset and I was trying to help."

"Don't be sorry. I appreciate it. It's just . . ." I press my fingers to my face, trying to push back the creeping flush. "It was embarrassing."

"I didn't mean to embarrass you."

I glance up and meet his eyes. "I know that."

"It's not like that stuff is yours." His lips spread into a mischievous smile, both eyebrows popped into his messy hair. "Wait. *Is* that stuff yours?"

"What? No!"

He laughs and nudges my arm with his and I find myself laughing too. A few minutes ago, after the vacuum and the penile paraphernalia, I didn't think my mouth could bend itself into a smile, much less emit a laugh.

"Seriously," he says as he finishes off his scone. "If you want to tell me, I'll listen, but I won't ask."

I grab the container that holds the sugar packets and start separating them. Sweet'n Low, Equal, Splenda, raw sugar. "It's not a big deal."

"Which usually means that it is."

I smile a little at that as I slide a pink packet in with its mates. Then I start on the blue and let my words spill out quickly. "I messed around with Josh at a party and he was dating Jenny Kalinski. She found out and her friend Sloane is the one putting all that stuff on my locker."

He sits back. "Ah. And I'm guessing from the way that you've been dicing Josh into little pieces with your eyes all week that you didn't know he had a girlfriend."

I shake my head.

"So it's not your fault."

"I shouldn't have believed him. I thought he was a decent guy."

"But he's the one who lied." His tone raises a little, something sharp edging his usually smooth voice.

"I know, but . . . I still hurt someone. You wouldn't understand." I stuff the last brown packet into the container. "The whole thing just made me feel cheap. It made me feel no better than that woman who—" I stop myself just in time, biting on my lip so hard, tears sting my eyes. Sam remains silent, and when I look up at him, his jaw is clenched, a muscle jumping near his temple. His fingers are bloodless on his cup.

"It's Josh's fault too," he says, his voice gravelly. "You weren't the only one who made a bad decision. The guy lied, probably talked you into it—"

"He didn't—"

"And he was probably using you to fill up some pathetic midlife crisis hole and didn't give a damn who he hurt."

I sit back in my chair and stare at him. His eyes are a little hazy and I don't know what to say. It's nice he's defending me, but it feels like something else is going on.

"Midlife crisis?" I question, grinning a little in an effort to lighten the mood.

He presses his eyes closed, shaking his head. "You know what I mean." Then a ghost of a smile drifts over his mouth. "A quarter-life crisis, then."

I smile, relieved to see him do the same.

He clears his throat and focuses on a toddler at the next table who's shredding his napkin, forming a pile of papery snow on the table. After a few seconds, he asks, "So, do you like Josh?"

I almost laugh. "Josh? Um. No."

"So why did you hook up with him?"

I blow out a breath, disturbing a strand of hair so it grazes my cheek.

"Were you drunk?" Sam asks when I remain silent.

"No. I don't drink."

He hands me a Splenda and I stick the little yellow packet in with the others. "Why not?" he asks.

"I just don't. I don't like how I feel when I do. I hate that loose my-head-is-floating-three-feet-above-my-body sensation. It makes me feel like I need to heave into a paper bag."

"Okay. So why Josh?"

I press my fingertips to my thumb until they whiten,

remembering Josh's breath on my skin, the way he temporarily unsnarled the mess in my head. "Why does a girl need to be either madly in love or drunk to kiss a guy?"

He frowns, his forehead creased in thought like he's pondering black holes. "Um. She doesn't."

"That's right. She doesn't, and I was neither. Josh was there. He was nice. He was a distraction, all right? That's it."

"A distraction."

"Yes." I pull on the ends of my hair, working my fingers through a tangle.

"From what?"

I continue to detangle my hair, stalling from giving an answer because I don't have one. Kat's asked me the same question a million times, and I don't have an answer for her, either.

"Do you want to talk about something else?" Sam asks.

"God, yes." I let a nervous laugh slip from my throat.

He leans back lazily, propping his ankle on his knee. "Enough of this heavy shit. Tell me something about you I would never guess."

"Something you'd never guess?"

"Yeah, like a funny quirk or a weird phobia or obsession. Although I already know you have a compulsion toward organization."

"I do not."

He holds up the color-coordinated sugar container. "Would you like to ask Suzanne for a job?"

I laugh and yank the container out of his hands. "All right. But you first. Tell me something unexpected about you."

He smiles and taps his chin in thought before jutting his forefinger into the air. "I'm afraid of spiders."

"Wrong. So am I. So is half the world. Try again."

"Damn, you're bossy."

"Come on, Baker Boy, quit stalling."

He laughs, then purses his lips while he thinks for while. In the café, the breakfast crowd thins out as the sun lifts higher into the sky. Finally, a small smile cuts into his cheeks and he drops his eyes. He looks almost shy.

"All right, here's something. The only people who know this are Livy and my friend Ajay, and he's weird enough that he doesn't judge me."

"I'm intrigued."

He draws a breath and presses his fingertips together. "Last year, we read *Romeo and Juliet* in my English class. It wasn't the first time I had read it, but for some reason I became obsessed with it. This past summer, I watched every film version a million times and I dragged Livy to any live performance I could find."

"That's it? A lot of people like Shakespeare."

He shakes his head. "I even drove down to this rinky-dink

town in south Georgia from Atlanta and back in one night to see a production—if you could even call it that—at some po-dunk theater that served beer and peanuts. It was the *only* thing I read for four months. When I finished it, I'd just flip back to the beginning and start again. I can quote the whole thing from memory. I'm okay with admitting I took it to an unhealthy level."

"Why did you love it so much? Don't tell me you're a sappy romantic."

He smiles grimly. "It wasn't the romance. I know that's what it's about for most people, but not for me. And I'm sorry, but that play is anything but romantic."

"Then what?"

He props his elbows on the table, his gaze turned inward. "It sounds stupid, but I think it was just about how sad it was. It was comforting. My parents were going through all this shit right when we studied the play and . . . I don't know. It made me feel less alone. Like if two people who loved each other that much still managed to fuck everything up, then maybe the way my parents destroyed each other wasn't so bad. It was like this weird sort of hope in reverse."

"You liked that there are no happy endings. For anyone."

He shrugs. "I guess I'm better suited for Shakespeare's trag-edies." He smiles, but it doesn't reach his eyes. "I got over it."

Looking at him now, I'm pretty sure he's not over it. Not even close. I want to ask him what happened with his parents, but if he's anything like me, that question is more unpleasant than a stomach virus. So I swallow my curiosity.

"Sorry," he says, pulling on his ear. "I didn't mean to get so morose. I should've just told you that I still sleep with the stuffed duck I had as a kid."

I laugh. "Do you?"

He shrugs as he studies my face. "Okay, your turn."

I shift in my seat, not sure I have anything interesting to tell that I'm willing to part with. "There's nothing unexpected about me."

He leans forward and gives me a lopsided grin. "Everything about you is unexpected."

He holds my gaze, locking me in place. I'm relieved when he finally slides his eyes away and clears his throat, but I keep watching him, half hoping he'll press me for an answer.

"Do you want to go back to school?" he asks.

Without hesitation, I shake my head. I may barely remember my own name right now, but I know I don't want to go back to school. "No. Can we . . ." My gaze drifts to a server writing lunch specials on a chalkboard. I look back at Sam, his expression curious. "Can we go to your house and hang out? Watch a movie or something?" The words fall from my mouth like rain—I felt them coming, smelled them in the air, but there was nothing I could do to stop them.

Sam's mouth drops open a little. "You want to go back to my house?"

"Is that all right?" I swallow as I wait for his reply. I'm not even sure what I want it to be. I'm just about to revoke my request when his brows dip into his eyes and he answers.

"Yeah. Sure. Why not?" He stands so quickly, his chair cracks onto the floor, scaring the toddler into spilling his paper snow on the ground. "Crap," Sam mutters, and runs a hand down his face. The toddler starts wailing and Sam bends to pick up the chair and the paper. "It's okay, little man."

I kneel to help him, accepting a thank-you from the boy's harried-looking mother. When we finish, I edge Sam's hard stomach with my elbow, trying to play off his sudden nervousness. "Don't get any ideas, Sam Bennett. I just want to hang out."

Pink splashes over his cheekbones as he throws up his hands in surrender. He smiles that lopsided grin. "I wouldn't dream of getting any ideas."

CHAPTER TWELVE

Sam

Okay, I would dream of getting ideas. In fact, I've dreamed up several ideas in the past week since I've met Hadley St. Clair, and none of them are of the PG-13-rated variety. It's not like I haven't heard that she's fooled around with a few guys in school, but what that entails exactly, I don't know, nor do I want to. It's none of my business, right? This girl is beyond off-limits, but suddenly the whole idea of her with Josh—or any other douchebag—makes the back of my neck itch.

As I drive Hadley to my house, I start really brooding over the whole thing. Josh has never mentioned specifics about him and Hadley, but I'm almost positive Jenny is the cheerleader he's been mooning over during lunch all week. If he liked her so damn much, why the hell did he mess around with Hadley? And why the hell do I care?

We pull into my driveway, and Hadley jumps in her seat as I

jerk the keys from the ignition. Her movement startles me out of my fog, and I turn to look at her. A lawnmower cranks up next door and we sit in its rumble as I try to figure out why the hell I'm so furious with Josh, want to slash Sloane's tires, want to crush every guy who even looks at Hadley below the neck.

"Sam?"

Her expression is open, but behind her eyes, there's this whisper of uncertainty. Then she smiles a little and it's like a clap of thunder. I feel an almost painful jolt in my gut coupled with this vision of Hadley in my house again, this time pressed up against me on the couch while we watch some lame movie I can't even remember the name of because she's taking up all the space in my brain and the only thing I can think about is *Dear-sweet-Lord-please-just-let-me-touch-her.*

Holy shit, Sam.

And just like that, I know I can't invite her in my house.

Ever.

"Um . . . you know what?" I say. "I just remembered that I have to turn in this paper for Humanities. It's already late."

Her eyes darken, but I swear I see a flash of relief. "Oh. Okay, that's fine. We can go back to school."

"I'm really sorry."

"Don't worry about it." She gives me another smile before turning her face away toward the window.

We drive back to school, letting some song I don't even like all that much fill the awkward silence that's sprung up between us. God, I hate this. I should've kept walking when I saw her at her locker this morning. She didn't need me to swoop in to save her from a bunch of sex toys. I would've felt like an asshat, but at least I wouldn't be such an angsty cliché right now.

When I pull into the school lot, we say goodbye. She thanks me for helping her and I thank her for taking me to the Green-Eyed Girl and it's all so polite and weird that I want to punch a hole in my dashboard. I watch her duck into the building, a cavern in my chest so huge, I'm sure my next breath will flip me inside out.

I drum my fingers on the steering wheel, trying to figure out what to do next, how to get rid of this torrent of clashing emotions in my gut. School is the last place I want to be. Besides, if I see Josh right now, it'll just remind me what a complete idiot I am. I check the clock. A little before noon.

I should just go home. Pump some loud, angry music through the house, cook something complicated that'll take me hours, and make Livy happy. Or I could find a batting cage and hit until my arms ache. Playing with the guys on Wednesday was enough to prove I could use the practice.

But I know I won't do either of those things.

Forty minutes later, I'm sitting outside Nicole's house in Nashville.

The first time I slept with Nicole was the night everything blew up. Livy was an incoherent mess and I had driven her to her friend Caitlin's house. Mom and Dad weren't talking to me, and when they weren't alternating between screaming and tears, they were smothering Livy like they were afraid the air in the house would kill her.

Nicole and I had hung out a few times in groups. She was friends with Sara, and Ajay wanted me to get with her so we could be one of those nauseating inseparable foursomes. I'd never felt much when I was with her. She was beautiful, she was fun, but there was no real connection between us. She used non-words like "supposably" and "irregardless." I think she did this mostly to annoy me, because she was in the top five of our class.

That night, she called at exactly the wrong moment. Or maybe the right one, I don't know. Either way, I unloaded everything on her and she told me to come over. When I got to her house, her parents weren't home, because they're both real estate agents and are never home. She didn't say a word. She just took my hand and led me into her bedroom. This became a regular occurrence for the next few weeks. Things got too thick at home, I'd get Livy to a friend's house and I'd always end up at Nicole's. I don't even know her middle name.

Hadley's is Jane. I'm not sure how the hell I know that.

Now I punch the glowing orange circle next to Nicole's front door so hard, my thumbnail splits.

"Sam Bennett, oh my God," Nicole says as she opens the door, her eyes wide with surprise. "What are you doing here?"

"Hey, Nic. How are you?"

"I'm great now. How'd you know I have early release from school?"

"Lucky guess." Or not. I texted Ajay on my way here and asked him and then ignored him as he proceeded to blow up my phone with a bajillion versions of *What the hell are you doing?*

She opens the door wider and I slip past her. She looks incredible, as always. Slick, straight blond hair, green eyes like a cat. Smooth, tanned skin that I remember felt like silk under my fingers.

"You look good," she says as she closes the door.

"Thanks. You too."

"To what do I owe this visit?" She leans against the wall, her hips popped out into the space between us.

I shrug and look around her house. It's still dark and woodsy and open, like one of those ritzy lodges at ski resorts. "Just wanted to say hey."

"After four months?"

"I just got back into town last week."

She purses her lips and pushes herself off the wall. "Well, well. Welcome home."

I follow her into the living room, drawing cedar and a left-over smoky scent from the wood-burning stove into my lungs. We sit on her blue and red plaid couch and watch one of those house renovation shows she always loved, chitchat mindlessly about baseball and her theater group and school. It's always easy with Nicole. Nothing complicated, nothing twisted or con-trived or hidden. Simple.

And predictable. After a while, she clicks off the TV, leans into me, and sweeps her lips over mine. I pull her closer and squeeze my eyes closed as I kiss her. She tastes like watermelon lip balm, a trace of clove cigarettes. We end up on her blue and white striped bed, our clothes on the floor and my hands in her hair. Her room is exactly the same, the floor littered with screen-plays and SAT prep books and her million pairs of shoes.

"I missed you," she whispers into my ear as she slides on top of me, straddling my hips.

I have a sudden flash of Josh's lying face and I almost swear out loud. Not exactly the image I want in my mind at this par-ticular moment. But there he is and then there's my mom's ly-ing face and my own lying face and then there's Hadley's dark eyes, and even Livy worms her way into my rapidly clouding thoughts. I know I should stop this. I should just kiss Nicole one more time and leave, but the creeping oblivion on the edge of my thoughts is like a drug.

Fighting through Nicole's warm breath on my neck, I find a moment of clarity, a piece of truth that I need to give her because I can't seem to give it to anyone else. I push her hair back from her face so I can see her. "Nic. I don't think I can give you anything other than this. I'm just not . . . I just can't."

We stare at each other for a few seconds, our bodies pulled taut with anticipation. Then she reaches for the condom on the nightstand. She tears it open and leans in close to my ear again. "I didn't exactly ask."

Soon I'm lost in her skin and scents and sounds. She could be anyone. I could be anyone. There's only a mass of sensations between us. There are no minds or hearts or effed-up twists of fate or blame or guilt. Colors don't even exist here. Just shade after shade of gray, with me hiding in between them.

CHAPTER THIRTEEN

Hadley

Mom always said she never understood Dad's and my obsession with swimming. A runner since she was a girl, she couldn't fathom pushing your body to the limit without sweat, without the wind in your face and shifting scenery to prove that you're attaining something, getting somewhere. She came to all of my meets, but whenever they confined her to an indoor pool, Dad clad in his West Nashville Wahoos hoodie and whistle and determined brows, Mom would sit in the bleachers and try to look interested, devoted to me but not so much to the sport itself. I don't think she so much as blinked when I quit competing.

But for me, swimming is freedom. I love the feeling of weightlessness with control, speed without impact. The water hems me in above and below, and I can cut my body through the pool and fly.

Tonight the water is a relief. *Stroke-stroke-stroke-breathe.*

Stroke-stroke-stroke-breathe. Twenty-four freestyle strokes per fifty meters. Not bad. Not great, either, but after months with avoidance as my only motivation, I'm probably a little out of shape. A tiny sliver of water edges into my goggles, but I keep moving, extending my arms to their full length and willing my body forward. If I stop and surface, my eyes will automatically swing to the clock on the cement block wall. If I see the time, no doubt tick-ticking toward the mandatory St. Clair dinner, I'll have to go home, because there's this part of me that sort of *wants* to be there just to see if my mother will actually show up. And if I go home, I'll probably just walk into an empty kitchen, waiting around with Jinx for one of my parents to stumble through the door with takeout.

For the past two weeks since the vacuum incident, I feel like I catch only little glimpses of Mom. A blur of color as she whips into the kitchen in the morning for coffee, and then whips back out. A quick peek when she gets home long after dinner right before she disappears into her room. She haunts the house, more memory than flesh.

Any words spoken between my parents are either about who can pick up the dry-cleaning or my mother setting passive-aggressive bombs for Dad to walk right through, turning our house into a minefield.

Oh, I love digging soggy food out of the sink's drain.

Oh, I wish I taught college so I could work three hours a day a few times a week.

Oh, I just read this fascinating article in American Literary History. *Jason, didn't you submit a piece to them a while ago? Whatever happened with that?*

Dad meets all of this with heavy sighs, hands raked down his face, and even an hour-long call to Liam, my parents' therapist, during which I overheard phrases like *coping mechanism* and *acute stress.* But he doesn't speak to my mother about it. No arguing or blaming or name-calling. Everything's quiet and razor-sharp.

So I keep swimming.

When I'm about 250 meters in, a girl dives into the lane next to me as I turn. She carves through the water gracefully and soon we're swimming side by side, spurred on by each other's presence and speed. The old thrill of competition surges through me, that familiar rush of adrenaline and anxiety and determination. My lungs burn as my body pivots perfectly with each stroke, but this girl keeps pace with me, edging me by a half a head by the time we've gone 200 meters. At 400, my body feels boneless as I plunge into the wall a split second after she does, surprised that she also stops, as if there were an agreement on the length of our race.

I gulp the chlorinated air, pulling off my goggles and purple swim cap. Intrigued, I turn to face my competitor and suck in a little stream of water as my gaze locks onto Sam Bennett's sister.

"Oh," she breathes out, her eyes wide on mine, her own chest heaving up and down from her effort and, now, I can tell, her surprise. She grabs an inhaler from on top of a towel on the ledge and sticks it in her mouth. I watch her take a few puffs.

"Hey," I say when she gets a breath. "Livy, right?"

She nods, sliding a hand over her wet hair, and looks away from me.

"Are you okay?"

She nods again.

"I'm Hadley. We met a couple weeks ago at Wasabi's."

"I remember." She takes another drag on her inhaler before hanging one hand on the edge of the pool. Her other hand taps out a rhythm on the water's blue surface. "You're Sam's friend."

I frown at this, not sure whether to agree or deny or just pretend I didn't hear her. I don't think Sam considers me his friend. Since our breakfast at the Green-Eyed Girl, I've seen him every day at school, but aside from the occasional wave in the hallway and our businesslike conversations whenever Ms. Artigas gives us time to work on our project in class, our relationship consists of polite smiles and a flock of birds careening through my stomach every time he taps his pen against his full bottom lip.

I know he didn't have a Humanities paper to turn in that morning. He was completely bullshitting me. But honestly, his excuse was a relief. As I sat in his car outside his house, I could feel the red panic sliding up my neck and settling into my face at the thought of being alone with him again.

"You're a great swimmer," I say to Livy. "At least at freestyle. Do you swim competitively?"

She shakes her head. "I just like swimming."

"Me too." I try to catch her glance, but she's well practiced at avoiding eye contact, looking in my direction in a way that convinces me she's interested but wary.

"Woodmont has a great team," I say. "You should try out."

"Maybe." She hauls herself out of the pool, her shoulders and slim legs leanly muscled just like a swimmer's.

I look up at her, the fluorescent lights behind her turning her into a silhouette. In the open-swim pool, a few human cannonballs slam their bodies into the water. She dries off while I climb out and do the same. Livy pulls on a pair of track pants and a huge, ratty Harrison High Baseball T-shirt that has to be Sam's. She has the same blue eyes, same elegant cheekbones, same full mouth that probably spreads into the same lopsided grin when she lets herself smile.

"Why aren't you on the team?" she asks.

"I used to be on a team at my school in Nashville, and my

dad used to coach my neighborhood team when I was a kid." I wrap my towel around my shoulders. "But . . . well, I just needed a break."

She nods and swings her backpack onto her shoulders so hard that the strap flies up and slaps her in the face.

"I need to go," she says, rubbing at her cheek.

"Sure . . ." But she's already walking away, her head tucked in to her chest. I can't figure out any of these damn Bennetts.

In the locker room, I rinse off and change into jeans and a long-sleeved thermal shirt and hoodie. I nod a goodbye to Henry Murphy, the lifeguard on duty with whom I shared a little moment in the supply closet back in August. When I pass, he lifts a flirty eyebrow along with one corner of his flirty mouth. Henry was the first guy I kissed whom I had absolutely zero interest in dating. I had just started teaching the five-year-old class at the Y, and whenever he walked by, his shaggy auburn hair in his eyes, he made my heart hammer in my chest. When we ran into each other in the closet one hot afternoon, both of us hunting for a kickboard or whistle or I can't even remember what, we slammed together like two magnets.

I remember the way I melted into him, all hard edges and sharp corners rounded out by the touch of someone who wanted nothing more from me than what I was willing to give.

He asked me out after that, but I surprised myself by saying no. He was a nice enough guy, if a little cocky, and a senior at Franklin High. Incredibly cute, an amazing kisser, but when it came down to it, I didn't like him. What's more, I realized that I didn't want to like him. Liking him would mean talking to him, listening to him, trusting him.

Outside, the cold fall air stings my lungs, and I breathe it in, letting it steel me for whatever I'm about to face at home. On my way down the sidewalk, I spot Livy near the bike rack, sitting on her heels by a bright blue bike, digging through her backpack.

"Is everything all right?" I ask as I pass by.

Her head snaps up and she falls back onto her butt.

"Sorry!" I jog over to her. "I didn't mean to scare you."

She waves a hand as she stands and brushes off her pants. "It's fine."

"Is something wrong with your bike?" I crouch down and see that the front tire is completely flat, a large rock gashed into the black rubber. "Uh-oh."

"Yeah."

"Do you need a ride?"

"I just need to call Sam, but I . . ." She rifles through her bag again. "I think I left my phone at home."

"You can use mine. Or I can drive you. It's not far, right?"

"No, but that's okay." She rubs her forehead, the same way Sam does. She still hasn't looked at me once. "I'll just walk."

"It's dark and there's not a sidewalk. Let me drive you. I don't mind."

"I can't . . . I don't think . . ." She fumbles for her words, her face pinking up even in the dim light. She clutches her inhaler in a tight fist.

"Livy, I just want to make sure you get home all right. Please, let me drive you."

She finally, finally looks at me. "Okay."

I give her a relieved smile. "I think we can fit your bike in the back of my car."

She unlocks her bike and we pile it into my CR-V. She's quiet on the drive to her house, crammed against the door and staring out the window. She radiates unhappiness. I feel like I could reach out a hand and swipe some off her.

"Sam told me you guys just moved here," I say, and she nods. "When we moved from Nashville, I was miserable."

"You were?" she asks, head still turned toward the window.

"Totally. I felt sort of lost, you know? New town, new house, new school, my family was completely different. My first night here, I couldn't even make up my bed. I just fell asleep on the bare mattress. It was a lot to deal with. I don't think I would've survived it if I didn't have my best friend, Kat."

I pull into her neighborhood and notice, out of the corner of my eye, that she's turned her head toward me.

"You were sad?" she asks.

"Yeah. I guess I was."

"Sam helps me a lot. He's sort of like my best friend, I guess."

"He seems like a great brother." I turn in to her driveway and put the car in park.

She nods, smiling. "He's the best. He'd do anything for me." She looks down and fiddles with the zipper on her jacket. "It has been pretty hard. My mom is hardly ever home, and we're not close. I miss my dad."

"Is he far away?"

"Boston."

"Do you get to see him very often?"

"Not really. We've only seen him once since he moved up there."

"That sucks. I miss my dad too." I say it just to try to connect a thin line between Livy and me, let her know she's not alone, but as soon as I say it, I know it's true. I miss both of my parents.

Livy lifts her head and stares at her front door, her lower lip quivering like a leaf in the rain. "My mom cheated on my dad."

All the air in the car is suddenly gone. My fingers whiten around the steering wheel, and when I finally get a breath, it burns all the way down my throat. It's a few long seconds before I realize Livy is watching me, her head cocked to one side.

"I'm so sorry," I manage to say.

She nods and opens her door. "Maybe I shouldn't have said anything." She pauses with her body half out of the car. "I thought Sam told you."

"No. He didn't." I get out to help her with her bike, glad for the cover of darkness to hide the water welling up in my eyes. *God, Hadley.* How is it possible that this sort of thing still affects me so much?

"Listen, Livy," I say after I finally get myself together enough to speak. "I know you have Sam, but I'm around if you ever need someone else to talk to, about anything. We could swim or go to a movie. Sam told me you're an amazing film critic." A little smile lifts her mouth. "Whatever you want."

Her smiles widens, but it drops quickly into a frown. She grips the handles on her bike. "Maybe. I'm just not sure . . ." Her voice trails off as the front door opens.

"Livy?"

Sam jogs down the front walk. "What's going on?" He stops in front of his sister, his eyes widening on me. "Oh. Hey."

"Hey. I just gave Livy ride home from the Y." I smooth my still-damp-and-tangled hair and try not to look at Sam, which is proving more difficult than I'd like. He's barefoot in dark jeans and a slim-fitting plaid button-up, sleeves rolled to his elbows. He looks good. Too good.

Livy tilts her bike toward him and explains about the flat tire.

"Aw, Liv. I'm sorry." Sam bends down to inspect the tire. "We'll get a new one on tomorrow." He props the bike against the garage.

"Thanks for the ride, Hadley."

"Anytime." Livy gives me shy smile. Sam's gaze shifts back and forth between us, the hint of a question on his lips. Livy waves and walks up the path, disappearing inside.

Sam watches her go, his mouth open a little. "What . . ." He shakes his head as if to clear it. "Um. Thanks for driving her home."

"It was no problem. She's really sweet."

"Yeah." He hangs his hand on the back of his neck and looks at me. God, this boy stares too much.

"Oh, I keep forgetting to give this back to you." I open my car's back door and find what I'm looking for on the floor. "Here."

He grins as his hand closes on the neatly folded green and white striped apron he slipped over my head in his kitchen a few weeks ago. "Thanks. Although this really did look better on you."

I laugh and look down.

"Listen, Hadley." He flips his finger under a fold in the apron. "About the last time we—"

"Samuel!" A male voice splits through his words, and I let out the breath I didn't realize I was holding. "A glaringly loud beeping is disrupting the zenlike state I attained after kicking your incompetent-at-Assassin's-Creed ass."

"Just take the pizza out of the oven!" Sam yells toward the house.

"What pizza?" A tall boy fills the doorway and starts toward us. "I don't recall any pizza."

Sam scratches his chin. "Could it be the one you threatened me into making?"

The boy reaches us, his black hair sticking out at crazy angles. "Threatened? Me? Never. Cajoled, perhaps, but never threatened."

"I believe you said you'd find my autographed Chipper Jones rookie card and soak it in olive oil unless I provided you with homemade pizza. That's a threat, my friend."

"Psh. You're delusional." The guy turns his nearly black eyes toward me. "And who is this?"

I can't help but laugh at the way he's looking at me. Any minute, I expect the word *enchanté* to roll out of his mouth.

"I'm Hadley."

His eyes crinkle into a grin, his teeth blindingly white against his smooth, brown skin. "Of course you are."

"Don't mind this idiot." Sam shoves his friend in the shoulder.

"And this idiot is?" I ask, playing along.

"Ajay Desai." He extends his hand and I take it. "Longtime confidant of one Samuel Prescott Bennett."

"Prescott?" I crook an eyebrow at Sam.

"God." He shakes his head, but smiles. "I need to get Your Majesty's pizza before it burns. I'll be right back." He shoots Ajay a look I can't read before running into the house.

"Hungry?" Ajay asks, that little grin still on his face.

"Oh. Um . . . my parents are expecting me home." I glance at my phone. I'm not meeting Kat until seven thirty, but I'm already eleven minutes late for dinner. I watch the second hand tick over the clock app's tiny icon, envisioning an empty house oblivious to my absence.

"It's impossible to fully appreciate the art of eating until you've feasted on a Sam Bennett pizza."

"I've had his coffeecake."

"Also a noteworthy experience." He jerks his head toward the house. "Come on. Join us."

"No, that's okay. Sam didn't invite me."

"I'm inviting you and I'm more Sam than he is sometimes." He slings an arm over my shoulder and starts toward the house.

"It'll be good for him. I insist."

I dig my heels into the ground. "Really. I don't think he wants me here." And I don't think I want to go eat with a guy who looks at me like he's known me for years one minute and lies his way out of hanging out with me the next, not to mention that whole weird scene with his mother.

Ajay stops and turns so he's facing me, his expression suddenly serious. "Really. He does want you here." He comes behind me and puts his hands on my shoulders, propelling me forward. "He just doesn't know it yet."

I grate Parmesan cheese over the pizza while laughter trickles in from the living room. It takes all my willpower not to dump the whole pie in the trash, kick everyone out, and end the misery now.

"Ajay! That guy just killed me," Hadley says, a teasing edge to her voice. "That's not fair. I didn't know that button was for the gun!"

"All's fair in love and Assassin's Creed, my darling," my so-called best friend says.

"Oh, it is so on. He's going down."

"Jesus Christ." I slice the cutter through the pizza and throw triangles onto plates.

Livy smiles as she fills cups with ice.

"You're sure you're okay with this?" I ask her.

She shrugs. "Sure."

"Really?"

"Yeah."

"Come on, Livy. Enough with the monosyllabic answers."

She pops a hand onto her hip. "Fine. It's a little weird, okay? But she's nice and . . . I don't know. She made me feel better earlier."

"What do you mean?"

Another shrug. "She knows how we feel, Sam. She gets it."

"Uh. Yeah. And do you remember *why* she gets it?"

Livy slams a glass down on the counter so hard, an ice cube jumps out.

"Everything all right in there?" Ajay calls.

"Shut it," I call back.

"Guess not."

Livy huffs through her nose. I usually tease her about sounding like a rhinoceros when she gets mad, but I think I'll keep that little tidbit to myself right now.

"I'm not stupid, Sam," she whisper-yells at me. "I remember who she is."

"I never said you didn't." I plunk a pile of napkins next to the plates.

"Yes, you did."

She wheezes a little and I freeze.

"God." She catches my look. "I'm not going to pop a lung."

"What's going on, little elf?" Ajay asks, gliding into the kitchen.

"What's going on is that I, at least according to my all-knowing brother, am a child." Then she spins on her heels and stomps out of the room like the oh-so-mature teenager that she is.

"Damn." Ajay slips onto a barstool. "You're finally the mold on her favorite muffin, eh?"

I flick a rogue piece of pepperoni at him. It lands on the arm of his blue thermal and leaves a slimy orange grease circle.

"Hey! Jesus, Samuel." He grabs a napkin and wipes while I feign innocence.

"Where's Hadley?" I ask.

"She's outside on the phone with her dad. Apparently she was supposed to be home for dinner."

"You should've let her go."

He tosses the napkin down and folds his arms. "And you should be thanking me."

"Thanking you? For what? Most-awkward-Friday-night-ever?"

"It's only awkward if you make it so."

"Life makes it so."

"Only for you."

"And Livy."

He leans forward, his face serious. "Sam. You need to let Livy make her own decisions."

"I don't make her decisions for her."

"No, you just wrap her up in a little cocoon so nothing can ever touch her."

I swallow the ass-chewing I feel like doling out right now. "I can't believe you invited Hadley inside."

"Sure you can."

"If my mom comes home, she's going to shit a brick."

He sticks out his lower lip, mocking me like I'm some freaking kid complaining that my ice cream fell off its cone.

"Ajay, remember what happened when I had coffee with her? You know why I can't get close to her. Why I can't afford to let this happen."

"Oh, I remember. You told me you like her."

"I never said that."

"Eh." He flips a hand through the air. "You told me without words."

I press my fingers to my temples. "You're giving me a migraine."

"You don't get migraines."

"Well, consider yourself a walking catalytic event."

"I'm flattered, Samuel. Truly."

I tear a chunk out of my pizza. Damn good, if I do say so

myself. "Look, it's not just about who she is or the papers on her door. I'm not sure about any of this anymore."

"Any of what?"

I take another bite and chew slowly. I think about my parents and me and Livy, all part of the same unit, but separate. Like pieces of a once-functioning clock taken apart and left strewn out on a table. Broken. All because twenty years ago, two people believed they would love each other forever.

"Nothing." I swallow hard. "Never mind."

"You know, Sam, just because you're scared to like someone doesn't make the like go away."

"But *not* liking someone might."

He makes a derisive sound, similar to Livy's rhino huff.

"All right, then, Dr. Phil," I say. "If you think I like her—and I'm not saying that I do—why are you flirting with her?"

He grins. "Me?"

"Yes, Mr. Girlfriend-of-a-Year."

His face falls south. "Ah. Yes. Well. See, Sara and I are in the middle of a tiny—just a little one, really, minuscule—hiatus."

"What? Why?"

He blows out a huge breath. "I just . . . I got tired of feeling awful about myself around her, you know?"

"I do know. I'm just surprised. I thought you'd all but flushed your own ass down the toilet when it came to Sara."

He frowns at me but doesn't disagree, which is a huge red flag that Ajay's dead serious about this break.

"So why'd you stay with her for so long?" I ask.

He purses his lips. Finally, he exhales loudly. "I don't know, Sam. You know I've always been a little . . ."

"Weird?" I grin at him.

"I was going to say eccentric, but yes, fine. Fill in the blank with the appropriate synonym." He shrugs. "Sara has her good moments. She can be really sweet—"

"Oh, sweet as pie as long as she's perched on her throne, minions bowing low."

He shoots me a withering look. "Listen, she put up with my quirks and I put up with her inhuman lack of compassion. I guess I convinced myself that's what you do in a relationship—you compromise, right? And it worked for a while. Until it didn't."

"What changed?"

He looks down and grips the counter with both hands. "Do you know why she was acting strange after we copul—I mean, slept together?"

I stick my tongue in my cheek to keep from laughing and shake my head.

"She said I didn't talk enough."

"Huh?"

He snaps his fingers. "Exactly."

"You mean, like, *during* sex?"

He nods.

"Did she want to discuss Middle Eastern politics or something?"

He laughs, but it's halfhearted. "I wish. She said she wanted me to talk about . . ." He leans forward again, lowers his voice. "Her body and how good it felt."

"Like . . . dirty talk?"

He shrugs and actually blushes. "It was this epiphanic moment. I realized how little she really knew me."

"Aw, man." I laugh long and loud. Ajay Desai is good at a lot of things. Need a geometry tutor? Call Ajay. Advice about how to execute panty-dropping charm? Ajay is your man. Power tools? Ajay "the Tool Man" Desai. But he's a romantic. One of the last true gentlemen. Talking dirty is not something I would imagine Ajay to ever, ever, ever excel at. Thank God.

"What's so funny?" Hadley asks as she comes into the kitchen. Livy trails in behind her and sticks her tongue out at me. Nice.

"My love life," Ajay says. "Or current lack thereof."

I bust up again.

"Yes, yes. It's just hilarious. Laugh it up. I'm not the one calling up a pretty blonde—"

I cough so loudly, it echoes off the countertops, and level Ajay with a glare that could melt glaciers. Luckily, Livy's rooting around in the pantry, probably hunting for that nasty canned Parmesan she likes. But from the way Hadley catches my eye, turns red, and then slides her gaze to her phone, she picked up on Ajay's comment. And it shouldn't bother me, right? Who cares if she knows about Nicole? Not me. Nope.

"Here." I hand her a plate. "Eat up."

"Thanks." She bites into the pizza. A long, gooey string of cheese extends out from her beautiful mouth, which I am definitely not staring at. "Wow. Amazing, Sam."

I shrug and smile stupidly for a moment before I realize Ajay is grinning at me like the goddamn Cheshire Cat. I clear my throat and finish off my pizza just standing there while Livy and Hadley take theirs to the table like civilized people.

After we're all fed and Ajay and Hadley clean up (and flick soap bubbles into each other's hair, but hey, that's normal platonic behavior, right?), Ajay retrieves a copy of the *Nashville Scene* from his messenger bag and flops down next to Livy on the couch. "All right, campers. What shall we do tonight?"

"Tonight?" Hadley asks from the doorway into the kitchen, glancing at her phone. "I don't think—"

"No, no, my lovely. You're stuck with us now." Ajay shoots her a wink over the paper, and I sort of want to rip his eyelashes off.

She just smirks at his charms. "I have to meet my friend soon."

"Friend? Of the male or female persuasion?"

"Female," she says slowly, and Livy snorts a laugh. "Interested?"

Ajay chuckles but doesn't answer. Instead, he flips through the *Scene*, Nashville's guide to all goings-on in the city. Hadley smiles and fiddles with her phone, wandering back into the kitchen.

"You can go if you need to," I say, following her.

She glances up, her expression a mystery. "Thanks for the permission."

"I didn't mean it like that, but Ajay can be very persuasive. If you need to escape, I'd do it while he's distracted."

She tucks her phone into her back pocket and folds her arms over her chest. Her eyes roam all over my face, brows crinkled, like she's trying to dig under the surface of my blank expression. At least, I think it's blank.

"Right," she finally says. "Right. I'll just go now." She starts toward the hallway and I get this sick feeling in my stomach. "Tell Ajay and Livy bye for me."

"Wait—" But she's already out the front door, a flash of hair and tight jeans. I catch up with her in the driveway, the cold air biting at my bare feet. "Hadley, wait."

She whirls around, eyes flashing. "What?"

"Are you mad about something?"

"No. Of course not." She opens her car door and stops. She seems to deflate a little, her shoulders descending from her ears, but then she slams the door shut. "Okay, yes. I am. Listen, Sam. If you don't want to be friends with me, fine. But I'd rather you be straight about it."

I step back a little. "Why would you think I don't—"

"Really?" She folds her arms again and pops out her hip. "The last time I was at your house, you all but shoved me out the door, and I know you didn't have a Humanities paper due the other week. But you show up at my locker and help me and take me to breakfast and tell me things I'm almost positive you don't tell many people. It's just getting a little hard to keep up with your mood swings."

I sigh. "It's not that I don't want to be friends with you."

"Then what is it?" Her voice is soft and quiet. She's inches away—her familiar smell mixed with chlorine, her long hair sweeping against my forearm, her pulse pounding under the smooth skin at her throat.

And all I want to do is touch her.

Any part of her. I'd settle for the soft skin above her elbow, the long slope where her neck meets her shoulder, the lines on the palm of her hand.

My head feels like I just tossed back four shots of tequila. I'm freaking swaying on my feet here and it's not because she's standing close enough that I can see these tiny amber flecks in her dark eyes I've never noticed before, or even that I'm tired of keeping secrets.

Fuck the secrets.

It's because I want her *closer.*

I scrub a hand down my face so hard, my nails dig into my skin. "It's just a weird time right now . . . with the move and my parents and Livy. I'm sorry. You're right, I've been an asshole."

She frowns and opens her mouth to say something, but then Ajay is heading toward us, his timing impeccable as always. Livy files out behind him with my shoes tucked under her arm and her camera around her neck. She's donned her usual black apparel and I notice she's sprayed a thick section of her blond hair hot pink.

"What are you doing?" I ask.

"Sorry to interrupt your little tryst, Samuel," Ajay says, "but we have a show to catch."

"A show?"

"Aren't you two doing a project for *Much Ado?*"

"Yeah," I say slowly, catching Hadley's questioning glance. It's always best to proceed with caution when dealing with Ajay's plans.

He claps his hands. "The Circle Players are putting it on at the Shamblin. Right this very minute." He checks his phone. "Well, not this very minute, but in less than an hour."

"It's Friday night, Age. I doubt we'll get tickets."

"Fear not. I already called and they have plenty of tickets left."

"That probably means it sucks."

He grins. "The only thing better than an excellent Shakespeare production is a shitty one. Are you game, fair lady?" he asks Hadley.

"I don't think so." She lifts her gaze to mine for a split second before sliding it away. "I have plans with Kat."

"Bring her." Ajay takes her elbow and tries to move her toward his Jeep. He fails.

"No. Really. Another time."

"Hadley." A little voice in my head is screaming, *Shut up, you effing moron!* "Come with us. We need to see the play performed, right?"

She shoots me an exasperated look, and I don't blame her. But still, my mouth opens again. "I want you to come. Who else will ridicule Benedick and Beatrice with me? Sure, Livy's a well-practiced cynic, but she refuses to mock Shakespeare."

"It's true," Livy says. "Goes against my artistic sensibilities. Please come, Hadley. I don't want to be alone with these idiots all night."

"My IQ is a baby's breath shy of genius level," Ajay says, "and that's the second time tonight I've been called an idiot."

"I doubt it will be the last," Hadley says with a little laugh, but her eyes are on Livy. She walks over to her and takes the pink lock between her fingers. "Hey, this looks great."

Livy's eyes light up. "Really? You want one?"

Hadley twists a piece of her own hair and inspects it. "You think it'll show up? My hair's so dark."

"I think so." Livy digs into her cavernous bag and pulls out the can of spray dye. "It's really bright and it washes out easily."

"Do it." Hadley grins. I stand there, transfixed, while she lets my sister glaze a long section of her hair pink, right there in the driveway. Livy's expression has those soft lines to it that I haven't seen since my parents were together and we traveled down to Atlanta to watch the Braves play for Opening Day. Right before we found out about my mom.

"You look amazing," Livy says with a real smile.

"Yes, everyone is beautiful and dazzling and glittery," Ajay drawls. "Now, are you coming, my fairy queen?"

Hadley rolls her eyes but smiles her amazing smile—a singular dimple in her left cheek, one bottom tooth just barely overlapping the other. "All right." She gets out her phone. "But we have to pick up Kat."

"Done." Ajay holds out his arm for her to take. "Shall we?"

Hadley mutters something under her breath I can't make out, but takes his arm. She throws me a soft glance over her shoulder and I meet it, hold it, pull it into my own until she takes it away again.

"He's shameless," Livy says, sliding next to me. "You think he likes her?"

"No." I watch as Ajay waggles his eyebrows at me while he opens the car door for Hadley. "He's doing it to piss me off."

"Now, why would that piss you off?"

For a split second, I think her question is a serious one. But there's this funny glint in her eye—curious and a little teasing—and I realize, possibly for the first time, that she really isn't as young as I like to think she is.

I sling my arm around her shoulders and tell her what she's already guessed. "Because he knows me a little too well."

CHAPTER FIFTEEN

Hadley

"Why are we doing this?" Kat says when I call her about our plans.

I glance up from the passenger seat in Ajay's car to where Sam is slipping on his ratty Vans in the driveway. "I have that project with him and we need to see the play."

"And?"

"And what?"

"Come on, Hadley. Since when do you hang out with guys other than to—"

"I guess since right now." Lately, Kat's playful references to the number of guys at Woodmont with whom I've locked lips grate on my nerves. I always laugh it off or change the subject, but it's getting old. "Just come with me. Please?"

"I didn't think you were friends with him," she says after a long pause.

"I'm not. I mean, maybe I am. I don't know. It's weird."

"*Eldritch?*"

"Har, har."

"All right, fine. I'll come, but you owe me a pack of peanut butter M&M's and a Channing Tatum movie marathon."

"Please don't make me watch *The Vow* again."

"Are you kidding me? That one's first on the list."

I groan. "Fine. Done."

"Hey, maybe this will be a turning point." Her words are muffled in a way that I can tell she's slicking on lipgloss. "If anyone can inspire you to believe in real, honest-to-God love stories again, it's William Shakespeare."

I snort, loud and clear, before I hang up.

By the time we pick up Kat, we have thirty minutes to get to Nashville, get tickets, and get in our seats. Livy is prone to carsickness, so we let her sit in the front of Ajay's book-filled Jeep Cherokee. Because I know the idea of constantly bumping into a guy she just officially met while flying down I-65 would completely freak Kat out, I'm wedged between her and Sam in the back.

"Do you run a library out of your car?" I ask Ajay, to get my mind off Sam's warm skin pressing into my shoulder and thigh.

"What?"

"Did you not notice there are at least twenty books in here?"

He laughs as Livy pulls a book out from under her butt and waves it in his face.

"Care to sign up for a membership?" he asks, swatting her away.

"Ajay's car is his overflow space," Sam says.

"Overflow?" Kat asks.

Sam nods. "He refuses to check books out of the library. Says he needs to own them to really experience them. His room is like one giant ream of paper."

"The experience doesn't end when you finish a story," Ajay says. The lilting tone to his voice that I'd gotten used to over the past couple of hours vanishes and turns serious. "The physical book is like a memento. Plus, I'm a collector."

"So it's important to own two copies of *The Brothers Kara-mazov*?" I ask, holding the proof in my hands.

"New translations, my dear."

"He has a third stuffed in his closet," Sam says.

"Wow. You and my dad should meet. You're like his dream student." I flip through one of the books, feeling Sam shift closer to the door.

"Sure," Ajay finally says after a few seconds, before clearing his throat. "So, Kat, I noticed the button on your bag."

Kat looks down at her burnt orange hobo bag. On it she's fastened a green button with a picture of a pig and the words I DON'T EAT ANYTHING WITH A FACE encircling its head.

"What about it?" she asks.

"Is it true?" Ajay asks. "You're a faceless eater?"

Kat laughs. "If by 'faceless eater' you mean vegetarian, then yes."

"Would you mind explaining your reasons?"

"Here we go," Sam says.

"What?" I ask him.

"Ajay loves debating vegetarianism."

"I don't debate," Ajay says. "I discuss."

"Right."

"Are you a vegetarian?" Kat asks.

"Me?" Ajay says while shifting lanes. "Oh, no, no, no. I relish my saturated-fat-ridden farm friends far too much."

"That's gross," Livy says.

Ajay grins at her. "But my mom is and she's always trying to get my dad and me to see the light or what have you, so I respect it. I know a lot about it."

Kat laughs again. "I don't mind sharing."

"All right, but when he starts talking about methane and cows, I'd be ready with a subject change," Sam says before turning toward the window.

"I just really love animals," Kat says, shrugging. "I respect them, I guess."

"Pigs in particular," I say. Kat harbors a borderline obsession with pigs. "Every Christmas since I've known her, she asks her parents for a piglet. To no avail."

Livy laughs, turning in her seat to face us. "Pigs?"

"Um . . . well . . ." Kat flushes and hems and haws and I ready myself to swoop in with a subject change. But then she catches Ajay's glance in the rearview mirror and, I swear to God, the girl melts next to me. "Yes, pigs. When I was little, I read *Charlotte's Web* the same week I went to a petting zoo. A sow had just had her piglets and . . ." She sighs wistfully. "They were so tiny and adorable and needy. I just couldn't get over it. You know, the whole slaughter-the-cute-little-piggy-for-bacon thing."

"Mmm . . . bacon," Sam murmurs to the window, and I choke back a laugh.

"A couple of years ago, I decided to try not eating meat." Kat fiddles with the button. "I don't even really miss it, although my mom still tries slipping me beef every now and then. She's terrified I'm going to become anemic or develop a B_{12} deficiency."

Ajay smiles and nods, sliding his gaze to hers in the mirror again.

While Kat and Ajay exchange thoughts on the ethical treatment of animals and the health benefits of Tofurky for Thanksgiving, I watch Sam watch the night fade into a deeper dark. The city outside passes by in a blur of black and muted color. Streetlights from the highway flicker over his face, illuminating his pensive expression every fifty feet or so, then throwing him back into shadow. His body is smashed against the door while one hand flicks a button on his shirt repeatedly.

I'm not exactly sure what happened back in his driveway. When I called him on his lie, I expected a laugh, a shrug, a *whatever*. Actually, that's not true. That's what I *hoped* he'd do, thus proving he's a dick who couldn't care less about messing with a girl's head. Instead, he looked confused and genuinely regretful.

Flying down the highway now, it hits me.

I'm not the one calling up a pretty blonde . . .

All his weird behavior, all his hedging. There's another girl. He's got a girlfriend back in Atlanta or wherever and here I am, batting my stupid lashes at him and inviting myself to his house and practically begging him to be friends with me.

Good God.

I feel ill.

By the time we get to the Shamblin Theater, I already want to go home, but I follow everyone inside. We file into our seats while Kat, now sporting her own pink streak, chatters up a storm with Ajay and Livy, which is totally freaking me out. When we sit down, my arm collides into Sam's on the armrest we'll share. He gives me a smile and gestures for me to take the armrest. I try not to smile back, but I fail. His simple, considerate gesture stirs up a hive of bees in my stomach.

My mind flashes to a memory of my parents. I was maybe eight or nine and Dad had placed light blue sticky notes containing clues leading to Mom's Valentine's Day present all over the house. In the coffeepot, the refrigerator, the microwave, even in the DVD drive. He always did something extravagant a few days or weeks before February 14.

"Real romance can't be scheduled by a calendar," he had said as I watched him slide two tickets to *Wicked* in New York City for the following weekend into a copy of *The Wizard of Oz*. Mom actually cried a little when she found them. God, even my prepubescent heart fluttered.

The lights in the Shamblin blink on and off. I settle into my seat, picturing my parents at home right now. Dad, pouting over my absence, will soon shut himself in his study to edit his articles or grade papers while Mom, if she's even home, watches *Scandal* and fantasizes about replacing her husband's toothpaste with hemorrhoid cream.

That's a real, honest-to-God love story.

Throughout the play, I feel Sam's eyes drift over to my face more than once, but he never says a word. We never nudge each other and mock Benedick's and Beatrice's cynicism-turnedpuddly-love or point out that the actor playing Claudio seems to have no scruples about upstaging his fellow thespians during their lines. In fact, Sam barely speaks to anyone until the five of us are squashed into a booth at Fido, a hipster coffee shop in Hillsboro Village, sharing massive slices of cheesecake with thick, foamy cappuccinos.

"I like this," Sam says close to my ear so I can hear him above the cacophony of the busy café. He twirls my pink strand of hair between his fingers. "Very Katy Perry."

"Damn, I was going for Gwen Stefani."

He keeps his eyes on my hair, his thumb smoothing over the texture again and again. I want to knock his hand away, but my arms feel locked in my lap.

"Nah. Livy's Gwen. Or maybe Kat. Blond hair and all." He drops my hair so that it falls onto his arm, the pink like a neon light against his smooth skin. "It was cool of you to let Livy color it."

My phone buzzes against my leg in my bag. I dig through a tube of lip balm, my graphing calculator, wallet, and a copy of Rilke's *Letters to a Young Poet* I'd forgotten was even in there before my hand closes around the phone. *Dad* flashes across the screen. I tap *Ignore.*

"I wasn't trying to be nice." I look across the booth to where Livy's snapping pictures of Kat and Ajay fighting—and by fighting, I mean flirting — over the last bite of key lime cheesecake. I tilt my head and watch my best friend for a few seconds before turning back to Sam. "I just really, really like hot pink hair."

Sam smiles and flips his fork over his knuckles, studying me with softly narrowed eyes. "You know, you never told me something unexpected about yourself."

"I thought you said everything about me was unexpected," I say without thinking. Warmth crawls up my neck and I take a bite of turtle cheesecake. I'm flirting with him. He has a girlfriend stashed away somewhere and I'm freaking flirting with him.

Sam makes a *whoo* shape with his mouth. "Okay, I'll rephrase. Tell me something you've never told anyone."

"Why?"

"Because I have a narcissistic need to feel special and unique?"

"I can verify that statement's truth," Ajay says, grinning wryly. Sam startles and sits up straight, like he forgot we weren't alone.

"I don't think that statement is true at all," Livy says. Sam grins at her.

"Regardless." Ajay looks at me pointedly. "I'd be interested in this rare bit of information as well."

"Me too," Kat says.

"You already know everything about me," I say.

"I doubt that. We all have secrets."

"Is that right, Kitty Kat? And what, pray tell, are your hidden demons?"

"Kitty Kat?" Ajay's eyes crinkle into a smile. "I like that. Meow."

"Oh, God," she says, dropping her head into her hands. "Not you too."

He laughs and nudges her shoulder playfully. "We'll all do it. Each of us shares something we've never told anyone before."

"Kat and Hadley just met you, Age," Sam says. "I mean, I know you think you can charm your way into an old lady's will, but I'm not sure even you can extract that kind of information."

"You expected Hadley to pour out her soul to you, Don Juan." Ajay smirks at his friend and Sam smirks right back, a silent war that can only be waged between two people who've known each other longer than they haven't.

"I'll do it," Kat says, and my mouth drops open. What parasitic life form has taken over my best friend?

"Excellent." Ajay turns so his entire body is facing Kat. "Go."

She fiddles with her napkin, twisting it into a cottony wreath. "All right . . . well . . . um." Ah. There she is. "I keep a journal about . . ." She flicks her eye to me and I smile. "My dad. Actually, it's *to* my dad."

"Your dad?" Ajay asks, eyebrows up.

She nods. "He left when I was ten and he's a complete jerk, but . . . he's still my dad, you know, and he knows nothing about me. So once a week I write to him in this journal. Just stupid stuff really. What I'm doing at school, what music I like, my best time at a swim meet."

I tap her foot under the table. I didn't know this about Kat, but somehow it doesn't surprise me. She's always been more forgiving toward her father than I would be in her situation. When she was nine, the guy said she looked like a whore when she dressed as Catwoman for Halloween. But Kat, though damaged by him, rarely wanders beyond her usual "He's a jerk" assessments. I'm glad to know she can express herself in writing, but I can't keep my heart from shuddering. I think of my own dad's journal to me and whether or not he still writes in it.

"I like it. Subtly revealing." Ajay holds Kat's gaze as he says, "Sam. Go."

Sam hesitates, eyebrows cinched in thought. Finally, he chuckles. "I sucked my thumb until I was ten."

Ajay's eyes pop and I spit a mouthful of lukewarm coffee back into my mug.

"Seriously?" I ask.

He shrugs, totally unfazed.

"It's true," Livy says, giggling. "When he watched TV, he

173

used to lie on the floor so that the coffee table blocked him from Mom's view on the couch and go to town. It's amazing he's not bucktoothed."

"Wow," Ajay says, eyes glittering. "I'm nonplussed. I'm flabbergasted. I'm humming with anticipation of future manipulation."

"All right, pot-stirrer," Sam says to Ajay. "Your turn."

"Me? A magician never reveals his secrets."

"Oh, no." Kat pokes his arm gently with her fork. "Spill it."

He slides the fork from her fingers and rubs his arm. "Okay, okay. No need for violence." He grins at her. She grins back.

Ajay pushes his fingertips together and takes a deep breath. "Okay. I cried—"

"Oh, this is gonna be good," Sam says, his leg pressing against mine under the table.

Ajay narrows his eyes at him. "I cried when I read the last scene in *Harry Potter and the Deathly Hallows*. You know, when Harry kneels down in front of his kid and calls him Albus Severus? Gah. Totally bawled."

"Who didn't?" Livy asks.

Sam lifts a hand. "But only because I had already wept a river when Voldemort dropped dead. *Loved* that guy."

Under the table, I bat his knee with mine and he laughs. Our eyes lock and his laughter fades into something softer. His eyes sweep over my face, exploring like fingers.

Click.

"Livy, what the hell?" Sam asks, blinking. I inch away from him, painfully aware of the myriad of emotions that just bled out of my face. I meet Kat's raised eyebrows and look away.

Livy lowers her camera lens from our faces and inspects the digital view, an odd look on her face I can't place.

"Sorry," she mutters without glancing up. "Good lighting in here."

"Yawn." Ajay reaches over Kat to snap the lens cap onto Livy's camera. "Little elf. Deepest, darkest secret. Go."

Livy's face drains of all color and she looks down at her lap. Sam's leg jerks next to me and Ajay yells, "Ow!" Then his whole face opens up. "Oh. Um. I'm getting more coffee. Anyone else?"

He stands and Kat hands him her cup while we exchange bewildered looks. Next to Kat, Livy fiddles with her camera, her body smashed against the wall.

Ajay returns with two steaming mugs, sliding one in front of Kat. They lean toward each other, talking quietly, and I wonder if she's asking him what the hell that was all about. I could ask Sam, but looking at Livy's face, still pale, I swallow my questions.

My phone buzzes again.

"Do you need to get that?" Sam asks as I check the screen.

I shake my head. "It's just my dad again."

He inhales deeply. "Shouldn't you talk to him?"

"Nah. He's just mad that I skipped out on dinner. I don't want to talk to him right now." I power down my phone. Dad will just have to get over it.

"Hey! Sam!" A female voice filters through the din and finds us. Something flickers in Sam's expressions as he pulls his gaze from mine to look up. I do the same.

"Ajay's here too," the voice says.

"Oh, fan-freaking-tastic," Ajay mumbles, pinching his lower lip with his fingers as he turns around. Kat frowns at him while two girls approach our table. One is tall and leggy and busty and blond, and the other is shorter with more sharp angles underneath her brown hair. Livy's eyes are wide. She flicks the lens off her camera.

"Hey, guys," the blonde says casually, her eyes on Sam.

"Hey, Nic." Sam sits back in the booth, his leg still pressed against mine. "What's up, Sara?" This to the brunette, who is currently glaring at Ajay.

"What are you doing?" she asks, a hip cocked and arms folded.

"I'm hanging out with my friends. What does it look like?"

"And who's this?" She jerks her chin toward Kat, who is

176

clearly sitting a little closer than necessary to Ajay. She flushes and scoots toward Livy.

"One of the aforementioned friends," Ajay says calmly.

"Right." Sara's gray eyes roam over Kat like they would an annoying insect. "A little whore for the hole I left when you dumped me, is that it?"

"Excuse me?" The words are out of my mouth without thinking. I can already feel angry red dots blotching my neck, and I start to stand, but Ajay beats me to it.

Wordlessly, but with a scowl that could cut glass, he takes her arm and walks with her outside. Her mouth is already moving, and an irate line zigzags between her eyes. Livy snaps a picture of their retreat.

"Livy, come on," Sam says, and she spreads a hand innocently.

"Sorry about her," the blond girl says. "Sara doesn't take rejection very well."

I ignore her and get out of the booth, rounding the table to slide into Ajay's vacated seat next to Kat. Her face is still bright red, her fingers white on the edge of the table.

The girl clears her throat and I shoot her an annoyed look.

"Oh. Um. This is Nicole," Sam says. "Nic, this is Kat and Hadley. Friends from Woodmont."

"Hi," Nicole says brightly, collapsing into my empty seat

next to Sam. Kat gives her a wan smile because she's too nice to do anything less, but I look away. This girl hasn't done anything to me, but I can feel my face settling into a tight, bitchy expression. I can't help it, because I know this is her. The "pretty blonde." She's pressed so close against Sam, she might as well be straddling him.

"Livy, you look so grown up," Nicole says. "How are you?"

"I'm fine, thanks." A little smile tugs at one corner of Livy's mouth. "You?"

Nicole bumps her shoulder into Sam's. "Oh, I'm always good." She shifts her green eyes over us. "Did you guys just come from a costume party or something?"

"What?" Sam asks.

"The pink hair."

"Oh." Livy shrugs. "No, we just did it for fun."

"Right. Fun. I know all about that." She laughs and bumps into Sam. Again. She's practically purring. He smiles slightly and clears his throat. His gaze passes over mine and he looks away quickly, but not before the tips of his ears turn as pink as my hair.

Ajay strolls languidly back to the table, but his expression is pinched in frustration. "Nicole, Sara said she'd meet you outside."

"Already?" Nicole rolls her eyes as she stands. "I wanted cake. God, Ajay. Can't you just skip all this drama and make her happy?" She swats him playfully on the chest. "You know, like you could tell her . . . Oh, I know! Just talk about her boobs a lot when you two are—"

"Nicole!" A red-faced Sam scrambles out of the booth.

"What?" she asks, all wide-eyed confusion. "Isn't that what this is about?"

"No. Jesus." They move away from the table and into a corner next to a plastic bin filled with used dishes. His expression is maddeningly unreadable, but they keep *touching*. He lays a hand on her shoulder. She leans into him, her ample chest colliding with his. He shakes his head and steps back, but touches her elbow. She rolls herself onto her toes and kisses his cheek.

Touch, touch, touch.

My breathing feels shallow. I watch Sam watch Nicole walk away before he turns and talks quietly with Ajay, who seems on the verge of laughing. I force myself to focus on Kat.

"Are you all right?" I ask her.

"Sure. Why wouldn't I be?" She taps the tines on her fork.

"Oh, I don't know. Maybe because you cry when your dentist lectures you about flossing and that girl was a total bitch."

She shrugs. "Yeah, she was. But she's got nothing to do with me, right? Clearly, she's Ajay's ex. And I just met him three hours ago."

179

"Right, but—"

"Let's just go, okay? I think the guys are ready." She wiggles against my hip until I let her out of the booth. Livy raises her eyebrows at me, but I shake my head, just as confused.

The ride home is quiet. Before we left, Ajay apologized to Kat for Sara's behavior. Kat waved him off casually, but her fists were clenched into the strap of her bag and her mouth was smashed into a colorless line.

Sam sits in the front, Livy having insisted on sitting in between Kat and me, risking a queasy stomach. Some invisible line has been drawn, girls against boys. What we are battling over, I'm not even sure, but images of Sam and Nicole swim sloppy laps in my head.

By the time we pull into Sam's driveway, I'm feeling both completely stupid and vindicated. Kat was so sure something was pulling me toward Sam Bennett—something deeper than his chiseled arms and cerulean eyes—but all that's between us is an English project and a cantaloupe-chested blonde.

We pile out of the car and mutter goodbyes. I refuse to look at Sam, but he hovers around me in the driveway. I can't imagine what he might have to say, and neither do I care. Livy finally pushes him inside and I turn to find Kat talking with Ajay, leaning against his car.

"Are you ready?" I ask her.

She looks up, a rare flash of irritation in her eyes. "I guess."

"Are you sure you're all right?"

Her whole body locks up. She mutters something to Ajay and then walks over to me. "I'm. Fine. It wasn't a big deal."

"I know that, but you're usually pretty sensitive about that kind of stuff."

"Right. Poor, inexperienced Kat. Hadley, just because I'm not accustomed to being called a slut on a daily basis doesn't mean I'm going to fall to pieces at the first sign of conflict."

I take a step back, her sharps words ringing in my ears. I swallow hard, waiting for an apology, but it doesn't come. She just stares at me, shock and something that looks a lot like relief mingling in her expression.

"Everything all right, ladies?" Ajay asks, approaching warily.

"Fine," Kat says.

"Ajay, would you mind giving Kat a ride home?"

Her eyes taper into slits, but she says nothing.

"Sure. It's on the way."

Kat opens her mouth, but I mutter a *thanks* and turn my back on her, too tired and irritated to care what else she has to say.

CHAPTER SIXTEEN

Hadley

Sam. Nicole. Sam's hand on Nicole's shoulder. Nicole's fountain of blond hair down her back. Nicole's tanned legs under her tiny little denim skirt. Nicole's lips on Sam's cheek.

I can't stop this relentless march of thoughts as I unlock my front door. The house is quiet, my parents already asleep. I stumble through the pitch-black downstairs and notice that the little lamp on the hall table, usually burning bright all night, is turned off. Dropping my keys next to the lamp, I flick it on before I trudge upstairs.

Sam . . . Nicole . . . Sam . . .

I pass Mom and Dad's room, and all thoughts of Sam and Nicole vanish. The door is wide open, the room a dark cavern.

"Mom?" I call as I step inside.

Nothing. I snap on the overhead light, blinking into the glaring brightness.

The room is empty, the bed neatly made and layered with designer pillows. Everything is in its place. Everything except my parents.

My pulse picks up as I walk down the silent hall to the guest room.

Empty.

My room.

Empty.

Dad's study.

Empty.

By the time I get downstairs, my hands are shaking. The living room is empty, the kitchen is empty, the garage is empty. I dig my phone out of my bag and it takes me three tries before I successfully power it up. The voicemail alert pings and I tap on the message.

"Hadley, it's Dad. Listen, it's around ten and I'm going out for a while. Your mom can explain, but everything's fine. Call me if you want—"

A fog glazes over my vision as I delete the message and tap *Mom*.

"Hello, you've reached Annie St. Clair at Sony—"

When I hear her voice, one tear leaks out. I call Dad but get the same thing, businesslike words that turn my parents into nothing more than wards, strangers even. I swallow hard, over and over, trying to push the water back, but I can't get my breath. My fingertips feel fizzy and my insides twist into tight coils. I slide down the cool stainless steel of the refrigerator until I hit the ground. The microwave clock glows blue, the little colon flashing rhythmically toward midnight.

Jinx slinks into the kitchen, mewing and sniffing at my shoe. She pads up my legs and nuzzles under my chin, and for some reason, this breaks the dam. I let out a sob that makes her tail snap straight, but she stays on my lap, peering at my face quizzically. My crying gets louder and messier, but Jinx doesn't seem to mind. She presses closer, curling up on my legs with her back to me like she's trying to give me some privacy, but purring a little louder than normal so I know she's there.

How many times have I sat in this kitchen, alone, clinging to my cat while I waited for my parents to get home? But never in the middle of the night. Never had my solitude felt so much like literal abandonment.

I'm not sure how long we sit there. Eventually, my crying quiets, but the tears keep coming, a silent race down my cheeks.

Then I hear the automatic garage door go up. A few seconds later, Dad walks in, his clothes rumpled, his hair a disheveled mess. When he sees me on the floor, he jerks backwards to keep from stepping on me.

"Hadley. Honey, what are you doing?"

His words are like fire, drying up every single tear. I pull myself to my feet and Jinx scampers to her water bowl. "What am *I* doing? What the hell are *you* doing?"

He startles at my tone. He opens his mouth, but snaps it shut again as he takes in my clenched hands, my shoulders pressing up against my ears.

"I left you a voicemail to let you know I'd be out for a while. Your mom and I . . ." He rakes a hand over his head. "Well, we argued and we both needed some space—"

"I called you and you didn't answer."

He pulls out his phone and frowns, tapping the screen almost frantically. "Oh, honey, I'm sorry. The battery's dead."

"You're sorry?"

"I thought your mother would've—"

"You're *sorry?*" I repeat, louder this time.

He tilts his head at me, his brows furrowed. "What is wrong with you?"

"Are you serious?" My knees wobble and I know I'm losing my grip on whatever got me through the last hour. "I come home and everything was dark, Dad. Everyone was gone. What do you think is wrong with me?"

"What are you talking about?"

"You left."

"I . . . yes. I did. But only for a while, honey. Where's—"

"And Mom left."

He flinches and turns, staring into the still-open garage door at the glaringly empty space next to his own car. "She what?"

"Mom's not here, Dad. Gone. No note or anything. And you were gone and no one was answering their phones and I . . ." His form blurs in my vision, but I can see him pale, his mouth fall open. I wipe at my eyes. "I can't do this. I am *so tired* of this." In the hallway, I find my bag. I sling it over my shoulder and head for the front door.

"Hadley."

I throw the door open and it cracks against the wall.

"Hadley Jane, you get back here! What has gotten into you?"

Dad follows me outside, but I keep moving, nearly running to my car while clawing through my bag for my keys. I mutter a curse when I realize they're still on the hall table.

"Hadley. Come inside. This is ridiculous. It's nearly one in the morning!"

I flip him off. I'm not sure if he can even see me in the dark, but that one finger shoved into the air as I walk off down the sidewalk succeeds in holding back the river of tears welling in my eyes right now.

He calls my name a few more times, but eventually I get far enough away that he gives up. I stop at the end of my street and sink to my knees. The quiet is so thick, I can taste it. I find my phone and stare at it, clicking the top button and igniting a picture of me and Kat at a Vanderbilt football game more than a year ago, our faces covered in black and gold paint. My fingers move on their own and land on a name. I hit *Call* and press the phone to my ear, the space between each ring like a thousand years.

Finally, a click.

"Hadley, hey."

"Sam?"

"Uh, yeah. What's up?"

"Can . . . can you come pick me up?"

CHAPTER SEVENTEEN

Sam

"Pick you up?" I sit up in bed and rub my eyes. I hold my phone away from me and squint at the time. 1:16 a.m. What the hell? "From where? Are you okay?"

She doesn't answer right away, just breathes into the phone. Deep, rib-cracking breaths.

"Hadley?"

"Please."

Her tone makes my guts curl up. I fling the covers back and pull on some jeans. It takes me a few seconds to get a shirt over my head while gripping the phone, but I can't put it down. On the other end, Hadley's breathing gets a lot thicker.

"Okay, where are you?"

"On the corner near my house."

"Stay on the phone with me," I say after she gives me her address. I don't even bother being quiet as I leave. Mom sleeps with earplugs, a habit left over from living with my dad's chain-saw snoring for twenty years. Even if she did catch me leaving, I doubt she'd give a shit.

As I start my car and back out of the driveway, Hadley starts full-on crying. It's quiet, gentle, even, but it's there, filling up the distance between us with all sorts of weird. So I start talking. Well, babbling really. I tell her about my first memories of Livy as a baby and how I used to try to hide her in my closet because I hated all the attention my parents gave her. I tell her about my dad teaching me how to throw a changeup, how I met Ajay on the first day of first grade when our moms got into an argument in the carpool line.

I keep talking until I spot her sitting on the curb, her whole body washed golden from the streetlight. As I slow the car, she stands, phone still mashed onto her ear. Her face is tear-stained and pale, her hair wrapped in a messy ponytail. She flops inside and I slide her phone from her ear, dropping it onto my lap along with mine.

We sit. A dog starts barking, really throwing all he's got into it. Hadley jolts in her seat, her body tensing like a spooked cat. The dog barks for what feels like thirty damn minutes and I'm about to go find a shotgun when he finally shuts up. Hadley relaxes and leans into my shoulder a little. I lean back. She still smells like coffee from our time in Fido.

Quieter night sounds fill in the space around us. Hadley's very still, posture almost impossibly straight. Her fingers move up and down the zipper of her hoodie. It takes me a few seconds to realize she's counting the teeth.

"My parents were gone," she finally says.

"What do you mean?"

She tells me about coming home to her dark, empty house.

"That should be one thing you can count on, right? You come home late at night and at least one of your parents should be there. It just hit me how ..." She takes a deep breath, her gaze turning inward.

"How what?"

"How different things are now. My parents. Everything."

I swallow hard, try to think of something else to talk about, but she keeps going.

"It's our whole family for the past six months." Tears well up and she wipes her eyes. I want to press my hand to her mouth, turn up the music, roll down the windows, and drive seventy miles an hour.

Because I know what's coming.

"My dad had an affair," she says, real quiet. "He screwed around with one of his students for a *year*, and now my mom is practically a ghost. I mean, she hasn't been the same since we found out, but it's just getting worse and worse. Lately, I barely see her. She doesn't talk to anyone, and I . . . I don't know. I don't know what she's thinking."

God, I had really hoped she'd never, ever tell me this. Because now I can't play dumb—I can't pretend like I never made the connection. This tiny sliver of time has officially changed me from clueless asshat to dickhead liar.

"Um . . . Hadley . . ."

She turns toward me. Her cheeks are all pinked up and when her gaze lands on mine, she sort of softens. I have to sit on my hands to keep from touching her. There's no way in hell I can tell her anything when she's looking at me like that.

"Thanks for coming to get me," she says. "I'm sorry I called you. I just didn't feel like being alone."

"It's fine." My voice sounds scratchy, so I clear my throat. "It's no problem."

Something buzzes and I remember that I have Hadley's phone in my lap. I lift it up—*Dad* lights up the screen, blinding in the dark. I angle it toward her and she groans and rolls her eyes.

"Shouldn't you talk to him?"

She shakes her head, lips pressed flat.

"He probably just wants to know where you are."

Nothing.

I breathe out heavily. The phone stops vibrating and registers the missed call. Seconds later, it rings again. *Dad.* She flicks her eyes to the phone before meeting my gaze.

"All right," I say, rubbing my forehead with the back of my hand. "I'll talk to him, just so he knows that you're here and safe. Is that all right?" Jesus, I don't want to do this, but the last thing I need is for Jason-effing-St. Clair to show up outside my car looking for his daughter.

She frowns, but nods.

I slide my thumb over the phone. "Hello?"

"Had— Wait. Who the hell is this?" His voice is smoother than I remember from that awful rainy day back in April, my mom freaking out and Livy's lungs slamming shut, but it's still nauseatingly familiar and comes back to me like a hard slap.

Whoa, whoa. Let's all just calm down. Cora, there's no need to get hysterical.

"A friend of Hadley's." I shake my head to clear it of the memory. "We're—"

"Put my daughter on the phone."

I glance at Hadley. She mouths *no.*

"Um. We're at . . . Waffle House. She had to go to the bathroom."

"Dammit," he mutters. "Is she okay?"

"I'm not really sure."

He sighs loudly. "Her mother and I fought earlier. I only left to give her some space. I didn't know she was going to—" He stops abruptly. Thank God. "Is Hadley back yet?"

She reaches out and squeezes my forearm.

"No."

"I'm sorry, who are you again?"

I swallow hard. "Sam."

"I've never heard her mention you."

I have no freaking clue what I should say to that, so I settle for the sanest, simplest explanation. "We have English together."

"Fine. Sam." His voice drops low and gets a little shaky. "Just . . . get her home safely, all right?"

"I will." I hang up before he can say anything else. My fingers bleed white on her phone and I take several deep breaths. "He said he didn't know your mom—"

"I heard him." She slips her fingers free from my arm. She takes her phone back and slides it into her bag before dropping her head into her hands. "Sam, I really, really don't want to go home right now."

I'm pretty damn sure I should take her home. It's the middle of the night and her dad is pissed and sad and all sorts of other real human emotions I don't want to even think about right now. And her mom . . . Jesus. This is such an effing cluster and if I were smart I'd let Hadley rant a little more, deposit her on her doorstep, and get the hell out of Dodge.

But I think I've proven multiple times over the past several months that I'm a total dumb shit. Looking at Hadley now, her eyes all puffy but still deep and gorgeous, I sure as hell don't want her to go home either.

"Buckle up," I tell her, and throw the car in drive.

CHAPTER EIGHTEEN

Hadley

We end up back in Nashville. While Sam drives, I fall asleep, my head pressed against the cool glass of the car window. The chilly night air tickling my face and Sam's gentle voice calling my name wake me.

"Where are we?" I ask as I unfold myself from the car.

"Love Circle."

"Excuse me?"

He laughs and shuts my door. "You've never been here?"

I look around, trying to get my bearings. We're parked on the side of the road. A hill. Below us, I see darkened houses spiraling down toward a highway. Looks like West End Avenue, a major road in Nashville. Directly in front of us is another huge hill, grassy and looming in the dark, with rough stone steps slicing a path to the top.

"I don't think so."

"This place is great." He opens his trunk and retrieves a woolly, ruby-colored blanket. "Technically, it's a neighborhood—the main street is called Love Circle and winds up the hill—but *this* hill is why people come here all the time. The view is amazing."

We start up the rocky stairs. At the top, there's a flat grassy area. The entire city of Nashville spreads out in front of us, lit up and alive and warm. I can see the Vanderbilt Stadium and the electric high-rises in downtown. The Batman Building—I think it's actually the AT&T building, but its blue lights and spires on either side look like something right out of Gotham City—blinks in the distance. The sky is so huge. Even in the dark, I can imagine it filled with kites, a swath of rainbow against the black.

"This is beautiful. I can't believe I've never been here."

"I used to come up here all the time after baseball practice, especially a bad one. Clear my head." Sam spreads the blanket and settles onto it, propping his elbows up on his knees.

"How did you get into baseball?" I ask, eager to get my mind off my parents and whatever comes next. I sit down beside Sam and tuck my legs under me. The night is pretty mild for November, but a cold breeze picks up and cuts through my thermal shirt. I zip up my hoodie.

"I guess the same way any kid does. Throwing a ball around with my dad in the backyard."

"He taught you how to pitch, right?"

A little smile dances over his mouth. "You remember that, huh?"

"I wasn't that out of it."

"Yeah, you kinda were. I mean, with good reason, but I probably could've told you that my name was Seraphina and I was your fairy godmother and you wouldn't have questioned me."

I toss him a hard look and he throws up his hands. "Yes, my dad taught me to pitch. He was in the minors for a while with the Brewers' farm team. That's how he ended up in Nashville —he played for the Sounds. He met my mom when he was on the road in North Carolina, where she went to college. They met in some bar he went to after a game."

"A bar? Really?"

"I know, right? Not exactly the makings of a happily-ever-after, but they got married two years later." He shrugs, picking at a clump of clovers.

"Did he ever play in the majors?"

"He got called up a few times. Right around the time I was born, he blew out his elbow. Had surgery and could've gone back after physical therapy, but by that point, Mom was pregnant with Livy and he decided to give it up. He coached at Belmont until he moved to Boston."

I shiver as the wind picks up again, bringing with it the

smell of dead leaves and Sam's day-old cologne. "Livy told me about your mom . . . why your dad left."

He sucks in a breath through his teeth. "She did?"

"It must be hard, with your dad gone." His shoulders drop and I shift a little closer to him.

"It's not great," he finally says after a pause. "Livy and I both wanted to go with him, but he didn't want us to."

"Why not?"

He pulls at his ear and looks up at the inky, moonless sky. "The whole thing came out because Livy and I caught my mom."

This time, I suck in a breath. "Wait. You mean . . ."

"Yeah. *Caught* her, caught her."

"Sam." A cold fist closes around my heart. "God."

"The day it happened, Livy got sick and had to leave school early, but my parents weren't answering their phones. I was third on the list, so I picked her up and brought her home. I remember it was raining." He claws at the clover again, decimating the little patch in a matter of seconds.

"God," I say again.

"Livy went completely batshit crazy. Cussing, screaming, crying, followed by a huge asthma attack that almost landed her in the hospital. Then . . ." He swallows so hard, I hear the gulp in his throat. "Let's just say it was bad. A couple months later, Dad decided to leave. Said he needed some space from all of us. How it all came out, it's like Livy and me sort of remind him of it, you know? He says he knows it's not our fault, but he *acts* like it is."

I don't know what to say. Things have been horrible in my house, but my mom never blamed me. For a brief, awful moment, I almost wish she did, because that would at least be *something*.

"The thing is," he goes on, "I expected all of these explosions when he left. I thought Mom would beg him to stay, thought Livy would freak out again. Hell, I even thought I would cry a little. But none of that happened. He was just gone, this memory I can't even remember clearly. I felt sort of lost, like I couldn't get my bearings or something."

I reach out a hand to his and he lets me take it.

"The house was really quiet after he left." Sam stares down at our intertwined fingers. "It still is. My mom barely talks to me . . . though I guess I don't really blame her."

Questions flood into my mind, but I stay quiet. In fact, the whole universe seems to have fallen silent.

"I guess the world really does end with a whimper," he says after a moment. "A whole lot of quiet, a million things left unsaid until it's too late to say them."

I nod even though he's not looking at me. His hurt rolls off him in hot waves, and it's so familiar I can hardly get a breath. There's this dizzying sense of connectedness to him. Something fragile and new and nervous. As I sit with Sam on top of this hill, everything in my life seems so much less scary.

"T. S. Eliot," I murmur.

"What?"

"T. S. Eliot. He wrote, 'This is the way the world ends. Not with a bang but a whimper.'"

"Right. Eliot wrote that." He inhales and blows it out through puffed cheeks. He shakes his head at the city. "Of course he did."

At the sound of his flat voice, my stomach goes cold. I can feel him pulling back from me, fraying the connection. He starts to get up. Before I can stop myself, my hand is in midflight, reaching out to grab his arm and pull him back down. "No."

"What?"

"I'm not going to let you do that again. Not this time."

"Do what?"

I pause for a beat before answering, knowing I should shut up, knowing there's a Nicole somewhere in his life, knowing I don't want this. I *can't* want this. "Push me away."

He drags his hair back. "Hadley. I don't want to. But this . . . it's complicated."

"What is? It's just you and me. Why is that so complicated?"

He opens his mouth and snaps it shut again.

"Nicole?" I ask.

"No. Nicole and I aren't together."

"But . . . but you were?"

He narrows his eyes, thinking, before looking at me. "In a way. But she's not . . . Look, she's really great and a good friend, but we don't like each other like that."

Relief pours through me, and suddenly I need him closer. Unlike with Josh or any other guy, it's not about filling some void or only having fun. It's about Sam. It's about me. It's an overflow of whatever this unspoken, unseen thing is between us, and I realize that I do want it. I want *him*.

I push myself up to my knees and inch forward. My stomach flutters as I close my hands around the collar of his jacket. The ends of his hair curl around his neck and tease my fingers. He's so close that I can feel his shallow, warm breaths sweep over my face, smell his piney, boyish scent.

"Hadley, maybe we should—"

I cut him off with a brush of my lips over the corner of his mouth. His breath hitches and my head feels light and dizzy. His hand drifts up, sliding over my face before moving to work the elastic out of my ponytail. My hair curtains around us and his fingers press into my hips. He pulls me against him and my breath vanishes, replaced with his when our lips finally meet.

CHAPTER NINETEEN

Sam

Her kiss is a starter pistol at a marathon. My body springs into action before my brain can even register what the hell is going on. My arms wrap her up, my mouth tastes and teases her lips and neck and collarbone. She pushes closer, her fingers working a button on my shirt before she slides her hands inside over my shoulders. She feels amazing this close — sweet and wild all at once.

Then everything that is her and me piles up in my head like rocks from an avalanche.

"Wait." I take hold of her wrists. She makes a sound of protest and I know I must be completely insane, but I force myself to push her away.

"What's wrong?" Her voice is thick with our kiss.

"It's just ... Hadley, this has been a really weird night. Maybe we shouldn't ... Listen, I don't want to be some distraction for you."

She frowns and her shoulders drop a little, but she doesn't pull away from me. Instead, she leans into my hand that I hadn't even realized had snuck up to her cheek. "You're not. You're not a distraction."

"Then what am I?" I'm not sure what I want her to say. Any answer will only complicate this whole mess even more. What can possibly come out of her mouth that will make this work, make either of us someone other than who we are?

She tilts her head and puts her soft hand on my face, letting her fingertips glide down to my neck, to my chest. She flattens her palm there, the heat of her hand searing through my shirt. "You're . . ." She pauses and I take a breath, my heart thumping madly. "I don't know. It sounds stupid, but . . . you're like home."

And that's when I know I've finally lost this battle with myself. I don't care who I am, I don't care what our parents did or how I'll explain everything to her. I only care about being with her, right now up on this hill. I feel her in my gut and in my bones and that deep, hollow place in my chest.

Home.

I pull her onto my lap and a little gasp of surprise escapes her throat. "That doesn't sound stupid." I slide my hand to the nape of her neck and hold her there, look at her, inhale her. Closer, closer. Then her mouth is on mine and her hands lace through my hair. My fingers move on their own, unzipping her hoodie and slipping under her shirt, pressing against the warm skin of her lower back. She sighs my name against my lips and with that sound—that tiny, one-syllable word—any doubts still holding me above water snap, and I go under.

The knocking on my door the next morning is deafening.

"What?" I grumble, stuffing my head under the pillow.

"Sam? It's almost ten."

Mom. Awesome.

"I just went to bed thirty minutes ago." Not exactly true, but from the way my eyelids are glued over my eyeballs, it feels true.

"Your father called the house. He's been trying to reach you on your phone."

I groan and roll over, grabbing my phone from the nightstand and checking the missed calls. Dad. Ajay. Dad. Dad. "I had it on silent."

"May I come in?"

God, please, no. "Fine."

She opens the door and stands in the entryway. Her blond hair is loose around her face and she's nursing what I would guess is probably her third cup of tea.

"Does he want me to call him?" I ask.

She sighs and sips. "Yes, and I don't appreciate you putting me in that position, Sam."

"What position?"

"Your father called the house."

"So you mean the position where you have to talk to the guy you had two kids with?"

She closes her eyes for a good ten seconds and runs a thumb down her ear. "No. I mean having to hunt you down to get you to speak to your father."

"You didn't hunt." I throw the covers back and get up, spreading my arms out. "I'm in my natural habitat. And I wasn't ignoring him, I was sleeping."

"All right, fine. Just call him." She turns to go but then stops, looking back over her shoulder so I can only see her profile. "How's that project going with the St. Clair girl?"

"Fine," I say, white-knuckling my phone.

"She still doesn't know? She hasn't said anything?"

I frown at her tone—it's that sticky, probing tone she uses when she's trying to weasel some sort of damning information out of me. I'm well acquainted with this tone. "She's said many things, but nothing relevant to you."

She turns around to face me. "I don't want you to see her outside of school, all right?"

Memories of last night and Hadley's fingers gliding over my stomach flood back. I feel my damn face heat up and look away. "You've already told me this."

"I mean it, Sam."

"Okay. Fine." I toss some clothes into the hamper and start moving around my room, a clear indication that I'm done talking. Luckily, Mom doesn't make a habit of sticking around in my presence any longer than she has to.

I shower and then call Dad. A predictably awkward conversation takes place, during which he splutters vague ideas about Livy and me heading up to Boston for Christmas. Something we both know will never happen. After we hang up, I can picture him in his barely furnished apartment, checking the obligatory weekly phone call to his progeny off his to-do list.

I flop back on my bed and finally let my thoughts take over.

I kissed Hadley.

I did more than that. I liked it. I couldn't get enough of it, of her. We stayed on that hill until night started fading into a gray morning, kissing and talking, over and over. By the time I took her home and crawled into bed, my lips were totally numb and I felt drunk. The weird thing is, even with all the crap surrounding us, all the fucked-up history, I don't regret a single minute.

I pick up my phone and send her a quick text. I just want to know she's real, that it all really happened. Then I find Ajay's number, knowing he's going to flip his proverbial shit when he hears about my night, but a text pops up from Josh Ellison.

Last minute game at school fields. 11AM. U in?

Beyond the regular Wednesday games, Josh and I haven't talked much since I found out what happened between him and Hadley. When I saw him the day after she and I skipped school, I had calmed down enough to know nothing good could come of me confronting him.

But now things feel different. Sure, Hadley still doesn't need me to fight any battle for her, but maybe *I* need it. Hell, maybe I just plain want to. Plus, it'll be a relief to blow off some steam on the mound and get my mind off Hadley. My fingers itch to call her, to hear her voice, but I know she's dealing with her parents today.

I tap out a message to Josh. *Sounds good. See u then.*

In search of something interesting for her hope-in-black-and-white photo project, Livy comes with me to the game.

"I think I've already settled on a subject," she says in the car on the way over, "but I want to make sure."

"What's your subject?"

"Uh-uh. Not telling."

"Why not?"

"Because it's not a sure thing yet. I just said that."

"Sorry, Ansel Adams."

She snaps a picture of me. "Now, that is a face that reeks of hope." She laughs as she checks out the digital display.

I pull on her still-pink hair.

"How's Hadley?" she asks after she swats me away.

I nearly swerve off the road. "Why are you asking me that?"

She shrugs and flips her camera lens on and off, on and off. "I heard you on the phone with her last night. And I heard you leave. And I heard you come back this morning."

"Oh. Right. Um. I think she's okay. I haven't talked to her today, though."

"You like her, don't you?"

"Why would you say that?"

She gives me a look dripping in sarcasm.

I breathe out heavily as we pull into the school. "Yes. I like her. I've tried not to, but I do."

"And she likes you, right?"

The memory of Hadley's mouth brushes across my jaw and I shiver. "Pretty sure she does."

Livy nods, her lips pursed into a little knot. For the first time in a long time, I can't tell what she's thinking.

"Does that bother you?" I finally ask.

She fiddles with her camera lens. "I'm not sure. I feel like it should, but I . . . I like her too, you know? And like you said, none of what happened was *her* fault."

"Hey," I say when her lower lip starts jittering. "None of it was yours, either."

"Or yours?" She lifts her blue eyes to mine.

I press my lips together, but shake my head. "Or mine."

"But it makes me nervous, Sam. I mean, how . . . what are you going to . . ." She trails off, knowing the same unanswerable questions are in my head too.

"I don't know, Liv." She squeezes my hand, comforting me. It's a nice feeling, knowing she's behind me. I've never really thought of my baby sister as someone who could help me. It's always been the other way around, but I'd be lying if I said I didn't feel better from her just listening to me. "Let me know if you get any brilliant ideas."

She smiles and nods once. "Will do."

Before the game, I check my phone, but Hadley hasn't texted back. I try to push it out of my mind. She's fine. She's got her parents to deal with. She's busy. The guys split up and I end up pitching on Josh's team. It feels amazing, hurling the ball down the stretch, the pull in my shoulder and arm, the sound of the ball *thwacking* into the catcher's glove, the lighthearted curses from the guys when they strike out, my own embarrassed laugh when they smack a double into center.

About halfway through the game, the cheerleaders show up on the next field over, practicing for some competition they have in a few weeks. Josh cranes his neck toward them, a familiar expression on his face. It's not the kind of look guys get when we're checking out hot girls. It's the kind we get when we're looking at one particular girl—a girl we actually like.

"Josh, what's up with you?" I ask. Our team is batting and he and I are in the dugout, our arms dangling over the railing.

"Nothing, man." His eyes are still glued to the pixie-haired girl as she vaults into the air.

"Her name's Jenny?"

He swivels his head toward me. "Who?"

I nod toward the field. "She was your girlfriend, right?"

"Yeah." He narrows his eyes at my tone. I cringe a little, realizing I'm using that same tone Mom tried with me earlier. The I'm-going-to-weed-you-out tone.

"I'm guessing you wish that were still the case."

He exhales, then blows a bubble with his bright pink gum. It pops and the residue coats his upper lip. "Yeah, I guess I do."

"What happened?" *Smooth, Sam. Very smooth.*

"I fucked up. We'd been dating for a few weeks and she wanted me to meet her parents."

"So?"

He snorts a bitter laugh. "Dude, her parents are both record label executives and live in this gated, rich-ass neighborhood. Each house has its own freaking zip code. My mom works two jobs and I've never even met my dad. He took off before the strip turned blue."

I don't say anything, but I get this feeling in my gut like I inhaled a bag of Cheetos for breakfast.

"I freaked out and bailed at the last minute on the dinner Jenny planned. We had a huge fight, and I ended up at that party. I saw Hadley and she was . . . Christ, she was there and she's hot and I drank too much and my head was totally messed up. Then Jenny shows up and I was . . . well . . . occupied when she got there and I guess Sloane saw Hadley come out of the room we were in."

My hands ball into fists. The idea of Josh with Hadley in a room makes me want to hit something. Hard. But as Josh casts another wistful eye at Jenny, my anger starts fizzling out. A foul ball soars into the dugout, narrowly missing beaning Josh in the head.

"You put Hadley in a really shitty position," I say as he flips off Matt, the batter.

"I know, man. I didn't mean to. I've told Sloane to lay off, that it wasn't Hadley's fault."

"Why'd you have to lie to her?"

"I don't know. I told you. I just wanted . . . I thought I needed . . ." His eyes drift back to Jenny before whispering weakly, "I don't know."

I stay silent and watch as Josh yanks up a bat and heads to the batter's box. When someone pisses you off, it's so easy to forget they still have blood under their skin. Yeah, he acted like a dick, no doubt about it.

But.

And this is a big *but,* because I'd like nothing more than to make this all his fault. *But,* his mistake had a reason behind it —something that flipped a switch and changed him into a smooth-talking assclown without any common sense or a conscience.

I scan the outfield and spot Livy on the other side of the fence, viewing the game through her camera as she walks the perimeter, her pink streak catching the sun. I think about our parents, who sure as hell didn't have a fairy-tale marriage. Their conversational style consisted of loaded statements and comparisons of who did more around the house or for Livy and me. Long before my mom pulled the trigger on the gun that killed their marriage, they were effing miserable.

I check my phone again and there's a text from Hadley. Looking up to find Livy, I see Josh smack a line drive down the third base line, a thing of beauty. I glance back down at Hadley's text. My heart bolts into a sprint, feeling like I just clicked the safety off a loaded gun.

CHAPTER TWENTY

Hadley

I'm already awake, lying in bed and staring at the undulating shadows the midmorning sun is casting on my wall, when my door creaks open. I roll over, expecting to see only Jinx's tail flicking at the air as she saunters toward me, but it's not my cat.

It's my mother.

I sit up, never shifting my eyes off of her. She looks tired, dressed in jeans and a navy sweater, her brown boots pulled up to mid-calf. The house was quiet when Sam dropped me off near dawn, and only my dad's car was in the garage, so I'm not sure when she got home. From the metallic, cold-weather smell she brings into my room, I'm guessing probably not too long ago.

Mom sits on the edge of my bed. Her eyes drift over my room, over swim trophies and honor roll certificates and pictures of Kat and me thumbtacked to my bulletin board. Over the one framed picture of our family I couldn't bring myself to put away—the three of us smiling and laughing at the Kite Festival two years ago.

She looks down at her hands, her thumb circling over her bare left ring finger.

"You're leaving, aren't you?" The question slips from my throat, but I don't even feel like I need to ask it. She certainly doesn't need to answer. The fact is like a living thing pushing in between us and taking up all the space in the room.

She presses both hands to her mouth and exhales slowly. "I'm sorry about last night. I should've left a note or called you, but I was upset and tired and I . . . I need a break, Hadley. I need some time."

Her words crack something inside me. This isn't how this is supposed to go. We're supposed to deal with this—Mom and me together. Crying together. Getting mad together. *Anything* together. "Why doesn't *he* leave? This is his fault. You shouldn't have to leave."

"He offered. *I* need to go, Hadley. I need out of this house for a while, away from . . ."

"From me," I fill in for her. It doesn't even matter if that's not what she was going to say. That's what it *feels* like. I want to beg her to stay. Beg her not to leave me alone, but she's already gone. She's been gone for six months.

"No. Honey, *no.* You've done nothing wrong. I know I'm not

handling this the right way, but I . . . I don't know what else to do at this point." She turns toward me, ducking her head so she snags my eyes with hers. "Your father and I love you. Nothing can change that, okay? Ever."

I nod, feeling more like a complication to their problems than loved.

"I'll be at a hotel nearby." She gets up, stretching out a hand to smooth over my hair, but from where she's standing, she can't quite reach, and her arm falls back to her side. At the door, she turns back. "I'll call you soon." Then she clicks the door closed behind her. I listen to her footsteps recede down the hall, clomp down the stairs, thump over the hardwood in the kitchen, and fade away.

I'm still balled up in my blankets when my phone pings on my nightstand. I clench my teeth as I reach for it. It's probably Kat. Our little spat last night seems like forever ago, but I'm still not sure I'm ready to talk to her yet.

But it's not Kat.

It's Sam.

Hey. I'm here if you need me.

That's all it says. I stare at his message and my chest tightens up even more.

If you need me.

Oh, God. A wave of panic washes over me and I lie back

down. I press the heels of my palms into my eyes, remember-ing the way he kissed me, how his fingertips studied me like I was an intricate piece of art. Last night was the first time in so long that I've felt comfortable in my own skin. I wasn't worried or scared or angry. I was just . . . me. But now my mother is gone, really gone, and something old and dark and ugly is creeping up on me again, and I want to talk to Sam so badly my teeth ache.

And that scares the crap out of me.

Sitting up, my fingers scramble over my phone. Ready or not, I tap Kat's name. She answers and I start talking before she can stop me. I pretend that the last ten minutes of our previous conversation never happened and fill her in on everything about Mom.

"Wow, Hadley. I had no idea things had gotten that bad. Why didn't you tell me?"

I pick at a loose thread on my comforter. "I didn't tell anyone."

"Do you want me to come over?"

"Thanks, but I'm fine."

"Sure." Several short intakes of breath buzz in my ear, evi-dence Kat is trying to figure out how to say something awkward.

"What? Just say it."

"Okay. Sorry. It's just . . . is she, like, *leaving* leaving? For good?"

I flop back onto the bed. A thin layer of dust is coating the ceiling fan. "I don't know, Kat."

"What can I do?"

"Just talk to me for a while."

"About what?"

"Anything."

"Okay. How's your dad handling—"

"Except that."

"All right, fine. Well . . ." She drawls the word into about three syllables and I can tell her lips are curling into a shy smile. "Ajay drove me home last night."

"Yes, this I know. And?"

"And we sat in his car and talked until almost two in the morning."

"Really. You like him?"

"I don't know. Maybe. But, God, he's completely delicious."

I laugh, even though it feels almost like swearing in church on a day like today. "Now *that* deserves a meow."

"Please don't."

"What's up with that Sara girl?"

"Oh. *Her.* They just broke up and she's not happy about it. At all."

"You don't say."

"I'm serious," Kat says, oblivious to my sarcasm. "He hinted that it's all pretty recent and he's still sort of recovering, but has no interest in getting back with her."

"What about *Rob?*"

She sighs. "I don't know. Rob is still Rob, but he seems even more unattainable after talking to Ajay. I'm not sure the real Rob could measure up with the guy in my head."

"I could've told you that two years ago."

Kat laughs. "Anyway, Ajay asked for my number."

"Of course he did."

"Although I doubt he'll use it."

"I'm sure he will."

"He just seems like an entirely different breed of boy and I'm just . . . I don't know. Me."

"Obviously he likes you enough to get your number, Kat. But Sam did mention that Ajay has an unusual style of courting." Last night, Sam and I talked about everything from my disastrous experimentation with the violin when I was seven to Sam's weird phobia of horses, including our best friends' clear interest in each other.

Kat snorts a laugh. "Courting?"

"That's the word Sam used."

"Huh. I sort of like the sound of that."

She babbles on happily, but I'm distracted, my mind drifting back to Mom's empty left ring finger. When did she stop wearing her wedding band? Did Dad notice? Is he still wearing his?

"Anyway, Ajay said Sam's family has been through a hard time," Kat says. "You know anything about that?"

The question rips my thoughts off the diamond and sapphire band I used to covet as a little girl. "Um, yeah, actually. His mom . . ." I pause, chewing on my lower lip as Sam's story floats back to me.

"His mom what?" Kat asks.

"Well . . . his mom sort of cheated on his dad."

"Really? Huh."

"Huh what?"

"Well, that's weird, isn't it? Both of your parents had affairs."

"Lots of people have affairs," I say, but it's a whisper. Lots of people *do* have affairs. But it doesn't feel like that when it happens to your family. You feel like the only one. Alone in this weird reality that no one can really understand.

"When did he tell you all this?" Kat asks.

"We hung out last night."

"What? When?"

Before I can answer, Dad calls my name from downstairs.

"I need to go," I say, my stomach knotting up.

"Wait, why were you out with Sam?"

I blow out a breath, unsure if I want to talk about Sam yet. But I know Kat. She'll literally haunt my every step until I give her details. So I tell her everything about last night.

When I'm done, there's a long pause. Too long for Kat. "Hadley, he's a nice guy," she finally says. Her voice is all wrong. She sounds . . . mad.

"I know that."

"I thought you were sort of friends with him."

I frown, totally confused. "I am."

"But you made out with him. Which you and I both know pretty much means you'll never talk to him again."

"Why would I never talk to him again? I like—"

"Do you talk to Josh? Or Henry? Or whoever else I may not even know about?"

"Kat, what the hell?"

But she keeps going, sounding close to tears. "I just don't get this, Had. Why do you have to do this with every guy you meet? You're acting like a—"

She cuts herself off with a huge sigh, but we both know what she was about to say. I knew Kat took major issue with some of the stuff I've done with guys, but I never believed she really looked down on me for it.

"I need to go," I say, and then I end the call before she can respond.

My hands shake and my heart thunders as I get out of bed and throw on jeans and a sweater. I don't even bother to brush my hair. I find Dad in the kitchen, sipping coffee at the table and leafing through the paper as if it's any other Saturday. A light green box sits next to him, a sticker with a dark-green-lidded eye on it sealing it closed.

"Hi, honey," he says a little too brightly. He nods toward the box. "I didn't know if you'd eaten breakfast yet, but I got your favorite cupcakes. I thought you might—"

"Cupcakes?"

He lifts his mug but doesn't drink, eyeing me over the rim. His wedding ring catches the recessed lights, briefly glowing white.

"They're just cupcakes, Hadley."

My throat aches and I swallow what feels like a hundred unsatisfying gulps of air. They are *not* just cupcakes. Yesterday maybe they were just cupcakes. Six months ago, just cupcakes. Today they're a placation. A desperate scramble at anything to cover up the fact that he screwed up and Mom is gone.

"You think that's all it takes?" I ask. "Some chocolate and I'll just nod and say okay and sit down and dig in and smile like nothing happened?"

"Of course not." He releases a sigh, squeezing his fingers into his eyes. "Jesus Christ. This is hard enough, Hadley. I don't need this right now."

Anger at Kat bubbles up to join my anger at this man standing in front of me, and it all boils over. "And I do? This is all your fault. You know that, right?"

"Hadley. Stop."

"No. I've spent months *stopping*, trying to forget what you did. What you did to us and her and me. I'm so tired of it. I'm tired of you pretending like this is fixable!"

"You won't even try. Neither of you will. At least I'm trying." His voice has that dangerous, quiet quality it used to get when I got in trouble as a kid. And that's all this is to him—me being a brat. Surely I'll snap out of it one day and come back to him.

"Mom wouldn't have left if it weren't for you. None of this would've happened if you had just kept it in your goddamn pants."

His mouth drops open. Before he can say anything else, I turn my back on him and head outside, pacing in circles in the driveway. The day is cool and crisp, the leaves beautifully dying in bright reds and yellows. I take out my phone and look at Sam's text again, choking down tears and doubts in one gulp. I tap the message box and start typing.

Can I see you later today?

I hit *Send*. I tell myself that I don't need him.

But he's the only person I want right now.

CHAPTER TWENTY-ONE

Sam

I wait for her on the tiny merry-go-round at the park across the street from my house. The air smells metallic, all cold weather and rusty swing chains. I lie down, my back pressed on top of the freezing, dingy red metal while my feet pull me in a lazy circle.

My stomach rolls right along with the rest of me, but it's got nothing to do with the merry-go-round. Livy tried to get me to eat something before I left, but I couldn't even choke down a swallow of water. I keep running through last night in my head, scrounging for that precise moment I should've stopped everything and taken Hadley home. But I can't find it, and honestly, I don't look all that hard. Now with every cell in my body anticipating seeing Hadley again, I'm an effing mess of excitement and terror.

A soft sound brushes over the bits of recycled rubber that

make up the floor of the playground. I stop my revolution and sit up too quickly. My vision blackens for a split second and then clears, revealing Hadley in a thick cream-colored cardigan over a black T-shirt and perfectly tight jeans. Her hair is loose and long and all but screaming at me to run my fingers through it.

She stops a few feet from me, her hands shoved in the pockets of her sweater. She looks down at her boots and pink splashes over her cheekbones. My gut stutters as I stand up.

"Hi," she says, so quietly I almost don't hear her.

"Hi."

"Hi," she says again through a deep breath.

I smile in response, relieved to see she's as uncertain as I am. Not upset or angry or regretful. Just a good old-fashioned ball of nerves. But then we stand there for what feels like hours in silence, and doubts creep in again.

I should tell her it was all a mistake.

Because it was.

Wasn't it?

"Wanna swing?" I ask.

She looks up and tilts her head at me, studying me through narrowed eyes. Impulsively—maybe insanely—I reach out and take her hand from her pocket, sliding my fingers over her palm to lace with hers. "It's just swinging, not an invitation to elope."

She laughs softly and lets me pull her to the green plastic seats swaying in the breeze. Soon we're airborne, climbing higher and higher into the sky and grinning at each other stupidly as the altitude seems to scrape away all the tension.

"Okay," I say, pumping my legs to gain more speed. "You ready for this?"

"For what?"

"On three, we jump off and see who lands the farthest away from the swings."

"No way!" She laughs as she soars backwards, her hair creating a dark curtain over her flushed features. "You're taller. You'll automatically win."

"Yeah, but you're lighter. You'll fly farther."

"All the more reason I'd rather not risk breaking my kneecaps."

"Just bend your knees a little when you land."

"I haven't jumped off a swing since I was, like, eight."

"That's sort of the point."

"No."

"Come on, Hadley. Let go a little." Rather than push her any more, I launch myself out of my swing and land with a *thwunk* on the crumbled rubber. My legs buckle and I go down, my body piling up in a heap of elbows and knees.

"Are you okay?" Hadley yells, still in motion.

I let out an exaggerated groan and shoot her a thumbs-up. "Your turn."

"No, Sam."

I roll myself up to sitting and prop my elbows on my knees. "You're really just going to let me win? I'm a privileged white male in America. Don't you think I have enough advantages already? Come on, St. Clair. Kick my ass."

She arches forward and then pushes back again. I watch her, totally mesmerized. The effect is weirdly hot as she gains more and more height. Then she's flying, her body a graceful line, arms in the air like a bird on the wind before she lands on all fours.

She's a least a couple feet farther away from the swings than I am.

"Atta girl," I say.

She laughs and flops onto her back, her chest rising and falling steadily.

"I haven't done this in forever," she says, staring at the sky.

I lie down and roll my body in her direction. It takes me three rotations to reach her. "What? Been to a park?"

"Played."

I stretch myself out next to her and realize I haven't either. I can't remember the last time I did something fun for the hell of it. Felt the wind in my hair and laughed at nothing and acted like a dumb shit just because I could.

I prop myself up on one elbow and look at her. The coppery sun ignites her brown eyes so they almost glow, her lashes a black fringe around them. She smiles and blinks heavily, her pulse rapid in the hollow of her throat, matching my own. I reach out and tuck a lock of her hair behind her ear. I try to slide my fingers down the long strand, but her hair is all tangly from the swing ride. I pull, but her damn hair has suddenly morphed into a thousand tentacles.

"Ow." She grimaces and I feel my ears burn red, but of course she's grimacing. A complete imbecile is glued in her hair right now.

"Sorry . . ." I tug gently and she inhales sharply. "Okay, I'm seriously stuck."

"Here, let me." She pushes my other hand away and locates the knot around my finger. She unravels the snarl of hair, obviously trying not to laugh.

Finally free of me, she pulls her hair over one shoulder and then tucks her hands under her head. She looks at me and gnaws at her lower lip, *still* biting off a laugh.

Uh-uh.

I lift my brows, smirking, and she releases a single giggle.

I lean toward her again.

Really. Slowly.

The closer I get, the more her lips curve upward. I stop an inch from her mouth and hear her breath hitch. I don't move any closer. I don't move farther away, either.

"Seriously?" She twists her mouth into a cute little knot.

"What?" I slide my thumb over her flushed cheek, and she shivers. "Did you want me to do something other than hover over you awkwardly?"

Her hand sneaks under my jacket and bunches around the hem of my T-shirt. Her cool fingers tease my hip.

"Hey." My body arches away from her a little. "That tickles."

"Two can play at this game, Mr. Bennett."

Her sweet breath fans across my mouth and I almost lose it right there. I slide the hand near her face down to her throat and around the back of her neck. Her eyes flutter closed briefly, but then she slips her hand even farther under my shirt, letting it trail up my back.

I stifle a groan and let my lower lip brush hers. Through some superhuman display of self-control, I don't kiss her. Not yet.

"Give up?" she whispers.

"Nope."

"You enjoy this torture, then?"

In answer, my mouth feathers over the corner of hers, first one side, then the other. She squirms underneath me. Then I trail over to her earlobe and tug it gently between my teeth, feeling maniacally triumphant when she emits a little squeak.

That sound totally does me in. Hand cupping her chin, I pull her face toward mine and finally press my lips to hers. I tease her mouth open and taste her. She tastes me back and that same heady mix from last night—something both soft and fierce—nearly smothers me.

She's just hooked one leg around my hip, wrapping me in pure freaking heaven, when my stomach growls against hers. She freezes, her mouth open on mine. Then she starts laughing. I let out a frustrated groan and bury my face in the slope where her neck meets her shoulder.

"Hungry?" she asks, still laughing.

"I don't know what you're talking about." She shuts up when I kiss her neck, literally some of my best work, but then my stomach whines even louder and she busts up again.

I roll off her and pat my gut. "Insistent little bastard, isn't he?"

"I have some cupcakes in my car."

I perk up at that. All my nervousness vanished with the first touch, and now my hunger—at least for something other than Hadley—takes over. "Yeah?"

"My dad got them this morning, but . . ."

I swallow around the sudden boulder in my throat. "Hadley, if you want to talk about—"

"I'll go get them." She pretty much catapults herself to her feet, pulling her sweater down over her hips and jogging away before I can say another word. Her form gets smaller and smaller in the late afternoon light until she reaches her car parked on the street.

When she gets back, her bag slung over her shoulder, her expression is a mask of impassivity. I don't ask about her mom. Maybe that makes me an asshole, but it's pretty obvious she doesn't want to talk about her family. God knows I don't.

An exhausted-looking woman with a brood of four red-heads arrives and takes over the playground, so we retreat to the picnic area at the edge of the park and sit cross-legged on top of a wooden table. Hadley pops open a box from the Green-Eyed Girl and offers me a chocolate cupcake the size of my hand. I devour it in two bites and start in on my second before she even gets the wrapper off her first. When she takes a big bite, choco-late frosting glazes her upper lip and chin.

"Messy much?" I ask, and try to thumb off the icing.

"Hey, I like it there." She swats me away.

"Yeah? It's sorta cute. Like a little prepubescent-boy-stache."

"I think you need one." Before I can react, she swipes a handful of frosting off an uneaten cupcake and smears it down my entire face.

My jaw drops in shock. A big glob of sugary goo falls off my nose and catches on my lower lip. I scrape it off with my forefinger and hold it up. "You did not just do that."

"Do what?"

She smirks at me like she's the cutest damn thing on two legs. Which she probably is, but that's beside the point when there's more frosting on my face than there is skin. Just as she opens her mouth to take another bite of her cupcake, I take aim and flick the icing off my finger. It smacks her squarely on the forehead.

After that, it's all-out war. I grab two more cupcakes and scramble to my feet, running to take cover behind a big oak tree. She stalks after me, a cupcake in each hand, and pelts me with little cake bullets that end up in my hair and all over my shirt. I barrel toward her and she squeals when I hook my arm around her waist and stuff a whole cupcake down the back of her sweater. The entire battle, I'm laughing so hard I can barely breathe. At one point, I'm pretty sure Hadley snorts some chocolate up her nose.

"Okay, okay! Truce!" I hold up my empty hands in surrender.

"Oh, thank God." She shakes out her fingers, sending tiny crumbles of cake flying to the ground.

I wipe my palms on my jeans. When I get them clean enough, I close my hands around the sleeves of her sweater and pull her closer so I can kiss a spot of chocolate off her cheek.

She laughs. "Tasty?"

"Mm-hm." I really just want to start licking every dot of icing I see on her, but considering there are now two wholesome families running around on the playground, I force myself to resist.

"We're a complete mess," she says, trying to slick some frosting out of my hair. "I think I have some napkins in my glove compartment."

We make our way to her car and wipe ourselves down with a bunch of scratchy brown napkins from Starbucks. Glancing across the street, I see my mom's car in our driveway. "I should go. Livy's probably starving and if I leave it to my mom, she'll be eating condensed soup or some shit like that for dinner."

"Oh, right." She looks down at her feet, worrying at her lower lip. "I need to go too."

There's a cold clench in my gut. I look toward my house again and try to figure out if there's any way I can smuggle her inside without my mom noticing. I squeeze my eyes shut, pissed off all over again at the crap between me and Hadley that she doesn't even know about. All the shit I can't hide from, even under a mountain of chocolate cupcakes.

I slip my hand to the nape of her neck and kiss her forehead. "This was really fun."

She nods and tilts her head up to meet my eyes. "It was more than fun."

"Amusing?"

"Pleasant?"

I shake my head. "Enjoyable?"

"Convivial?"

"Nice one. How about blissful?"

She laughs. "Are you trying to out-synonym me, Sam?"

"Oh. Yeah, actually I am." I scratch at my chin, scraping off some more icing. "Livy and I do this sometimes. Sorry, it's sort of a habit, I guess."

"Sounds like something I would do with my dad," she says quietly, squinting into the setting sun.

I pull her closer and press my face to the top of her head. She smells like grass and sugar. Her arms come around my back so that we're a just a tangle of chocolate and cotton and skin.

"Sam?" she asks after a few minutes, her voice muffled in my jacket.

"Hmm?"

"I want this."

I pull back so I can look at her. My stomach roils with the need to sit her down and tell her the truth, but the words jumble together in my head. My heart balls up like tinfoil, because I know this isn't about Livy anymore, if it ever was. It's not about our parents or those notes or who screwed who more than six months ago. I've kept my mouth shut because I want to hold on to this girl standing in front of me.

Hold on and run like hell.

So I tell her the only true thing I can.

"Me too."

CHAPTER TWENTY-TWO

Hadley

Kat slides into the seat next to me, startling me from the world of ridiculous misunderstandings in *Much Ado About Nothing.* My pen pops out of my hand and lands on the filthy cafeteria floor, which is stained with a couple decades' worth of mac and cheese and taco sauce.

"Oops." She crawls on all fours to get my rogue pen. "Sorry."

"Kat, gross. Just leave it."

"No, I got it." She hands me the pen, which I take gingerly between my thumb and forefinger.

"Blech." I drop it onto the table and retrieve one not coated in MRSA from my bag.

"You are such an old lady sometimes." Kat's mouth quirks into a diffident half smile. She's tried to talk to me several times in the past two weeks, but I've been unresponsive. I've got enough to think about without her making me feel like crap about Sam.

"Mm." I turn away from her, munching on a french fry. My eyes wander through the crowd, past the blue and gold spirit banners for tonight's football game, and find Sam across the room, tray piled with three grilled cheese sandwiches and two oranges. He weaves through the sea of tables toward me, but when he spots Kat and me sitting in a bubble of discomfort, he halts. I catch his eye, imploring him to come and mediate, but he shakes his head and mouths, *Talk to her,* before sitting down with Josh-freaking-Ellison.

"How are your parents?" Kat asks.

I take a deep breath without looking at her. The last two weeks have gone by in a blur of school, constant wondering about my mother, and avoiding Kat and my father. Only Sam has kept me from bludgeoning my head against a wall, and I've spent nearly every free minute with him. I've talked to Mom on the phone every day, but the conversation is strained and alternates between long silences and a barrage of meaningless questions like what sweater I'm wearing or whether or not I think the school's football team will make the playoffs.

Dad is a whole other ball of weird. We've barely spoken since our fight the day Mom left. He doesn't call when I miss dinner and hide out at Sam's. He doesn't insist on sushi Thursdays. He doesn't ask me about the Kite Festival. He doesn't tell me whether or not he and Mom talk, and I don't ask. I thought I'd be relieved on the day he finally backed off a little — instead I just feel hollow.

"Hadley," Kat says when I don't answer her.

I look down at my book, eyes scanning but seeing nothing.

"Listen, I'm sorry."

"Kat, do you even know what you're apologizing for?"

She frowns and looks away. Her cheeks twitch the way they do when she's about to cry.

"Yeah. I didn't think so." I turn back to *Much Ado,* but she covers the book with her hand.

"Hadley, stop."

"Stop what?"

"Just . . . *stop.* Stop acting like I'm a bitch who isn't on your side. Because I am. You just . . ." She exhales, deflating. "Look, I miss you, okay?"

"Right. You weren't too fond of me last time we talked. Besides, it's only been two weeks since—"

"No. It's been six months."

I stare at her, speechless.

She sighs, squirming in her seat as she tucks her hair behind both ears. "Listen, I know the circumstances sucked, but I was still excited when you moved here. Finally, we got to live in the same town. But you haven't been the same since all that stuff with your parents happened. I know that's expected, but sometimes I just wish . . ."

"What?"

"You're still you, but you're not. You quit swimming and started disappearing with guys like it was no big deal, which if that's really what you want to do, fine, but yeah, it sort of made me mad. People talked about you all the time and I felt like a little kid next to you. I don't even know what you're doing with these guys. Not that I want all the details, but how do I know you haven't had—"

"I haven't."

"But you never talk to me. Not about anything that matters."

I close my eyes. "I haven't done that."

She looks at me with eyebrows raised, like she's waiting for me to go on, but then nods. "See? That. Right there. No explanation. Just *yes* and *no* and *I don't know.*"

"Kat, come on—"

"And you're so pissed off. All. The. Time. And you like being that way. I feel . . . I don't know. Like you don't need me anymore."

I sigh, anger seeping out of me in a slow leak. "Kat, you're the only reason I haven't lost my sanity in all this. You know that, right?"

She shakes her head and shrugs. "I just miss you."

I reach over and wrap my arms around her. I don't know what else to do. "I'm right here," I say, but I'm not exactly sure what I mean by that. Who's here? The old Hadley, a girl who smiled easily and believed in trust and love and possibility? Or the new Hadley, this conflicted, angry girl I didn't even realize had infiltrated my body?

I pull back and try to smile. I know I should apologize too —for hanging up on her the day Mom left, for ignoring her for nearly two weeks. But something pulls the apology in deeper, yanking it into a complicated knot in my chest. One I'm not ready to try to unravel. Instead, I let the smile take over and change the subject. "You don't have to worry about me kissing a bunch of different guys anymore."

"Really?" Her eyes light up in a way that almost feels insulting. "Why not?"

She wanted me to talk to her, right? I take and deep breath and I tell her about Sam.

"Oh. My. God. Hadley!" Kat squeals, then her expression takes a plunge. "Oh, my God, Hadley. I'm the worst friend ever. Last time we talked. I gave you all that crap about him. I just figured—"

"It's okay."

"No, it's not. I'm so sorry. You really like him?"

I shrug and bite my lip. I could sear a steak on my face right now.

"You do! You really like him!"

"Sheesh, keep it down. It's not a big deal."

"Not a big deal? You, Hadley St. Clair, are blushing about a boy, and that's not a big deal?"

I press my hands to my cheeks. "Kat, I'm begging you."

"Is he a good kisser? He looks like he'd be a good kisser."

More heat creeps up my neck, and I smile but keep my mouth firmly shut.

"Wow." She grins broadly. "I mean, I-think-the-sky-is-falling wow."

"Wow what?" Sam asks from behind me.

We both jump and Kat emits a cute little yelp.

"Um . . ." I stammer as he brushes my hair back from my neck and sits down, tossing an orange between his hands. "Wow . . . that Rob . . . talked to Kat today."

Kat's eyes widen, but she nods, going with it.

"Rob Graham?" Sam asks, eyebrows low.

"Yeah, you know him?"

"He's in my gym class." He glances at Kat, clearly wary. "He's kind of a dick."

"Is he?" I ask. Kat's mouth drops open.

Sam steals a cold fry off my plate. "A locker room is a litmus test for douches. Rob's strip is acidic red. Trust me."

"What did he do?" I'm totally intrigued. Neither Kat nor I know Rob all that well. He and Kat have always gone to school together and he's on the swim team with her, but they've exchanged all of five words in the past five years.

Sam shrugs again, breaking the orange's skin with his thumbnail. "Nothing that I've witnessed. It's just his whole attitude, toward girls in particular. The other day I heard him telling some of the guys about a date with Rebecca Vansant. He told her that more than a handful is a waste. I mean, what guy actually says that to a girl? What an ass."

Given the fact that Rebecca has to wrangle on *two* sports bras during our own gym class, I decipher Rob's meaning pretty quickly. Kat's eyes widen and I wrinkle my nose in disgust while Sam winces apologetically.

"Forget Rob," I say. "He's not even real, remember? What about Ajay?" I waggle my eyebrows at Kat and she flushes pink.

"Um. I don't know. He hasn't called me."

Sam becomes extremely interested in his orange, peeling it like he's handling a newborn baby.

"Did you call him?" I ask Kat.

She just blinks at me.

"Sam?" I ask, drawing out his name and leaning toward him.

"What?"

"What's up with Ajay?"

He shrugs, shoving half the orange in his mouth.

"Sam Bennett." I pinch his thigh under the table.

"Hey, now." He grabs my fingers and pulls my arm around his neck. "If I did know something—and I'm not saying that I do—I couldn't tell you. Bros before—"

"Don't even think about finishing that sentence." I yank my arm back.

"I was going to say 'beautiful girls,' but you didn't let me finish."

"Right."

Kat looks stricken. Her eyebrows bunch together. I elbow Sam and motion toward her with my chin. He splays his hands in helplessness.

"I'm sure you'll hear from him soon," he finally says, but Kat nods and tries to shrug like she doesn't care.

"I've gotta go meet with Coach Torrenti. He wants to talk to Josh and me about some co-captain thing." He twirls a piece of my hair around his finger. "What are you doing tonight?"

"Nothing. Why?" I respond vaguely, distracted by Josh waving at Sam from across the cafeteria. Next to Jenny Kalinski. A slow cold coats my stomach.

Sam tips my chin toward his face, forcing my eyes on his. "We need to go on a real date."

"A date?"

"You've heard of them, right? Two people, soft music, romantic atmosphere."

"Are we going on a date or ballroom dancing?"

He pokes me in the ribs. "Maybe both. Tonight. You and me."

I blink at him and feel my face go slack. How did I end up as one half of a *you and me*? But he's smiling, studying my face with such care that all my questions dissolve.

"Okay," I say. "You and me."

"Wear something comfortable," he says, standing. "No skirts or jeans."

"Wait. Like sweatpants?"

"Just something . . . you know, comfy but not too loose."

"She has these really tight, stretchy yoga pants," Kat suggests, pointing at me with a baby carrot. "Although those pants have never experienced a downward-facing dog."

My face heats up as Sam presses his tongue to his top lip, clearly trying not to laugh. Kat crunches her carrot, oblivious that her words came out sounding vaguely dirty.

"Those sound like a great choice," Sam finally says, lifting his eyebrows at me.

"What are you up to?"

He grins and leans down to kiss me, citrus-scented fingers curling into my hair. "You'll have to wait and see."

"Yo, Bennett!" Josh calls. I swivel my head toward his voice and narrow my eyes into a glare. Unfortunately, Josh has mastered the art of avoiding my gaze, but Jenny's eyes find mine and for a split second we stare at each other. Her expression is hard to read, but it's not angry or even sad. It's just . . . curious.

Sam gives me a half smile and strolls off toward Josh and Jenny. My stomach finally freezes over. Sam told me about his conversation with Josh a couple weeks ago. When I see Josh in class and in the hallways, he has looked fairly miserable. Aside from nasty glares, Sloane has finally grown tired of her crusade against me, but I can't seem to release my anger. So he had a fight with his girlfriend. Big freaking deal. But I can tell there's something about Josh that Sam just understands or at least tries to understand. They're not exactly friends, but they're not *not* friends either. Honestly, it irritates me like sand in my swimsuit.

When I look up, Kat is staring at me. "What?" I start packing up my book and wrapping up the crusts from my sandwich.

"Nothing. It's just . . ." She shakes her head. "I just never thought I'd see you with a boyfriend."

"He's not my boyfriend."

"Right. Because that whole starry-eyed, red-cheeked thing is the same way you look at Josh Ellison."

"No, I save that for you," I say, batting my lashes.

Kat ignores me. "If he's not your boyfriend, what is he?"

I sit back, the cold from the cheap aluminum chair piercing through my shirt. I grab for the right words, but there are too many and not enough to choose from.

"Sam and me . . . we're . . . he's . . ." Oh, who am I kidding? I have no idea what I'm doing or what's really happening between us. At first it was scary, letting Sam in my life like this, but now . . . I don't know. Sam and me—we just *are*. Being together is terrifying and easy all at once.

"He's just *Sam*."

"Yeah, I know who he is. The weird thing is who you are when you're around him."

"What do you mean?"

"Well, I can tell you're nervous and scared about liking him, but at the same time, you're not. You're *happy*. It's totally bizarre."

I swallow, but manage to keep my expression blank. I don't want Kat to know how accurate her assessment is—how unmoored and content I feel with Sam. "It's hard to describe. I mean, why do you like Ajay?"

Immediately, I wish I could suck my question back into my mouth. Kat's face falls and I know she's not thinking about Sam anymore. "I don't like Ajay."

The bell rings and I sling my arm around Kat's shoulder as we wade through the masses toward the hallway. I breathe in her familiar smell—orange Tic-Tacs and fruity shampoo. It feels good to have my Kitty Kat back. "I'll be your date anytime, baby." I smack her cheek with a loud kiss.

"Thanks, honey, but you're really not my type." She reaches around me and pinches my butt. "Then again . . ."

We laugh our way to Music Appreciation, a fluff senior class during which we do nothing but listen to our own iPods while completing personal music preference surveys. Kat's laughter is short-lived. I can hear Adele crooning from her earbuds, see a definite slump in her shoulders. Rob was only ever a dream, and therefore pretty much innocuous. But Ajay is flesh and blood, capable of wreaking emotional havoc on my best friend.

Despite my misgivings, it's nice to think about things like Kat's crush and my date tonight. God, it's all so normal.

At the end of the day, the bell rings and releases us for the weekend. I push through the sea of bodies and head toward Kat's locker. When I get there, she's grinning and bouncing on her feet with a large cup in her hands. It's a combination of a honey-toned wood and some silver-colored metal, welded together with zigzags of shiny copper. It's strange and totally incredible.

"What's that?" I ask, relieved to see her smile.

She looks up, her eyes wild with excitement. "Oh my God, Had, look!" She thrusts the mug under my nose, and a little *oink* greets me.

"Holy crap!" I yelp and jump backwards. "What the hell is that?" A few kids stop their mad scramble for the exit to look at us. I step closer to Kat, ducking my head.

"It's a pig! A teacup pig!" She gazes into the cup, crooning. "Aren't you the cutest thing? Yes, you are. Yes, you are."

I peer into the cup and, yes, there is a *pig* curled up at the bottom, staring up at me with Wilbur don't-eat-me eyes. It's wrinkly and pale pink with black spots, and its tiny, shiny snout is about the size of my thumbnail.

"That's actually a living thing? It's so cute."

"I know. Oh my God, can you believe it? Do you think my mom will let me keep it? I've read about these little guys and they only grow to be, like, five pounds. That's doable, right? That's smaller than a cat. Totally doable. Oh, I need to get food and a crate and a maybe a heating lamp and—"

"Um, Kat?"

She startles, her euphoric eyes focusing on me. "What?"

"Where did this adorable, impossibly small pig come from?"

"Oh." She strokes the pig's head with one finger and it snorts. "He was in my locker, in this cup, just waiting for me. Were you waiting for me? Yes, you were. Yes. Someone knew you were just what I wanted. Yes, they did."

Immediately, I know who put the pig in her locker. The only person capable of this kind of quirky, designed-perfectly-for-Katherine-Johnson grand gesture.

"Ajay."

Her head snaps up. "You think?"

"Well, he knows about your pig obsession, and who else has the time to break into your locker in the middle of the day? Who else is crazy enough to tell you he likes you with a teacup pig?"

She blushes and smiles and then blushes and smiles some more as she hugs the cup to her chest. "Oh my God. If he did this, Hadley, if he really did this, I'm totally in love."

I laugh as she kisses the pig's snout and throw an arm around her shoulder. "Kitty Kat, if Ajay did this, I think *I'm* in love too."

Livy's room is a total mess. Glossy black-and-white photos strewn everywhere, magazines and books and homework and what looks like her entire wardrobe covering every surface. I think she might have tried to turn her closet into a darkroom, but I don't really want to know. Nothing has a place. Total opposite of Hadley. Total opposite of the way Livy used to be. As I shove aside a crumb-filled plate and sit on her bed, I feel a weight settle over me, as if her room is a glaring and chaotic metaphor for our exploded life.

"What's up?" She's sitting on the floor, leaning against her bed, a thick photography book propped up on her knees. Lately I've barely seen her without a camera around her neck. She even wears it in the house. Hadley and I fell asleep on the couch last week, and I swear I heard a *click* and then footsteps fading away. She disappears for hours on her bike, skulking around town like some voyeur. When I ask her what she's doing, she waves me off and says it's for her project. I would worry, but when she delicately tells me to piss off, she's smiling her old smile.

"Listen, Livy. I know I said I wouldn't tell Hadley about all of this, but things are different now."

Her fingers freeze on a page in midflip. My eyes slide around the room and locate her inhaler on her desk. Just in case.

"I have to tell her and I'm going to do it soon."

"You mean . . . you're going to *tell her* tell her?"

I sit down to floor next to her. "Yeah."

Livy lets her knees drop. Her book *thwacks* as it hits the floor.

"I have to, Liv. I feel like I'm lying to her."

She nods, then lifts her eyes to me. They're surprisingly dry. "She's going to hate you. Hate all of us. And what about Kat? Ajay's going to lose Kat before he even had a chance to get her, and you're going to lose Hadley and then you'll be miserable again and then I'll be miserable again and then everyone will just be miserable. What's the point?"

"Liv—"

"You can't let her hate you. Not you, Sam. Please."

She stares at me, her blue eyes wide and pleading. I know what she really wants me to do, but I'm not even about to open up that can.

Just then, the doorbell rings and Livy's eyes get even wider.

"Tonight?" she asks as I get up.

"I don't know. Maybe. But soon." When I reach the door, I turn back to look at her. Her shoulders are squared, jaw set. She looks so different from how she did even a month ago. Stronger. I feel my resolve tighten.

That resolve crumbles into nothing when I open the front door to find Hadley standing on my porch. She looks almost transcendent. Dressed all in black, wrapped in the coppery light of the late sun. Her hair is pulled back and her eyes literally light up when they land on me.

She's here an hour before I'm supposed to meet her, but I'm not really surprised. I know she hates being at home right now. Honestly, it's a bit of a relief —I still hadn't figured out how to pick her up for a date without coming face-to-face with her dad. Talk about a mood killer.

My arms go around her and she sort of melts into me. I rest my cheek on her head and we just stand there, wordless. I let myself imagine a different life with her, free of knots and lies and little slips of paper. I let myself believe what feels true— that she's just a girl and I'm just boy and we want to be together. We couldn't *not* be together, because being together was the only thing that made sense. The only thing that kept us both from disappearing.

★

I glance at Hadley in the passenger seat for the gazillionth time since we left my house. Her expression is relaxed and even a little excited. Every time she catches my eye, she sort of grins and her hand tightens on mine and the voice in my head screaming *Dumbass!* on a constant loop gets a little louder.

"What are we doing here?" Hadley asks as I pull into the parking lot of the Rock Your Face climbing gym.

"This place has a great snack counter. Thought we'd grab a soft pretzel here before we meet up with the baseball team for some beer-pong."

She whacks me on the arm, but cracks a grin. I grab my pack full of my own climbing gear, barely used for the past several months, and lead her inside.

"What size shoe do you wear?" I ask after I pay a guy with a poofy beard and a tattoo of Jesus Christ smoking weed on his neck. No shit.

"Seven." Hadley's eyes roam over the climbing walls, dotted here and there with climbers reaching for solid holds. One guy is bouldering on the low climbs, and the place smells like sweat and exercise mats and the mustiness of chalk.

"Need both of y'all to sign waivers," Toking-Jesus-tattoo guy says, handing us each a clipboard. The name tag on his shirt reads *Scott*.

I sign the sheet while Hadley reads every word of the waiver, her brows all wrinkled up in concentration.

"You guys cool?" Scott asks, motioning toward the walls. "I'm short-staffed tonight, so if you don't know how to belay, it's gonna be a while."

"We're good, man," I say. "We've done this a million times." I feel Hadley's eyes flick to me, but I keep mine on Scott.

He scratches at his poofy beard, surveying the busy walls. "All right. I'll circle around and check on you. But seriously, make sure you know what you're doing before you get up there."

"Sam, I don't—" Hadley starts, but I cut her off.

"Will do. Thanks."

Scott nods and Hadley shuts up, finally signing the damn waiver. If her thoroughness wasn't so damn cute, I'd totally rag her about it right now.

"Sorry," I tell her as we take her shoes and head over to a free space of wall. "They're pretty strict about safety at these places."

"Can't imagine why." She cranes her neck to watch a lady climbing about thirty feet off the ground.

"Don't worry. I know what I'm doing."

She nods and sits to change her shoes. I remove two harnesses, two belay devices, extra ropes, a chalk pouch, my shoes, some extra carabiners, and two full water bottles from my bag. Then I step into my harness and secure it around my hips.

"Your turn." I hold up the other harness.

"What about my soft pretzel?"

"If you keep looking at me like that, we won't get any climbing done," I say.

"Why's that?"

I catch her hand and press a kiss to her palm. Her fingers curve softly into my cheek. Somehow, those two little movements—the action and reaction—feel so intimate, it almost knocks the breath out of my lungs.

Hadley smiles softly and I kiss her hand once more before I secure the belay devices to our harnesses. I take the rope hanging from our section of the wall and thread it through the device. Then I hook Hadley into the other end of the rope.

"Ready?" I hook the chalk bag onto her harness with a carabiner.

She pops up her eyebrows and looks around. "Um. You do realize I've never done this before, right?"

"Yeah, I caught that."

"So what do I do?"

"You climb."

She smirks at me and I laugh and then explain about belaying. "I'm not holding you up. I'm just providing support if needed as you climb. When you're ready, you say 'On belay' and I say 'Belay on.' That means everything is in place to keep you

255

safe. When you're about to climb, you say 'Climbing' and I say 'Climb on.' Then you climb. You just do it. Stretch yourself, think through a move, visualize yourself executing it. Use the chalk to give you some grip."

Her eyes study the wall. After a minute, she dips a hand into the chalk bag, brows furrowed and lips drawn taut. I plant my feet as she slaps her hands together, sending puffs of white into the air.

"Um." She glances back at me. "On belay?"

I grin. "Belay on."

She turns back to the wall. "Climbing."

"Climb on."

She hikes her leg up, plants her foot on a hold, and is off. I watch her, threading the rope through the belay device as she gets higher, and try not to look at her ass. This is nearly impossible considering that's all there is to really look at and my eyes have taken on a mind of their own.

"You're doing good," I call. She grunts in response, pausing as she realizes there are no holds within easy reaching distance.

"Want me to beta?" I ask.

"To what?"

"Beta. Offer you advice on moves to try. Some people hate it.

Think it's a crutch and that it disrupts the natural flow of the climber's state of mind or something like that."

"And what do you think?"

"I think that's bullshit."

She laughs, a little out of breath. "Beta on."

We talk through some holds. She slips once and I lock up on the rope, but she gets back on pretty easily.

"You're like a cat up there," I say.

She stretches out a toned swimmer's leg and uses her quads instead of her arms to push herself up. I swallow hard and lock my gaze on the back of her head.

When she reaches the top, she lets out a cute little whoop. I don't even have to explain about rappelling down. She just does it. Her feet hit the ground and her eyes are all fiery.

"Nice job," I say as I unhook her from the rope. "Did you like it?"

She nods, and takes a slug of water. "Amazing."

"You ready to belay me?"

She lifts her eyebrows and I feel the tips of my ears bleed pink. I unhook my own rope, threading it through Hadley's device. I show her how to weave the rope to provide slack before I approach the wall.

"Do you climb a lot?" she asks as I grab my first hold.

"I used to, back when we lived in Nashville. My dad was big into climbing. We went to the gym there a lot, but we also took trips to climb outdoors. Whole different experience, climbing natural rock. I haven't climbed much since he moved, though."

"Do you miss it?"

I pause, my knees tucked under a crevice. I think about my dad, about baseball and climbing and camping and all the things he taught me how to do and love. Everything that seemed to disappear, at least in some form, when he left. I swing my body out, airborne for a brief flash before my hands hook around a hold.

"Not at the moment," I grunt.

Hadley whistles below me and I don't even try to keep the smile off my face.

"Can I ask you a question?" she says when I stop halfway up to catch my breath.

"Shoot."

She remains silent and I crane my neck around and down. "Hadley?

"Yeah. Just . . . um." She bites her lip. "Why do you hang out with Josh?"

I frown and turn back to the wall. "I wouldn't call it hanging out, exactly. We talk at school. Play ball."

"And?"

I exhale and reach for a hold, anything to keep moving up. "He did a dumbass thing, but he's not a bad guy."

The rope pulls up on my harness with a ball-cracking jerk. Hadley's got the rope anchored at her hip, her mouth a hard line.

"Hadley," I squeak. "Come on."

She purses her lips and lets go. I rappel down and walk over to her, widening my stance in front of her so we're eye level.

"What?" I ask. "What do you want me to say?"

"You don't care that he used me?" She folds her arms but lets me put my hands on her hips and pull her closer.

"Yeah, I care. He and I have had words on the subject. Trust me, when I first found out what happened, I wanted to string him up by something a hell of a lot more painful than his thumbs."

"But?"

I loop my fingers through her harness belt and hold on. "Hadley. Didn't you do the same thing? Use him, I mean?"

She stiffens and tries to pull back, but I'm hooked in.

"I'm not judging you, Hadley. I've been there ... I've ..." Nicole's face flashes in my mind, her clear green eyes laughing and nonchalant.

"I didn't lie," Hadley says.

"I know that. But . . ." I wipe my forehead on my arm, suddenly pouring sweat. "I mean, people don't do stupid shit just to do it. Don't you think there's always more to it?"

"You're saying that he had a good reason for lying?"

"I'm saying . . ." *Think, man. Careful.* "That Josh was going through some crap and he acted like a dick. It's not an excuse, but that kind of stuff has to be taken into account when we're dealing with other people and trying to find a little meaning behind all the bullshit."

Something soft flickers in her expression, but it's a sad softness. I tighten my grip on her. "Should I have just said he's a douche and I'm only pretending to be his friend so I can destroy his life from the inside?"

A tiny smile slips onto her mouth.

"You guys doing all right?" Scott approaches in battered Tevas. "You need to either climb or clear out. You're clogging up wall space."

"Right. Sorry, man." I take Hadley's elbow, grateful for the mandate.

She stumbles behind me, her head tilted to the side as she really looks at Scott's skin art for the first time.

"See something you like, darlin'?" His lips curl at her in a way that sort of makes me want to throat-punch him.

She laughs nervously. "Oh. Um. Sorry. Just . . . nice tattoo."

I try to pull her away before we get our asses kicked out, but Scott just grins, clearly pleased. "Yeah, well. I figured the dude made the stuff, so he'd be the first to partake, know what I mean?"

"Oh, yeah. My thoughts exactly."

"Okay, you guys still good?" Scott asks as he eyes a pair of dudes a few feet away trying to convince one of his employees to let them climb without a harness. Scott starts toward them before I can answer, calling over his shoulder. "Hey, seriously, no falling off and busting your heads open. I yak at the sight of blood."

"*My thoughts exactly?*" I echo when he's out of sight.

She laughs into her palms. "What was I supposed to say?"

"Nothing. You say nothing to the guy who willingly had a needle stuck in his freaking neck."

She smiles, but it's half-assed, and she wraps her harness straps around and around her finger.

"What's wrong?" I ask, even though I'm pretty damn sure I don't want to know.

She crosses her arms. "This Josh thing is really bothering me, Sam."

I stifle a groan and pull my expression into something resembling interest. Because seriously, I'd rather talk about the possibility that Jesus smoked a fat one at the Last Supper than have another conversation about Josh Ellison.

"I mean, I don't get it," she says, agitated. "Are he and Jenny back together?"

"I think they're working on it."

"But he's a liar."

Her voice is getting edgier and edgier. I scrub a hand through my hair so hard it hurts. "He lied. He's not a liar."

She frowns at my tone, but charges onward. "You really think there's a difference?"

"Yeah, I do."

"Why are you defending him?"

"I'm not! He messed up. So what? One bad choice doesn't mean he's an asshole forever."

"That's not what I'm saying. I just think—"

"Jesus Christ, Hadley, give it a rest! Can't you just . . ." *Let it go.* But the words die in my throat. Hadley's expression is a mix of anger and hurt, because I'm yelling. Freaking loud, grabbing the attention of half the gym.

"Shit, I'm sorry." I reach out for her hand. She lets me take it, mostly because I think I've shocked the fight out of her. "God, I'm sorry, Hadley. Please. I'm an ass."

"What's wrong with you?"

I wait a beat, ready for more stupid to fall out of my mouth. A confession would be really nice right now, just get it the hell over with, but it doesn't come because I'm a total pansy-ass. "Nothing. I'm tired, that's all."

Her mouth parts in unbelief. Cold shame fills me up—hell, I don't even believe me. "Had, I'm sorry."

She looks away, squinting at the other climbers. Her eyes land on a group of girls our age. They're yelping and egging each other on, the girl on the wall laughing so hard, she's now dangling from her rope like a sack of potatoes.

"Let's just climb, okay?" Hadley says, threading the rope through her device to give me some slack.

I think I say yes, or at least nod. Doesn't matter. I launch myself at the wall. Fucking Josh. Fucking parents. Fucking fuck. I take a different route this time, pushing everything from my mind that's not me and the next hold. I swallow down everything I need to deal with. Everything in my whole goddamn life. I reach the top in a shower of adrenaline and a decent amount of oblivion. I rappel back down and unhook my rope.

"Impressive." Hadley's voice is way more relaxed than before, but her smile is still tight.

"Go again?" I ask, fingers tingling to get back up there.

"Sure."

We both climb a few more routes. By the time eight o'clock

rolls around, my stomach is growling and my arms and legs are aching.

"What now?" Hadley asks when we get back into the car. She folds her arms around her knees, tucking herself away. Her hair sticks to the back of her neck, and her cheeks glow with the flush of exercise and excitement. Or maybe that's just plain old pissed off.

"Now." I lean toward her to brush a kiss below her ear, desperate to diffuse this tension. I linger there for a minute, trying to memorize the way her skin smells and feels under my mouth. She sort of shivers and lets out a huge sigh. "We go back to my house and I cook you dinner."

She smiles and leans into me, my temper tantrum forgotten.

For now.

CHAPTER TWENTY-FOUR

Hadley

My arms and legs and butt are already burning from using muscles I didn't even know I had. The warm water from the shower runs over my skin, washing away the leftover chalk and soothing the blister on my right thumb. My body feels almost broken, but my mind is weirdly clear and still humming with Sam's explosion.

I throw on the jeans and long-sleeved shirt from my bag and find him in the kitchen. His hair is darker from his own shower, droplets of water sliding off the ends and onto the shoulder of his snug black T-shirt. He looks up from ladling a thick soup from a slow cooker into two bowls, the muscles in his forearms rippling. A smile ghosts across his mouth and we stare at each other for a few long seconds.

"Chicken and dumplings?" I ask, glad for the distraction of food. He hands me the bowl on a plate with a thick slice of brown bread. I hop onto the barstool and he rounds the island to join me.

"Uh, yeah. Hope that's okay. I made it earlier today. It's not fancy, but it's good for sticking to your ribs after a workout. That's what my dad used to say, anyway."

I slip a spoonful into my mouth. "Holy crap."

"Holy crap good?"

I nod through a mouthful and he grins.

"It's Ajay's favorite. He loves it so much, he doesn't even use a spoon, just scoops up the broth and dumplings with a piece of bread."

"Ah. Good ol' Ajay." I rip off a hunk of bread. "Speaking of your verbose pal, what's up with him and Kat?"

Sam's spoon freezes in midflight to his mouth.

"Sam Bennett. Tell me he left that pig in her locker."

He lowers his spoon and turns to face me, a wry smile on his lips. "Now, that's not a sentence one would expect to hear every day, is it?"

"*Sam.*"

"I'm not at liberty to disclose such sensitive information."

"You do realize that your goofy grin is sort of giving you away."

He laughs and squeezes my knee. "Kat's in good hands, Hadley. That's all I can say."

"She better be, or I will personally ensure that Mr. Desai's ability to procreate is severely impaired."

"Duly noted."

After dinner, we end up curled under a blanket on Sam's bed, watching old episodes of *Friends* on his computer. We laugh at all the appropriate places, but it sounds forced, from both of us. I try to concentrate on the dialogue, on Sam's fingers idling up and down my arm, but my mind keeps drifting back to his outburst in the climbing gym. I've never seen Sam so worked up. I know he's struggling with his dad gone, and his relationship with his mom is borderline scary. He was *angry*, and I understand angry, but it all seemed directed at me . . .

I shiver in Sam's arms.

"Was this a good date?" he asks, startling me out of my thoughts.

I nod, my head nestled where his shoulder meets his chest. I breathe in his clean, soapy smell, letting the realness of him push out the doubts in my mind.

"Sorry we didn't go to a fancy restaurant or something. I wanted to do something memorable, something unique."

"No, I loved it. Scott was by far the highlight."

"Ha." He takes my hand and threads our fingers together. "I could waltz you around my room if you want."

I laugh and nuzzle in closer. "Maybe later. Right now, this is perfect."

"Yeah. Almost perfect."

"Almost?"

He inhales so sharply, it's nearly a gasp. "Hadley. I . . . I need to talk to you."

I prop myself up on my elbows. "What? What's wrong?" I ask, and his eyes fill with this deep sadness. He looked the same way at the gym when he realized he was yelling at me. I want to erase that look, soak it up with my skin and replace all of it with *us*. I touch his face and he closes his eyes.

I press my lips to his. He tenses briefly and then releases, like he's letting go of something heavy. He rolls me over onto my back and looks down at me, eyes roaming over my face. He slides his thumb over my lower lip and brings his mouth to mine again. His kisses are slow and soft, exploring my jaw, down my neck, and across my collarbone before traveling back to my lips, and I'm nearly panting by the time he increases the pressure. His tongue slips over mine, carefully at first and then hungrily. My body responds, greedy for him, for every part of him I can't reach. I hear our breathing, little sounds rolling out of our throats, driving our hands over each other's bodies.

Everything fades into the back of my mind. My parents. My nervousness over this fragile young thing between Sam and me.

His anger at the gym. Because this is right. *This.* His hands in my hair and his breath on my neck. This is what I want and I feel almost giddy just letting myself want it.

I pull up his shirt and he yanks it off. I run my hands over his smooth skin, glowing almost gold in the dim light. His leanly roped arms lift my own shirt and we're skin to skin, mouth to mouth, racing heart to racing heart. Everything is warm, everything is soft but urgent. His hips slide in between my legs and I gasp, the feel of him sending little shivers all the way down to my fingertips. I find the button on his jeans and flip it free, my fingers edging along his skin and into the elastic of his boxers.

He sucks in a breath.

I find his mouth again and tug his lower lip gently between my teeth. I push closer, the ache for him colliding with everything else. My hand dips lower.

"God . . . Hadley."

Then everything stops.

His hands encircle my wrists and he pulls them free, tucking them against his chest.

"*Wait.*"

His labored whisper barely filters through my own fog. My head spins, air pumping in and out of my lungs. "What? Why?"

"Hadley." His voice is soft in my ear, his breathing heavy. He kisses my cheek and lingers there.

"Don't you want this?" I ask.

He lets out a ragged sigh. "Yeah. Jesus, of course I do. But—"

"So I do too." I try to pull him closer. I need him closer. Nothing is close enough. I press a kiss to his throat and push my hips toward his.

"Hadley." He cups my face between his hands. "Don't. We're not doing this right now. We're not doing this at all."

That stops me. Stops the frantic pace of my heart, stops my hands from roaming. Stops everything. "Why not?"

He exhales and dips his forehead against mine. "Because this isn't right."

I push him back, now needing space between us. "What isn't right, Sam?"

"Us. Like this."

"Like *what?* What are you talking about?"

He smooths a hand over my hair. The gentle movement should calm me, but his expression, his tone, his vague words send a pang of foreboding into my chest. Not foreboding—*certainty* that I've been an idiot.

"Oh." I jerk away from him, untying my legs from around his hips, and sit up. "Oh my God. Okay. I get it."

He sits up and catches my wrist. "Shit. No, no. No, you don't get it. Can we just talk? Please, I need to tell you some things, but it's . . . it's really hard for me."

I swing my feet off the bed, my eyes already peeling through the dark room for my shirt. I find it and throw it over my head. It's on backwards, the tag scratching at my throat, but I don't even care. Embarrassment crawls over my skin and I yank my hand back when Sam tries to take it.

"Hadley, please. Please stay."

"Why?"

"Because . . . because I *need* you to stay."

I press a hand to my mouth and heave a few breaths. His expression is so earnest, so . . . I don't even know. That same sadness from before but with something new mixed in. With a jolt, I realize it's fear.

"Okay. Fine. Just let me . . . I need a minute."

His shoulders relax. "All right. Thank you."

Without another look at him, I make my way downstairs to the kitchen. It's dark except for the light over the stove, the golden glow reminding me of winter nights and cups of chamomile tea. I find a glass and fill it with water, gulping it down in three swallows. I fill the cup again and drink more slowly this time, trying to still my pounding heart. *Calm down. You can handle this. He's just a guy. He's just a guy.*

Tears threaten to crawl up my throat. The aching in my chest is almost unbearable as I try to hold them back, swallow them down with another gulp of water. I'm just about to set them loose when the overhead light flicks on. The glass slips from my hand, shattering at my feet in a dozen sharp, wet pieces.

"Oh!" A female voice cuts through my shock. "I'm sorry, I didn't mean to scare you."

I whip around and see Sam's mom digging in a narrow closet by the door. She emerges with a broom.

"I thought—" She startles as our gazes collide. She drops the broom, and everything in her face darkens and narrows. "Hadley."

"Hi." I step over the broken glass. "I'm sorry about your glass. You surprised me."

"Surprise." Her eyes roam over my rumpled hair and backwards shirt, but it's not a friendly study. Cora Bennett is beautiful—an older, more chiseled version of Livy—but her expression is hard and cold. "Yes, I'd say this is a surprise."

"Sam's upstairs. I was just getting a drink. I can clean this up." I try to slide past her and take the broom, but she moves to the doorway, holding up a hand to stop me. I'm not sure why this woman seems to dislike me so much. I've barely spoken ten words to her, but the almost feral look in her blue eyes is evidence enough. Right now, I don't have the energy to care why. I just want to get back to Sam, let him dump me with as much dignity as I can manage, and go home.

But she has other plans. Her slender body is a wall in front of me.

"Hadley, listen very carefully." Her voice is as smooth as velvet, but sharp around the edges. "I know this is hard to understand, but you and Sam? Trust me when I say it is not a good idea. I need you to leave my house and I need you to leave my son alone."

CHAPTER TWENTY-FIVE

Sam

Jesus, this is a disaster.

I listen as Hadley treads down the stairs, and flop back onto the bed. I think about my grandmother's fuzzy upper lip. SATs. A bag full of dirty jockstraps. Anything to get my pissed-off body to go back to normal after having Hadley wrapped around me for so long.

Christ.

I dig the heels of my hands into my eyes. The sight of her lying in my bed, tucked underneath me, looking so confused and earnest was exactly what I needed to push me over the edge of this whole ridiculous cliff I've been skirting for the past month.

I get up and pace around my room, flipping on my iPod in the process. It picks up midsong, the frantic rhythm matching my pulse.

I'm in full panic mode now. My palms are pouring water, my throat feels like I've been screaming obscenities at a Braves play-off game, and my mouth is watering because I seriously think I'm about to puke. I squeeze my fingers white on the sides of my dresser and try to get a damn grip. My mind runs circles around a thousand crappy ways to tell her, each one crappier than the previous crappy option.

Why did I think I could put this off until now? I should've known the longer I waited, the worse the outcome. Ajay told me. Hell, even Mom told me in her own hands-off way. Now I'm in too deep and I'm about to freaking drown.

The sound of glass breaking downstairs sends a cold stab through my veins. I grab my shirt and stuff it over my head as I fly down the steps. "Hadley, are you—"

Mom's form fills the doorway to the kitchen and her voice drifts back to me in one huge, nauseating wave. ". . . not a good idea. I need you to leave my house and I need you to leave my son alone."

What the hell?

"Mom!"

She whirls around, her eyes almost glowing, she's so pissed. "Sam, what is going on? Did I not make myself clear on this issue?"

I push past her to get to Hadley, who's standing open-mouthed, her face flushed red, yanking at her fingers so hard I'm scared she's going to rip them off.

"I think I need to go," she says.

"That would be wise." Mom's eyes are on me like a snake viewing its next meal.

"No, Hadley. We need to talk." I take her hand, but she pulls away.

Mom moves aside to let her pass, her arms folded in a bitchy knot over her chest. I follow Hadley upstairs to my room. She grabs her jacket and her bag with shaking hands, digging in the bottom for her keys.

"Hadley."

"Don't. Just stop." Her voice quivers, not with tears but with rage. "Why does she hate me so much? What did I do?"

"Nothing. It's not you. It's me. That sounds totally lame, but it's true. Her problem is with me. If you'd just sit down and let me talk, it'll make more sense." I reach for her, but she steps back.

"No. I don't want to talk right now. I just want to go home." She wipes at her eyes and is out the door before I can raise another protest.

Livy's door opens and she pads into the hall, eyes bleary from sleep. "What's going on?"

"Nothing," I say as Hadley passes her without a glance. "Go back to bed."

"Sam, did you tell—"

"Later, Livy."

Livy frowns, but nods when I squeeze her shoulder. I tail Hadley down the stairs like a damn puppy. She's already out the front door, closing it in my face. I fling it open and run after her, heading her off before she can slip into her car.

"Hadley, come on. Wait. Talk to me."

She whirls around. "God, enough with the talking, Sam! This is too much right now. I want to go home." She presses her fingers into her eyes and takes a shaky breath. When she speaks again, it's a whisper, almost a plea, which makes me feel like shit all over again. "I'm so tired of talking, Sam. Can we please just say good night?"

"Yeah. Yeah, okay." She lets me hug her, lets me press a kiss to her forehead, but she's like a rag doll in my arms. I'm almost scared she'll fall when I let her go. But of course she won't, and when she pulls away and drives off, I'm the one who has to lock my knees to keep them from buckling.

I make it back to the kitchen in a daze. Mom sits on one of the barstools. A glass of red wine swirls in one hand and she pulls her phone from her ear, tossing it onto the counter with a muttered curse. Christ, she's pissed.

"Dammit, Sam."

"Mom, you don't get it."

"What is there to get?"

I drag both hands through my hair. "I care about her."

She sips her wine, her expression stony. "Are you serious? I can't believe this." She points a finger at me. "This has gone far enough!"

My hands ball into tight fists because she's right. She has no idea how *far enough* this has really gone. But this whole scene—*her*, sitting there like none of this has anything to do with her—just pisses me off. My temper rises red and hot, ready to burn the shit out of anything in its path.

"I will not have you jeopardize our life here," Mom says. "My job is going well and Olivia's smiling for once."

"Yeah, you know why? She has friends, Hadley being one of them. She has something she's interested in. She knows Hadley and likes her, and yeah, it's messed up, but I'm figuring it out."

"You have no idea what you're doing. You're acting on whims, impulses, selfish desires, just like you always do, anyone else be damned. You think this is easy for me? If you hadn't—"

"If I hadn't *what?*"

Her eyes narrow, but she looks away. "You know what."

I sense Livy behind me, her steps as soft as her touch when I feel her hand close around the back of my shirt.

"This is such bullshit," I say. "You're the one who did this, Mom. You. You want someone to blame for your life, for your wrecked marriage, your disaster of a relationship with your daughter, look in the goddamn mirror."

"Samuel." Mom's eyes drop to Livy's arm around my waist, and she deflates. I recognize that softness in her features from when she used to sing at night and laugh while eating dinner. But it's not for me. It never is anymore. Her gaze passes right through me.

"Yeah. An angry kid lost it and stuck a bunch of papers all over a door," I say. Livy's grip tightens and I put my hand over hers. "But that angry kid just had his world obliterated when he walked in on his mother screwing someone who wasn't his father."

Mom's mouth drops open. Actual tears well up in her eyes. "I made mistakes. I understand that, and I do not need *my son* throwing them in my face. But you are the one lying now, Sam. You're leading that girl on, and she has no idea who you are or what you did."

We stare at each other for what feels like forever. Shit, she's right. I'm lying like I do it for a living. I'm *pretending* I'm a different person living a different life, just like Mom did. Just like Hadley's dad did. Her accusations ping around in my head, but I push them back and grab ahold of this pissed-off feeling that's never far from my reach.

"I don't give a shit what you think you know about Hadley

or about me or Livy or about this situation *you* put all of us in,"
I say. "Fuck your blame and fuck your fabulous new plan for
your fabulous new life."

Livy grabs my hand as I turn to leave. Behind me, sobs start
up as something long buried in my mother bubbles to the surface and breaks her open.

But I just don't care anymore.

CHAPTER TWENTY-SIX

Hadley

I don't go straight home. I drive all the way into Nashville, through the streets of my old neighborhood, past my old school, my old house, my old life. When I finally get home, I sit in the car for a while. My hands white-knuckle the steering wheel as I stare down my dark street spotted with orange circles from the streetlights. It's cold and my breath sends little white ghosts wandering into the air.

My phone vibrates in my bag and I find a few missed calls from Dad and a text from Kat filling the entire screen.

Ajay left the pig and he made that cup! We're going out tomorrow. Can you believe it? The pig's a boy, btw. I named him Charlie. Mom's freaking, but so far, he's still here. How was your date?

I feel my lips bend into a little smile, but they quickly fall back into a straight line as I text her back.

Give Charlie a kiss for me. Date was fine.

Fine. It was more than fine, and then it was something out of a prime-time drama. I don't understand anything that happened tonight. All I know is that I feel like I've lost something and I have no idea where to start looking for it because I don't even know what it is.

Jinx greets me when I walk in the door, mewing and swishing around my legs almost frantically. As I pick her up, a hysterical laugh bubbles up my throat. Because I'm seventeen and I'm basically one of those people who live alone with their cat. She mews again, loudly, her little body a tense ball in my arms.

"What's wrong, girl?" I ask her, scratching under her chin.

"Hadley?" Dad calls from the living room. "Can you come in here please?" he adds when I don't answer.

"Dad, I'm really tired."

"Hadley, please."

Mom.

Her voice splits through me like a crack of thunder. Still clutching Jinx, I hurry into the room to find them sitting on separate couches. Their expressions are grim, but something childlike leaps in my chest. I can hardly breathe, and I realize it's because I'm excited, hopeful even. Things have been awful since the affair came out, but I've hated Mom being completely gone. Without her here to make things at least resemble our normal family environment, this house feels like the last rung on the ladder into hell.

Jinx wiggles and I set her down. "Mom?"

She manages a smile, but her eyes look weary. Getting up, she pulls me into her arms. Her fingers press into my back almost desperately. I should feel relieved, but it's been so long since she's really touched me, nerves tighten in my stomach.

"Are you okay?" I ask. "Are you home to stay?"

Mom tosses a glance at my dad, who's clutching his phone and staring at his lap. "I'm okay. And yes, I'm home. But we need to talk to you, honey."

"All right." I let her lead me to the couch.

"Hadley," Dad says. "We . . ." He blows out a long breath and rubs his eyes. "Are you . . ." He looks at the ceiling, his throat bobbing with a hard swallow.

"Jason, I'll do it. I'll tell her."

"No. This is my fault. I need to tell her."

"*I* need to tell her. I need to face this too."

Dad and Mom square off, their expressions a mess of glares and pleas. Finally, he deflates and rests his head in one hand.

Meanwhile, my entire world is shrinking.

This is it, I think. This is why she came home. To tell me they've finally given up. Soon our house will fill up with *That's mine* and *That's yours* and *Hadley will stay with me on the weekends and every other Christmas.* I'm a minute from bolting, flinging myself into my car and texting Sam to meet me at Love Circle. Nothing can touch us up there, on top of the world.

"What's going on? You guys are scaring me."

Mom inhales deeply before speaking. "Honey, Cor—" She swallows and clears her throat. "Your father called me a while ago, right after he received a phone call from Cora Bennett."

I flinch, sinking farther into the cushions. "What? Why? Why is she calling you?" None of this makes sense.

"She called because she's concerned about her son," Mom says.

"Her son?"

"Are you friends with a boy named Sam?"

"Why are you asking me that? What does he have to do . . . with . . ." But Sam's name in Mom's voice sparks something in my head, and my questions fizzle out.

"Hadley," Dad says from his corner, eyes locked on the floor. "Cora Bennett was . . . she was the woman I had . . . with whom I was involved."

I blink at him. That's all I can do. Open and close my eyes. Any moment now, I'll open them to a different room, different people, different words.

Mom rests a hand on my arm, but I shake her off.

"Sam is . . . His mom is . . . No, this is crazy." I say. "This isn't the same Sam."

"Oh, honey, I'm so sorry."

"No, it's not possible. And even if it is, he can't know who I am. He would've told me."

"He knows," Dad says, his voice impossibly small. "From what his mother said on the phone, he's always known."

I need to tell you some things, but it's really hard for me.

"Oh, my God," I choke out raggedly. "*This* is who you screwed around with?" Dad flinches, but says nothing. All this time, I've always pictured some super young grad student who got pregnant in high school the first time she slept with her boyfriend, popping out this strange kid who would one day freak out and plaster dirty notes all over my front door. I never fathomed she was a sophisticated woman with a real family. A family with feelings and lives and hearts.

"Hadley," Mom says. "I really think it's better that we know this. We can get it all out in the open and put it behind us."

"We can never put this behind us!"

I cover my mouth with my hand, pushing back the sob that's fighting to break free. Mom presses next to me. She twirls a strand of my hair around her finger like she used to do while we watched a movie or just sat and talked.

"Honey, who is Sam to you?"

"He's . . . he's . . ." My God, how could I be so stupid? My mind flies over Sam's own story, about his father leaving, what Livy told me about why he left, the timing of it all that he so conveniently never let slip and I stupidly never asked about. How could I not have known?

I press my hands harder against my mouth. My nails dig into my cheeks.

Mom keeps twirling my hair, winding her finger up to my face. Her touch is soft and steady.

"I wish you would've told me about him," Mom says.

"And when would I have done that?"

"I know I've been . . . detached from your life for a while, but—"

"*Detached?* Is that what you call it?"

Her lips press flat. "I want things to change, Hadley."

"Mom, please don't." I disentangle her hand from my hair. I can't sit here and listen to her voice of reason after everything that's happened.

She grabs my hand again, the familiar scent of her jasmine shampoo wafting over me. "I know you're angry. With me, with your father, with this boy. But we love you so much, sweetie. We're so sorry. We all need to try and move on. This anger, it'll bury you, honey."

"Then let it!"

"Hadley," Dad says, standing.

Mom's eyes brim with tears, the first I've seen in months. "Sweetheart. You don't mean that. It's time to let it go."

Just get over it, Hadley.

"Like you have?" I say, snatching my hand back.

She frowns and looks down at her lap. "I know I haven't set the best example. But I'm here now. I'm ready to try."

I shake my head. Dad's voice says something else, but I'm not here anymore. Not in this room, in this house, in this life. I'm standing in front of a red door, papers flapping in the breeze. All I see are those words, that messy black scrawl like a thousand knives cutting through my skin, revealing a life I didn't even know was being lived right in front of me. A hidden life, with me in the dark.

Then it all connects with a sickening crack.

Sam wrote those notes.

My head swims and my eyes and nose sting. I'm floating up, up, up. Not on top of the world, but too far above it. I can't decide if I want to laugh or cry. This is really happening. The one guy I choose to trust, choose to give myself to, and he turns out to be nothing but a liar with an unfathomable connection to my family.

Someone who hurt my family.

Both my parents watch me, but I barely register their worried expressions. The enormity of the truth takes over everything. I fumble to standing. Jinx, lying at my feet, mews and bolts upright. I take the stairs two at time, but Mom follows me up and down the hall, past my parents' dark bedroom, past the guest room where her paisley duffel bag sits on the bed. In my doorway, I whirl around, preventing her from coming inside.

"Hadley—"

"You want to know who Sam Bennett is to me, Mom?"

She just stares at me, my own pain and confusion mirrored in her expression.

"He's no one. He's just a guy, like every other guy."

She steps back, and I close the door on my lie.

CHAPTER TWENTY-SEVEN

Sam

She's already here. I stand outside the Green-Eyed Girl, freezing, and watch her through the window dotted with colored leaf decals. She's sitting at the same table where we sat that day we skipped school. She cradles her coffee mug between both of her hands, her long hair braided and pulled over one shoulder. As much as I want to touch her, talk to her, hear her say my name, I'd give anything not to have to walk into this damn café right now.

Hadley called a few hours ago and, I swear to God, relief almost swallowed me. Since I woke up at the crack of dawn, I'd already called her twice, texted her three times, and was ready to risk a run-in with her dad by driving to her house. Mom was holed up in her room and Livy had disappeared after breakfast on her bike, so I roamed the house freely, chewing my nails down to the quick. When she finally called, I thought I'd feel better just hearing her voice, no matter what the words were.

I didn't.

"Have you talked to your mom lately?" I'd asked after her robotic greeting.

"Yeah, she's home now."

"Oh. Well, that's good, right?"

She didn't answer, so I pushed forward. "I'm really sorry about last night."

No response.

"Hadley?"

"Yeah. Can I see you later this afternoon?"

We worked out the details, but after I hung up, I felt like I'd chugged a two-liter of Coke on an empty stomach. I still do.

I open the door to the café. A blast of warm air hits me, along with scents of butter and espresso and, I swear, a hint of Hadley. I slide into the chair across from her. She looks up slowly, her expression unchanged. She doesn't meet my eyes.

"Hey," I say.

"Hey." She nods toward her drink. "You want something?"

I shake my head and plunge in. "Listen, last night was so screwed up, but I really wanted to talk to you. I understand it was weird with my mom and I don't blame you for wanting to get the hell out of there, but now I need you to listen —"

"Why is April the cruelest month, Sam?"

Her voice is almost tender, but the words explode in my ears. "What?"

"The first day we met, you were wearing a shirt that said 'April is the cruelest month.' I asked you if you believed that and you said yes. Why?"

Behind the counter, the milk steamer kicks into gear. A baby wails in the corner. A chair screeches across the tile floor. Suddenly, everything is chaos in my head. Too loud. Too wrong. Too late.

"Maybe it has something to do with this." She digs into her bag and retrieves a wrinkled slip of paper.

And everything slows down.

Crash.

In *Romeo and Juliet*, stars didn't cross. They collided.

Game over.

Hadley slides the paper across the table.

I don't need to look at it.

I know what it is.

Crash.

"You wrote that," she says. "You put that on my door." She finally lifts her eyes to mine and it takes all of my concentration not to look away. Because she's looking at me like I'm a stranger.

I've seen this look before.

I try to push back the memory of that day in April, but it comes bubbling up anyway. Jason St. Clair calling Mom, every ounce of color sucked from her face, his tense voice on the other end of the phone. Mom's eyes landed on me and they went completely dark—dead.

I can't believe you did that, Sam. I can't believe you did that to me, to that family.

Neither one of my parents ever looked at me the same again. Neither one of them bothered to contemplate why a kid would do such a thing. They never even *asked.*

Hadley doesn't ask why either. She doesn't even look at me for more than a few seconds before her eyes float away from me.

I want to shake her. I want to ask how the hell she found out, to explain, to deny it, to take her hands in mine and tell her that none of this matters, none of this is about *us.*

But I don't. I just sit there, watching her not looking at me, her hands trembling. I try to clear the crud from my mind, try to figure out the right thing to say, but there's nothing. Nothing but the ugly truth that I'm not who she thought I was.

She slides the note back toward her with two fingers and crushes it into her hand. Then she gets up and leaves without saying anything, without ever really looking at me, and I'm left with a mouthful of words that wouldn't have made a difference anyway.

CHAPTER TWENTY-EIGHT

Hadley

He stays inside the shop for almost an hour. He just sits there, staring into space, alternating between dropping his head in his hands and resting his chin in his palm, fingers picking at the scruff on his cheek. When he finally comes out, I edge down a little in the front seat of my car, torn between wanting to disappear and wanting him to see me so he'll know how much I hate him and love him and every blurry shade of gray in between.

But he doesn't look up.

He hovers on the sidewalk for a few seconds, holds the door open for a mother with twins strapped into a double stroller, picks up a yellow leaf, and runs his thumb over its smooth veins.

The leaf flutters to the ground and he makes his way to his car. When his back is to me, I finally release the sob I've been holding in since last night. I imagine all those tears covering me in a protective sheath that nothing will ever break through again.

The next morning, the smell of pancakes and sizzling bacon lures me from the mountain of warm blankets under which I've been hiding with Jinx. Last night, I didn't offer an explanation about why I refused dinner, and my parents didn't ask. It appears as though the obligatory family meal is now more of a recommendation. I used to hate those dinners, but as I had lain in bed, listening to my parents' even voices filtering up through the floorboards, I felt that kind of sadness you can't explain—a weird sort of déjà vu, homesickness for another life you can't even remember.

Now I shuffle into the kitchen, familiar scents and sounds wrapping around me. Every Sunday used to start like this— eggs and bacon and pancakes, Dad at the stove armed with a spatula and homemade batter. A St. Clair tradition that died an abrupt death, along with everything else, when news of Dad's affair made its ugly appearance.

Which is why I freeze in the doorway of the kitchen. It's not exactly the same. Mom's not here, but Dad has succeeded in destroying the kitchen with all of his previous fervor. He hovers over the stove, humming a song I can't place while he flips silver dollar pancakes onto plates already loaded with bacon and scrambled eggs.

"Dad?"

He whirls, batter-soaked spatula in hand. "Hadley. I'm sorry, did I wake you?"

"No."

"Good." He removes the last of the pancakes and flips off the gas stove. "Your mother should be down soon. I thought I'd make us all breakfast."

"No, thanks. I'll just . . . cereal. I came down for cereal."

"Oh. All right, then." He gives me a weak smile, trying to cover up his obvious disappointment, before filling two mugs with coffee.

After grabbing a bowl and a box of granola, I sit on a barstool while he sits at the table. He doesn't talk. Doesn't ask me about school or even Sam. The silence is so heavy, it's a deafening ring in my ears. Dad's laptop is on the counter, the browser open on a retail site.

Kites.

I slide it toward me. The online shopping cart is filled with stuff Dad needs to make a sled kite—line attachments, cross spar, wing spar, keel. A single tear escapes and I wipe it away, furious that I'm upset by this. Dad's making our kite. Without me. Why do I care? Didn't I tell him I didn't want to do it? Haven't I told him to get out of my face about the Kite Festival, about movie night, about sushi, about reading his stupid papers?

I have.

That's what I thought I wanted.

But I never really believed he'd listen.

I feel a hand on my back, and I turn to find Mom standing there in her faded purple robe. The one she's had since before I was born and reminds me of lazy Christmas mornings and snow days home from school. Her eyes flick from Dad's to mine to the computer screen, her mouth bending downward into a pitying frown as she smooths my hair back from my face.

"I'm going back to bed." I launch myself off the stool before she can stop me. Back in my room, I grab my phone. I find Sam's name, my hand trembling over the screen. A slow, hot current flows up from my feet and twitches into my fingers. I hurl the phone. Its protective case cracks against the pale blue walls and leaves a tiny dent. I'm tempted to unearth the phone and throw it again so I'll never be able to call him. So I'll never spend another second of my life in that place where I forget what he did.

Instead, I bury myself under my mountain of blankets again.

Here, I'm safe.

Here, I'm protected.

Here, I'm alone.

"That sick son of a bitch."

Kat's voice always sounds funny to me when she swears, like she's a little kid playing at being a grownup, but this time her tone is edged in pure fury. I close my locker on Monday morning and turn to face her. I haven't spoken to her since Friday when she discovered Charlie. We texted a few times over the weekend about her date, but I never called to tell her about Sam. She was high on Ajay Desai, and I couldn't bring myself to shoot her down quite yet.

"Who?" I ask, sliding my books in my bag before homeroom.

"Who? Are you serious?" She folds her arms and glares at me.

I blow out a breath. "How did you find out?"

"Ajay. He told me last night. He *knew* this whole time. Can you believe it? I hung up on him. They're both sick sons of bitches and I hope their dicks fall off and they go bald at twenty-one."

"God, that's a little harsh." Still, I crack a smile at the thought.

"That's the edited version."

"It's not Ajay's fault, Kat." We start heading down the hall. Sloane Waters catches my eye and smirks, her glossy lips reflecting the fluorescents and nearly blinding me. I look away.

"He didn't tell me. You're my best friend. He knew about this crazy *Twilight Zone* link you had to Sam, and he didn't tell me."

I stop and pull her into the doorway of an empty classroom. "This is not Ajay's fault."

"But—"

"No." I put my hands on her shoulders and shake her a little. "Ajay's a good guy and he adores you. He bought you a *pig*, for crying out loud. This . . . thing with me and Sam wasn't his to tell. This was Sam's doing. All Sam. Only Sam. Totally. Sam."

Her body slumps against the wall. I know she's crafted this pissed-off front out of some sort of loyalty to me. It's sweet, but I'm happy to release her from that obligation.

"Ajay did seem really sorry," she says. "He said Sam's pretty bummed. Like, really broken up about it. I mean, like, a shades-drawn, Bon-Iver-playing-constantly, spending-hours-at-the-batting-cages-hitting-ball-after-ball-after-ball kind of broken up. Can you believe—"

"No, I can't believe it. And I don't care."

She frowns, but stays mercifully silent.

"And you should call Ajay," I say. "Please. I'm sure Charlie wants to see him, at least. Give him a slimy, snorty kiss."

Kat smiles a puny smile. "How are you feeling about all of this?"

The warning bell rings and we join the throng. "I don't know. I guess I have to be fine with it, right?"

"No, you don't. This totally sucks. I really liked Sam. He was the miracle that pulled you out of your meaningless groping phase."

I try to think of a snarky retort, but I barely slept all weekend. I've got nothing.

"Did he say why he didn't tell you?" she asks.

I shake my head. "He just sat there."

"Have you talked to Livy?"

I freeze in midstride.

"Livy. God, I haven't even thought about her in all of this."

"I'm sure she's upset," Kat says. "She's so sweet, she's probably just as heartbroken as you are."

"Right." My head is starting to pound. I feel myself getting angrier and angrier, thinking of all the lives tangled up in the ridiculous farce that is me and Sam. It's like a Shakespearian comedy.

Except no one's laughing.

As third period English approaches, I start to freak out. There is no part of me that wants to see Sam, and honestly, I don't trust myself to keep my voice steady if we have to work on our project today. Halfway through second period, I get a pass and dive into the nearest bathroom. I force air in and out of my lungs, murmuring to myself under the fluorescent lights to get it together.

He's just a guy, Hadley.

He's just a guy.

I fling on the tap and splash some water on my face. This always seems to work in movies. Cool water equals calm. I'm on my third desperate dousing when the graffitied door creaks open. I glance up at the mirror and meet Jenny Kalinski's huge brown eyes.

That party seems like a lifetime ago. Since then, I've managed to avoid this moment. Shame coils tight in my stomach and I grip the side of the dingy sink to hold myself up.

"Hi," she says, sliding her ballet flats over the yellowed tile.

"Uh. Hi."

She glides to the sink and takes a bottle of contact solution out of her bag. "My contact is inside out." She proceeds to pluck a tiny clear disk right off her eyeball.

"Yeah. I hate when that happens."

"You wear contacts?"

"Oh. Um. No."

She squirts some solution into her palm and smiles like she

knows I'm drowning in my own nervous sweat here. "So, you and Sam?"

"What?"

"You and Sam Bennett? You're dating?"

"No."

She frowns. "Oh. I could've sworn Josh—"

"Well, Josh was wrong." It comes out a lot harsher than I meant. I press the heel of my hand into my eyes and push until I see color.

"I'm sorry," she says. "I didn't know."

God, now she's apologizing to me. I nod, my fingers itching for the door, my feet aching to run. I take a deep breath and force myself to look at her. She pops her contact back into her eye and blinks rapidly.

"Jenny. I . . ."

She slides her gaze to mine.

"I'm sorry," I say. "For that night. With Josh. I really didn't know you were together, but I shouldn't have—"

"Hadley, stop." She tosses the bottle into her bag and turns to face me. "It's okay. Only a few people knew we were dating. Summer romance and all. I know Josh well enough to know that he wasn't in a good place that night and acted like a total jackass."

"But Sloane—"

"Sloane already hated you and she thrives on drama. The girl could write a bestseller about all the crap she blows out of proportion for the hell of it. I didn't know she was going to do that stuff to your locker."

I lean against the sink and exhale. Her words sound nice. They even *feel* nice, but something's still gnawing at me. "But you're with Josh. Now, I mean."

She sighs, then purses her lips. "Yeah."

"But he lied. And he cheated on you."

"I know that."

"But you were so upset that night."

"Of course I was." She zips up her bag and slings it over her shoulder. "But I was upset long before I ever got to that stupid party."

"So why?"

"Because that's what I want, Hadley."

I just stare at her.

"You think I'm an idiot," Jenny says. "You think I'm one of those girls who make excuses when their boyfriend gives them a black eye or sleeps with their best friend."

"I just . . . I don't understand."

She hikes her bag higher on her shoulder. "I don't understand the things you do either."

Her voice is gentle, even kind, but I still flinch. I press my fingertips together to steady myself.

"You don't have to understand it," she continues. "I know Josh, with all of his faults. I know what he's been through, what scares him, what makes him nervous and happy and sad. And I know what happened that night wasn't about him trying to get laid."

"But—"

Jesus Christ, Hadley, give it a rest . . .

Sam's words come back to me, hard and real. I feel marooned, stranded on a desert island, watching the last rescue boat float away. Because everyone else is moving on. Everyone else is *letting it go.*

The warning bell for third period echoes against the tiled walls. "I'll see you later," Jenny says. As she passes me, I search her face for any signs of pain or doubt or even anger. There's nothing. Just a smooth, unlined surface.

Peace.

Something I haven't experienced in months.

But as Jenny leaves, the door screaming with age behind her, tears sting my eyes as I realize that isn't exactly true.

CHAPTER TWENTY-NINE

Sam

She won't even look at me.

Or talk to me.

Ms. Artigas, God bless her, picked today for us to work on our Shakespeare projects for the entire class period, so now Hadley and I are sitting in silence, as far apart as possible while still giving the appearance that we're collaborating.

Before I can even attempt a conversation, Hadley slaps a sticky note on my notebook.

We're done with scene 1. You work on 2. I'll work on 3.

"Hadley. Can we—"

"No. We cannot."

She flips her book open and angles away from me. I rub my eyes, which are burning from getting only milliseconds of sleep between bad dreams, Mom's silent treatment, and Livy's pendulum of emotions this weekend. It didn't help that I've slept on my floor for the past two nights, bent into my old camping sleeping bag from three years ago that's now too short for me, while Livy wheezed herself to sleep in my bed.

When I told her what happened with Hadley, she immediately reached for her inhaler and started gulping.

"Look, I should've said something sooner," I told her. "I shouldn't have let myself . . ." What? God knows I tried to stay away from Hadley. Or maybe I didn't. I don't even know anymore. The truth is, I regret a shit-ton of stuff that happened between us. I regret that she found out before I could explain. I regret that she's hurt and I wish I could make it all go away for her. But I didn't regret *Hadley*. It's no secret that there wasn't a lot about my life that got me up in the morning with anything other than a fake smile plastered on my face, if I even managed that.

But Hadley. She was the real smile under all my bullshit.

"But she thinks you're this complete jerk," Livy said, her fists bunched at her sides. "How can she think that? I can't let her think that."

"Livy, there's nothing you can do."

A muscle worked in her jaw, making her whole face appear hard and angry. She spent the rest of the weekend waxing and waning between pensively staring into space and looking like she wanted to rip the head off a puppy.

I didn't fare much better.

Now, sitting this close to Hadley, it's as if I'm looking at a beautiful hologram. I can see her, remember how her hair felt sliding through my fingers, taste her on my tongue. But if I try to touch her, to reach out, I know she'll disappear.

CHAPTER THIRTY

Hadley

My arms and legs slice through the water. Since everything happened with Sam, the pool is the only place I feel halfway normal. Here, I can turn off my brain and let my muscles take over.

Over the last few days, Mom and Dad have been talking more and more. She's home by five every day and they cook dinner. Sometimes, an actual joke or a smile slips out. They went to therapy three times this past week and came back each time *not* tied in knots. The air in the house is still thick enough to choke on sometimes, but they're both trying. Dad's giving me space and Mom's inching her way closer, both of them hovering on my edges and waiting for me to send up the white flag.

Thanksgiving was relatively normal. My grandparents came down from Lexington. My parents cooked a huge meal. We gathered around the table and I mumbled my way through the annual "What's everyone thankful for?" tradition. But the entire time, I felt like I was just watching everyone else, observing, as if they were characters in a TV show.

Two days after Thanksgiving, I'm swimming again, numbing myself with adrenaline and speed. After an hour of laps and a scalding-hot shower, I run into Henry on my way out of the locker room.

"Hey, Hadley." His chiseled chest drips wet from his own swim.

"Hey." I go to move around him, but he stops me with a hand on my arm.

"I've been meaning to ask you something for a while now."

"Oh?"

His lips curve into this half-smirk, half-smile thing that used to make my knees go soft. "Ever reconsider letting me take you to dinner?"

I tilt my head at him. "I don't think so, Henry. Sorry."

His smile dims, but only for a moment before it reignites. "Hey, no problem. I get it." He laughs and shakes some excess water out of his shaggy hair. "But there's always the supply closet."

"Excuse me?"

He shrugs and grins wider. I can't tell if he's adorably nervous or ridiculously cocksure. "Lately, you seem a little . . . I don't know . . . down. More so than usual." His eyes slide to my lips.

I back away from him into the wall. He follows me and hooks his finger in the hem of my fleece jacket, pulling at it gently.

"No big deal, Hadley. You just look like you could use a distraction."

For a brief moment, I consider it. I could use a distraction. A barrelful. A closetful. A world full of Henry-shaped distractions. I could close my eyes while he kissed me and pretend he was Sam—a different Sam in a different world with a different Hadley.

And that would be okay. But it wouldn't be enough.

It'll never be enough, and I'm done playing these games with guys. Because no matter what I've told myself, that's not what I want. Maybe at some point it was. I don't know anymore. But everything's different now.

I push his hand away. "I need to go, Henry."

His eyebrows pop up, like he's flabbergasted that St. Clair, the Patron Saint of Sluts, would turn down an offer to get freaky again in a closet that smells like mildew and rubber. He shrugs and moves back. "Sure. Offer stands, though."

I watch him disappear into the guys' locker room, feeling a dizzying mix of anger and sadness and relief. I heave a breath and make my way outside. The late afternoon sky blurs into smears of copper and lavender and pink, and the air smells faintly of burning leaves.

When I get to my car, I stumble to a halt. Leaning against it is a familiar bright blue bike and a familiar blond head streaked with purple.

"Livy."

Her head pops up. "Hi."

"What are you doing here?" I rummage through my bag to find my keys. It's hard to look at Livy—her bleeding-heart, Sam-like features feel like little thorns in my skin.

"I wanted to bring you this." She holds up a large tan envelope but makes no move to give it to me. She shifts from foot to foot. "Do you hate me?"

I sigh. "No, I don't hate you, Livy. I just don't know what to say."

"I don't want you to hate Sam, either."

The thought of hating Sam is so appealing. It would make everything so much easier. "You know I don't. But I don't trust him either."

She takes a step closer, her eyes brimming. "You can trust him, Hadley. He's not . . . he didn't . . ." She swallows a gulp of air. I can almost see it sliding down into her lungs, steeling her as she squares her shoulders. "I think, in the beginning, keeping quiet was his way of protecting you . . . and me. Before you were together, he didn't see the point of telling you. He thought it would only hurt everyone."

I shake my head. "And after?"

"He was going to tell you. He told me so. But come on, Hadley. Can you honestly say you don't know why it was hard for him? Why he was afraid to?"

I drop my gaze, choking on the knot in my throat. "Livy, I know you and Sam are still dealing with your dad being gone and what happened with our parents, but it's more than that for me. It's not only that he lied. I can't stop thinking about those papers on my door. You know about those, right?"

She doesn't respond. Just stares at me with huge eyes.

"You have no idea what it was like coming home to that. My dad and I were close. I thought I knew him inside and out. I thought he was the one person who would never, ever hurt me. Those notes, what they said, they were like a bullet in my heart. I understand that my dad's the one who had the affair and I understand that Sam didn't know me then, but I can't forget that he wrote them, that he would do something like that to someone's family, to my mom and me. We weren't the ones who hurt him."

"Hadley." Livy's crying now, but something in me balls up and closes.

"I don't want to talk about it anymore, Livy. Maybe I'll see you around."

I fumble with the remote on my keys, hitting the lock button several times before finally landing on *unlock*. Behind me, I hear Livy take a giant, painful-sounding breath.

"Sam didn't write those notes."

My car clicks unlocked. I don't get inside. I don't turn around. I freeze and her words flitter around in my head, trying to land.

"That day we caught my mom . . . I was so confused," she says to my back. "I felt like I was outside of my body. I went ballistic. I had a huge asthma attack, but afterward . . . I just remember feeling totally unhinged, and I couldn't settle down. Sam was really freaked and kept watching me and following me around the house, but he eventually fell asleep. It wasn't hard to find out your dad's name. I looked through my mom's phone after everyone else was in bed. She even had his address. I sat in my room, writing those notes all night long. I know it was a screwed-up thing to do."

I turn to look at her now. The envelope is at her feet and she's gripping her elbows like she's trying to hold herself together.

"I skipped school the next day. Rode my bike to your house with a bag full of paper and tape. Sam had no idea until afterward." Tears trail silently down her cheeks. "It was me, Hadley."

"And Sam took the blame."

She nods. "When your dad called my mom that night, I guess he broke it off pretty harshly. Mom was . . . God, she was such a mess. I've never seen her so hurt and angry. She found Sam and me in the kitchen and started yelling and crying." She pauses, looks up at the darkening sky. "Sam didn't even look at me. He didn't even ask. He just said he did it. Mom slapped him. Hard, across the face. Dad came home later and Mom told him everything. I'll never forget the way he looked at her—at all of us. Like we were strangers or something. Sam took his reaction pretty hard. They were always close, with baseball and climbing and stuff, and I still don't think he's over it. Those notes changed the way my parents saw Sam."

"But it wasn't the truth."

"It was the truth to them, and they both pulled away from him. And I let them do it."

"Oh, Livy," I whisper. I try to gather up the anger I felt toward Sam for those notes, but it's like trying to grab a handful of water.

"I'm sorry, Hadley," she cries. "I didn't mean to hurt you or your mom. I was just . . . I was so mad and all I could think about was hurting *them*. I didn't mean for Sam to take the blame. It just happened and I didn't know how to fix it. But it's been so hard on him. His relationship with Mom gets worse every day. She has no faith him. I don't think she even likes him. And now you. You're the only person who makes him really happy, and I couldn't let you believe that he did that to you. I know he still lied, but at least you know he didn't write those notes. You can hate me instead of him."

Fresh tears spill out of her blue eyes. I reach out and pull her into my arms. She doesn't resist, but falls against me heavily.

"Shhh," I tell her as she cries into my shoulder. "I don't hate you, Livy." And I don't. How could I? She was only thirteen when all of this happened. *Thirteen.* She saw her own mother having . . . God. Having *sex* with another man and then watched her family fall apart because of it. That's punishment enough. With her tiny fingers pressed into my back, something starts thinning out inside of me.

When Livy finally pulls away, both of our faces soaked, she leans down and picks up the envelope. "This is for you."

I take the thick package. "What is it?"

"Copies of the photographs I took for my project." She wipes her thumbs through the dripping mascara under both eyes. "I thought you might like them."

"Thanks. You okay?"

"I think so. It feels nice having someone other than me and Sam know the truth. Especially if that someone is you."

I manage a smile. "I should go."

"Will you talk to Sam now?"

"I don't know, Livy." I swallow thickly. "I just don't know right now."

Disappointment floods her features and she takes a drag on her inhaler.

"But thank you for telling me the truth." I squeeze her hand. "That was really brave."

She nods, scuffing her boots over the asphalt.

I hug her one more time and get in my car. She climbs onto her bike, feet poised to hurtle herself home.

"Hadley?"

"Yeah?"

She hesitates, and then nods toward the envelope. "I named my photography project *Absolution*." Then, the hint of a smile shimmers across her lips. "It gave me some hope."

CHAPTER THIRTY-ONE

Hadley

At least a dozen photographs span the area on my bed. I stare at them, my SAT vocab book hanging limply in my hands. I knew what the word meant when Livy said it, but reading the black-and-white print, staring at the black-and-white photographs, it feels almost too fresh, like skin sloughed raw with a harsh scrub.

Absolution: formal release from guilt, blame, or punishment.

Livy's photos are beautiful.

Four are scenes from her own world. Cora standing outside Sam's closed bedroom door, her hand on the doorknob with her head resting against the frame. A photo of a photo — the Bennett family, whole and intact, in front of Turner Field at a ball game in Atlanta. Sam's dad, a dark-headed version of his son, smiles out from the picture like a ghost. The original photo is torn in one corner and coffee-stained in another. There's one of Livy standing in front of a mirror, shot from an upward angle with the camera poised at her hip. She's dressed all in black, hair color-free and pushed away from her face. Her eyes are heavily lined and wide as she considers her reflection. Her blank expression is so hauntingly beautiful, it makes my chest hurt. There's another of Sam handing a cup of tea to his mother, her arm outstretched, their fingers mere millimeters from touching, eyes on each other, waiting for the other to speak.

Seven photos are of Sam and me.

I remember when Livy took the one from Fido. Our heads are bent close together over half-eaten cheesecake, clear I'm-obnoxiously-into-you grins on both of our faces. God, was I really that obvious?

In another, we're standing in his open front door, the streetlight throwing us into a gray shadow. His forehead is pressed to mine, our eyes closed, my fingers bunched into the hem of his T-shirt, his hands soft on either side of my neck. I stare at this one for a long time before moving on to the others.

Me grinning broadly while Sam cooks in that ridiculous green and white apron.

Me cuddled under Sam's arm while we watch a movie.

Me on a swing at the park after a picnic with Livy and Ajay, laughing while Sam pushes me, our hands and feet blurred colors in the setting sun.

Me and Sam asleep, tangled in an intimate knot on his couch.

I can't tear my eyes away from my own face, the way I look when Sam touches me and interacts with me. I'm almost unrecognizable. Laughing. Happy. Hopeful. It's all there in glossy black-and-white. I know it's me. I know it's Sam. But we're not *us*. In those pictures, we're something else entirely—we're the excitement of a moment and the possibility of a future.

The last photograph brings me back to reality.

It's my dad.

He's sitting alone at a table by the window in the Green-Eyed Girl. The angle is from within the café, somewhere in the vicinity of the Green-Eyed photographs. His favorite Montblanc pen is poised in his hand, but he's not writing. His chin is cupped in his hand and his eyes are distant and a little glassy, the way they get when he's trying to rearrange a sentence in his head before he writes it down. Something about his expression reveals a deep loneliness.

Or maybe that's just me, hoping that's how he feels.

Then I notice the notebook on the table, its fraying edges, and a familiar feather lying next to it. I pull the photo closer, squinting through the black-and-white to the hidden color.

Yes. It's the same snow-white feather I found in the backyard and gave my dad when I was five. The one he used as a bookmark in the red-covered journal he started writing to me when I was born. The one he said he planned to give to me when I turned eighteen.

What are you writing, Daddy?

I'm writing about you, sweetheart.

I had convinced myself that it had drifted into the background of his life like everything else after his affair. My mind and heart revolt. This photograph is old. Years old. It has to be. But Livy took this picture. *Livy,* who's only been in town for a few months. Posted on the wall to Dad's right is a flyer for Woodmont Elementary's Fall Festival, dated this year. Dad's jaw is peppered with the scruff I'd become accustomed to while Mom was gone but that would never have been allowed to flourish in the past.

The photograph is slick under my sweaty fingers as I grip it, wondering what he wrote down that day, what he wrote down for a thousand days before that. A desperation blooms in my chest. My eyes glide back to the pictures of me and Sam, and a raw sob chokes me.

Before I can set my tears free, a knock sounds on my door. I swallow hard.

"Hadley?" Dad calls when I don't respond. The door creaks open and he sticks his head inside, keeping his body in the hallway. He looks nervous. I've sniped at him to get out so many times, I guess I don't blame him.

"Had?" His eyes scan my face and he frowns. "Your mother and I are going out for dinner. Would you like to come?"

I shake my head.

He opens the door wider, his expression drenched in concern, but he dries it up quickly with a blank look. "You sure? You'll be okay on your own?"

No, I want to say, but I don't. I don't say anything.

He steps into the room, approaching my bed with the wariness of a hiker caught in a hungry grizzly's path.

"We won't be long," he says. "We're both tired of turkey leftovers and I—"

He freezes, his gaze falling on the photographs. My eyes follow him down as he sits on the bed. One by one, he picks up the pictures. Something both hot and cold creeps through my veins as he looks at me and Sam, at the woman he possibly loved, at her son and daughter.

I rip the photo of the Bennett family out of his hand. I gather all the pictures into my arms, hugging them to my chest. I don't want him to see these. They're me. My life, my heart. My own father ruined all of it. Our family. Mom. He ruined Livy. He ruined Sam, turned him into a liar. This boy who I think I might have loved and now I'm alone and he's alone and Dad doesn't even care. He doesn't even care—

"Hadley!" I jerk as Dad's hands encircle my arms to stop me.

My throat feels hoarse and thick, my eyes burning with tears as I realize I've been speaking aloud. Screaming. Every word that just swam through my head had fallen out of my mouth in a messy rush.

Dad's eyes are wild and shining. He keeps his grip on my arms. My head falls to my chest, deep sobs racking my body.

"Honey," he says, his voice a cracking, desperate. "I do care, but I don't know what to do or say anymore. Tell me what to do."

The tears spill over and I'm unable to tell him anything. Because really, what can he do? We can't go back. None of us can. Eventually, he releases me and rises to his feet.

He lets me go.

I hear his heavy sigh as he turns away. A myriad of emotions—panic, regret, loneliness, remorse, love—fill in the empty spaces inside me, and I pull myself off the bed. The photos float to the ground like black-and-white petals.

I'm so tired.

Tired of pretending I don't feel anything. Tired of pretending I haven't been hurtling toward this spot—this place where acceptance finally sneaks up on me and wraps me up in its arms —for months. Tired of pretending I don't miss my dad. Miss us. Miss my family. Miss Sam. Miss myself.

Miss, miss, miss . . .

My thoughts settle around Sam and I feel a wash of relief, just to let myself see his face behind my eyelids. I remember how his whole body trembled a little when I slid that note across the table at the Green-Eyed Girl. I kept waiting for him to give me some explanation, but when he didn't, I wasn't surprised. Sam Bennett wears his loneliness like a skin. He's resigned himself to it, believes he deserves it, thinks it's just the way things are and nothing will ever change it. He looked so small and young as I watched him leave, his whole frame weighed down by half a year of brokenness, of missing his parents, of trying to be superhuman for Livy. I cried that day because, deep down, I knew he loved me. But I couldn't bridge that gap between the anger and the acceptance. The broken trust and the *need* to let him be someone important to me.

Just like my dad. I know he loves me. I also know things will never be like they were between us. But they have to be *something*.

"Dad."

It's a whisper. I barely hear it myself. But he stops and turns. Something in that tiny word, in my face, must cue him in to how I'm feeling, because his expression shifts from weary to relieved in a blink. He crosses the room in two strides, wrapping his arms around me and cradling my head against his chest. I breathe out months of anger, breathe in his familiar smell—the same one I remember as a little girl when I'd fall asleep in the car and he'd carry me to my room. Paper and ink and wool sweaters and coffee.

We sink to the floor and sit against my bed, his arm around me. He hands me a tissue and I lean my head on his shoulder, gulping jagged breaths. I don't know how long we sit there, both of us sniffling and swallowing over knots in our throats. Outside, the day fades into twilight, filling my room with a soft lavender haze I've always loved. This time of day makes me believe in magic. Of living in between two possibilities and letting that be okay.

Mom's form appears in the doorway. She leans against the frame, her hands clasped in front of her. I can barely see her face in the dim light, but I can tell she's smiling. It's a sad smile, but it's there. She's here. We're all still here.

"Had," Dad says quietly. "It's not too late, is it? For us all to start over?"

So much has happened—so much hurt and lying and unforgiveness and time—that I'm not sure what to say. I know what I want my answer to be, but is it even possible? To go back or move forward or whatever the healthiest reaction to all this crap actually is?

So I don't answer right away. I pick up the photo of him at the café, my eyes settling on the open journal, on his poised pen, on the illegible scrawl blurred underneath it.

"Do I still get to read it?" I ask. "When I'm eighteen?"

He tightens his grip around me and I hear the smile in his voice. "Of course. It's yours."

I nod against him, my heart settling into a steady rhythm. Mom comes in and sits down on my other side, her arm around me, fingertips resting lightly on Dad's shoulder. My chest feels open and airy, that sort of peaceful, exhausted sensation you get after you've let go of a bunch of tears that should've been released a long time ago.

"Dad?"

"Mm?"

"It's not too late."

CHAPTER THIRTY-TWO

Sam

I used to think Benedick was a smart-mouthed dick who morphed into a whipped asshole with no concern for anything other than getting laid. The guy's ready to kill his best friend, all because of some girl who until about ten minutes before claimed to hate him.

Now I'm starting to understand him a little better.

I sit on my bed, *Much Ado* in my lap as I read over act 5, scene 2. He and Beatrice banter back and forth, quipping about how they first came to love each other. *Suffer love! A good epithet. I do suffer love indeed, for I love thee against my will.*

The words bounce against my chest, my own translation coming too easily. My hand moves across my notebook, dark blue ink bleeding onto the page in a mindless word vomit. I sit back, fingers aching, and reread what I wrote.

My heart is crushed within me. Here is the truth: You made me love you—your eyes and mouth and voice. You pulled me into your heart. You don't want me there and I don't want to be there, but it's where I will always live.

Jesus.

I stare down at the words I scribbled into my notebook and shake my head. I'm pretty damn sure Benedick is just flirting with Beatrice, a girl who loves him back and can actually stand the sight of him, but my pen took on a mind of its own, spilling out mush I didn't even know was inside me. I have no idea how the hell I got here, but I feel physically sick at the thought of Hadley, beautiful and existing and hating me.

I slap the play shut and rip the page from my notebook. Then I throw all three things across the room. The play crashes into a framed picture of me and Ajay playing Little League, sending the two of us sprawling. It feels good to slam things around and get pissed, little rebellions against my slowly dissolving heart.

I flop back on my bed, arm flung over my eyes, and hear a soft knock on my door.

"What?" I yell it. Rudely.

The door creaks open and I hear feet padding over the carpet toward me.

Mom.

I can tell by the sharp, unhindered sound of her steps. Livy always drags her toes. The bed depresses as she sits. I keep my face covered, waiting for her to speak.

She doesn't.

She just sits there and breathes my air.

I lift my head to look at her. She's staring at me, her eyes crinkled softly like she hasn't seen me in years.

"What?" I ask again.

Her body jolts at my harsh tone. "Sam, I—"

"Mom, I'm sorry. But I'm really not in the mood for another lecture about something I did or didn't do or a dream I had that you somehow extracted from my mind and saw all of my devious plans to crap all over your life." I sit up and pull my laptop closer, flipping it open so hard, I'm surprised it doesn't snap in two.

I busy myself on Twitter, reading inane tweets like *OMG, I have so much homework!* and *Craving Sonic tots somethin' fierce #hungry.*

"I guess I deserve that," Mom says after a few moments. Something about her tone makes me look up. Black shit smudges up under her eyes and she looks pale. Her hair is in a messy ponytail and her hands are trembling.

"Sam, I don't even know what to say."

I close my computer on the blissfully frivolous teenage world I seem to be no freaking part of. "Say about what?"

"About you." She covers her mouth with a trembling hand. "About us. About everything."

What the hell is there to say? I'm so done with this. Done with treading water in my own house, with my own family, always on guard for an attack when I ran out of defenses a long time ago. Maybe I haven't run out so much as I've stopped looking for more.

"I talked to Olivia," Mom says.

"Yeah? Did she actually talk back?"

Mom looks at me, pain coloring her irises like ink in water. She pulls on her earlobe and it's this tiny, familiar tic, her finger under her silver hoop earring, that snags my attention.

"She told me everything, Sam."

"Told you what?" My voice is still hard and almost cruel, but something in my chest starts shriveling up.

"I think you know what, sweetheart."

My stomach flips at her use of a term of affection. I almost open my mouth to refute everything and anything Livy might have told her. I've gotten used to Mom's scathing glare and I don't really feel like dealing with another change. Not after the crap week I've had.

But I stop myself. Livy's not a kid anymore. If she took the initiative to set the record straight, she had her reasons, and I'm done using her as an excuse to cover up my own shit.

"Why?" Mom says, eyes filling. "Why didn't you tell me? Why did you let me think it was you for so long?"

"Come on, Mom. Would it have really made a difference? Would you have treated Livy like a pariah too? Would you have blamed her for everything? She was thirteen and one wheeze away from landing herself in the hospital. She was confused enough already."

"Sam . . . I . . ." She presses both hands to her mouth and whispers through her fingers. "I'm so sorry."

I shake my head. I don't want her apologies. I want her faith and I'm not sure that's even possible anymore. "Who put that stuff on the St. Clairs' door isn't the point, Mom. Don't you get that? The point is that you never really owned what you did. You never seemed sorry, not even at *how* you got caught, just that you got caught at all. We were kids. We're still kids. No matter how we reacted, no matter who went nuts for a few days and who didn't, it was *your* mistake. You were the parent and you and dad both acted like we were to blame. Like I was to blame."

Her tears spill over. "I know. I just . . ." She reaches out for my hand and it takes all of my control not to yank it back. "I was going to tell your father. I was. In my own way and in my own time and I felt like you took that away from me. Or those notes did. Jason . . . he was so angry. He ended it before I could do or say anything and I . . . I was devastated."

I close my eyes and live in the dark for a too-short moment. Open them again. "Did you love him?"

She rubs her eyes, blows out a breath. "I think you know that your father and I hadn't been happy for a while. Truthfully, I'm not sure what I felt for Jason St. Clair or what he felt for me. I do know I was hurt and angry when it all blew up in my face. I was furious with you, and I needed someone to blame."

"And you found him," I say, almost to myself.

"I was wrong, honey. So wrong and I'm sorry."

I look up at her, meet her teary gaze. "*Don't* punish Livy for this. I swear to God, if you make her feel the tiniest smidgen of guilt, I'll take her and leave. I'll go to Dad's. I don't care if he wants us there or not."

She shakes her head vigorously. "Livy was so upset because she let you carry this for so long. She had to use her inhaler twice before she even got it all out. I understand that this was . . . this *is* all my fault and I know how unfair I've been to put all of that on you."

I feel the familiar blankness of my expression, but as Mom acknowledges how shitty things have been—her own role in creating and maintaining that shittiness—something loosens in my chest and blows away.

330

"I'm going to speak with your father. He needs to know the truth, Sam. I know you think it doesn't matter, but the truth always matters, honey."

"All right. Yeah. Fine." I drop my head in my hands, not looking forward to having this conversation again with Dad. At the same time, I know it's time. Long past time, and I'd be lying if I said I didn't feel a freaking tsunami of relief.

We sit there for a minute, a million unspoken words passing through the air between us. Finally, she says, "I'm sorry about Hadley, Sam. I didn't mean to treat her unfairly. I didn't want you to get hurt. That's why I called her parents."

I just nod. I don't want to talk about Hadley. Can't.

"I believe things can get better, Sam. I have to believe that."

Better. What is that?

"I'm sorry, sweetheart," she says again. And again and again until her words form a lump in my throat I can't swallow around.

"Okay, Mom. It's okay." She squeezes my hand. We both know it's not okay. Maybe it won't be for a while, but I guess it's a start. Maybe it's a step toward that nebulous place called *Better.* I can only hope that when we get there, we'll recognize it.

Livy comes in a few minutes later. She throws herself onto the bed and lays her head on my shoulder. She puts a tentative yet steady hand on Mom's. We huddle together, all of our eyes stinging, a cracked unit trying to feel whole. Trying to act whole.

I breathe in, breathe out.

Feels a little better.

CHAPTER THIRTY-THREE

Sam

A week later, I'm on the hill at Love Circle after sundown with Ajay. It's cold, the kind you can smell and taste on the back of your tongue. We're bundled into coats and sprawled out on the grass under a clear, star-packed sky, a faded blue Frisbee resting on my chest.

"You know," he says, "I was going to bring Kat here later tonight, but when I got to your house, you looked so desperately pathetic, I knew you needed a romantic evening. I am your one true love, after all."

My eyes glaze on all the stars so they almost bleed into one spread of light. "Bros before beautiful girls . . ."

Ajay snorts. "No. Kat's mom dragged her to some self-concept seminar." He checks his phone. "I'm meeting her in T-minus sixty-three minutes."

I swing the Frisbee around and connect with Ajay's gut. He lets out an exaggerated *oof.*

"Why did you want to come here, anyway?" he asks, rubbing his belly.

"I come here to think. I like it here." I only brought Ajay along because he showed up as I was leaving. I don't mention that coming here is my own version of self-flagellation. Punishment, as I remember the first time Hadley knelt in front of me, her fingertips and her eyes skimming my face like she was discovering something brand-new and intriguing. Something she wanted.

"I take it you haven't talked to her," Ajay says.

"Nope."

"Have you tried?"

"Nope."

"Should you?"

"Nope."

"Samuel, man up. Admit it, you're miserable."

I sit up and toss the Frisbee at his face, the closest version I can get to *manning up,* whatever the hell that means.

He bats it away and smirks. "Exactly."

"Age, I know you're trying to help, but just stop. Hadley doesn't want to talk to me, nor should she. I fucked up. Messed with her life, her family, her heart. Just leave it alone and go enjoy your own little romance, all right?"

I expect a snarky response, but none comes. He just looks at me, his brows furrowed in deep thought. He was ecstatic when I told him my parents knew the truth about the notes on Hadley's door, because, of course, Ajay's known all along.

"Finally!" he had shouted through the phone. "God, I've been so tired of carrying that around. Don't you feel better? Is Livy okay?"

"Yeah, she's good," I said, purposely ignoring his former question. The truth was, I did feel better about my family. Hopeful. But it wasn't enough. The whole Hadley thing had really screwed with my head and, if I was being honest, my heart. It was going to take more than Mom's apologies and Dad's assertions of love and commitment to me and Livy to heal up the bloody mess in my chest.

"Samuel," Ajay says now, "you're my best friend, and normally I cherish your idiotic, self-deprecating ways, but both you and Hadley need to get the hell over yourselves. You guys are like a pair of tragic lovers out of a Tolstoy novel."

"I don't see either one of our bodies mangled under a train."

"Close enough."

Before I can offer a pointless rebuttal, a branch snaps behind us and we both swivel around. I suck in a breath and blink a few hundred times before what I'm seeing registers.

Hadley.

"Hey," I say automatically, standing.

"Hey," she says. God, she looks amazing. Moonlight streaks across her face, paling her already ivory skin. Her hair is long and loose and spilling over a fitted gray pea coat, buttoned up against the chilly wind.

"What . . . what are you doing here?" I ask.

"She's here to see me, man," Ajay quips, elbowing me.

Neither Hadley nor I respond, our eyes locked on each other.

"Damn. Not even an obligatory smile. Okay. Too soon for humor." He slaps my back after snagging my keys from the grass. "I'll just go attend to my own little romance . . ." His voice trails off as he disappears over the side of the hill. I barely register the sound of my own car starting up and driving off, leaving me stranded on a hilltop with a girl whose expression I'm finding impossible to read at the moment.

"How'd you know I was here?" I ask. Then I realize that maybe she's not here for me at all. Maybe she's here in search of her own peace and solitude and is revolted to find me here, polluting her air once again. My gut clenches and I think through options about how the hell I'm going to get home, mentally tracking to the nearest bus stop.

"Livy told me. When I stopped by your house."

I exhale loudly as she steps closer. Closer. Closer, until we're only an arm's width apart.

"You went to my house?"

She nods.

"Why?"

She shrugs, hands in her coat pockets. "I guess I wanted to talk to you."

"Why, Hadley?"

She looks up, her lashes fluttering heavily as she blinks at me. "Livy told me everything. You know that, don't you?"

I literally stumble backwards, feeling like I've been punched. Of course Livy told her. Hell, she probably told her a week ago, before she even told Mom.

"Sam."

I take another step back, needing more space between us, because I'm either about to crumble to my knees or gulp her into my arms, neither of which is a good idea.

"I'm sorry . . ." I say. I should add more, explain every little crazy tick in my thought process from the first day I met her, but my throat closes up as she pushes through the distance between us.

"You could've told me the truth," she says softly. "I could've handled it."

"Maybe I couldn't. And it would've changed everything. You know it would. It *has* changed everything."

"You lied to me, Sam. You were one of the only people I trusted and you broke that. You broke us." Her voice cracks and I fist my hands, aching to hold her.

"I'm sorry. I am. I don't know why—" I snap my mouth shut. Because I do know why. I've always known why.

"Sorry doesn't change anything." Tears spill down her face. "You know how I felt about lying and you kept doing it, every day, over and over. I don't understand why you didn't—"

"Because I wanted to be with you, all right?" I yell it, my voice raspy. Her eyes widen and cloud up. "You're all I think about and I knew if I told you, you'd disappear. You'd hate me. That's why, okay? I know it's not right. I know I screwed everything up, but I *physically* couldn't tell you. I didn't care about your last name or what our parents did. I wanted you. I wanted us. You made all of this . . . I don't know. It sounds crazy, but you, in my life—knowing you almost made every-thing worth it."

I can't look at her. I shove my hands through my hair and pace in circles.

"Sam—"

"I want to be with you, Hadley, and I don't care what our

families have to say about it. It's not about them. Our parents have nothing to do with us."

"But they do. My dad's a part of me. Your mom's a part of you. Nothing will ever change that."

"We don't have to disown our families or our own stories. We just have to . . . I don't know." I hang both hands around my neck. "Move forward."

"How? How would an *us* work? You really expect us to pose for prom pictures in my foyer with my dad behind the camera? Will our moms shake hands at graduation? Will we head off to college and stay together? Will we get married and turn our ex-lover parents into in-laws and co-grandparents?" She snorts a laugh, but then her eyes fill as she slides them up to mine. "How, Sam?"

I realize she wants a real answer. She wants to know how. She wants an *us* just as much as I do, despite everything. I bridge the gap between us and slide my hands up her arms to cup her face, relieved as hell when she lets me. "We'll figure it out. If you can forgive me, we'll figure this out."

"Sam." She puts her hands on my chest. "This is about more than just you and me. What about Livy? What about my mom and your dad?"

"I don't know." I pull her closer, inhaling her scent. God,

she's like a drug. "I know I should care about all of that, but I just don't right now."

She presses her forehead to mine. "You will. I know you, Sam. You will care, and then where will we be?"

I don't answer. I can't. Our breath mingles as the night air hems us in against the rest of world. She's so close that I can feel her heart pounding against my chest. I slip a finger down her chin to the hollow of her throat, feeling the *thrum, thrum* of her pulse under my touch. She sighs, a shaky, desperate sound.

And then we're kissing, a mad scramble to gather up everything we both fear we've lost. There's nothing but lips and tongues and hands. Hadley trembling in my arms, her tears mingling with mine, my name falling from her mouth again, just like that first time we kissed in this very spot. The first time I went over the edge.

She breaks our kiss and dips her head onto my chest, heaving giant breaths.

"Hadley." I smooth her hair, but she doesn't respond. "Had."

She lifts her head and I search her face—her eyes, her mouth, the crease between her eyebrows—searching for any sign that she's ready to try this, that I haven't destroyed everything all over again.

"What does this mean?" I ask.

Her expression tightens, but she keeps her hands on my

chest, my jacket balled into her fists. "I don't know, but I . . . I don't think I'm ready for this, Sam. Maybe we can try to be—"

"Don't. Don't say we can be friends." I put my hands over hers, pressing them deeper into my chest. "I can't live in that in-between hell with you. Not you."

"Why not? If we try being friends, at least we'll see each other."

I shake my head. "I'm sorry. I can't. I'm done pretending. Seeing you and not being with you . . . it would be torture. It's too uncertain—"

"That's living, Sam. It's always uncertain."

I close my eyes, squeeze them until I see bursts of color in the blackness. "Hadley, please . . ."

Her hands tighten on mine. "So maybe we don't call it *friends,* or the middle, or that scary, gray in-between place. But I need time, Sam. I need time to figure this out for myself. To get to know my parents again. To figure out where I am in my own life."

I nod, biting my lip to keep from saying anything else. I know she's right. Same as Hadley, I need to get used to my family the way it is now, not the way it's been or the way I hoped it would be. I need time too.

But I don't want time. I want to do all that *with* Hadley.

I meet her gaze, watch her search mine, imploring me to

understand why she's asking this of me, of herself. I let my eyes have their fill of her features, not knowing the next time I'll get to look at her like this, so close and soft and beautiful.

I breathe in, breathe out, searching for *Better*—or at least the belief in it. Looking at Hadley, I can tell something has changed in her. It's in the gentle set of her shoulders and clear glance of her eyes. She believes in *Better.*

"Sam."

I close my eyes and pull her arms around my neck. I let her voice, wrapped in my name, fill me up. I let the feel of her fingers curling into my hair transfer some of the hope I see in her eyes. I let Hadley hurtle me forward, even as I feel her pulling back.

"Don't," I say, tightening my grip on her. "We don't have to do this."

"Do what?"

"Say goodbye." She sighs and sort of sinks against me, so I keep talking. Anything to keep her here as long as I can. "This is just you and me, remember? You said that to me, right here on this hill. Hadley and Sam. No last names. We can just be here. We can just be *us.*"

CHAPTER THIRTY-FOUR

Hadley

Infinite images, poetry and light, flood my mind with Sam's plea. I'm drowning in them. Or maybe they're drowning in me. Like Livy's photographs of us, all soft lines and possibility.

Two days ago, my parents and I dug out some old kites and flew them at Percy Warner Park in Nashville. Now, holding on to Sam, the breeze circling us like a blanket, I think about the way the lines felt both loose and taut in my hands, the way the wind picked up the kite and flung it here and there, how only my grip kept it from disappearing into the horizon.

Letting go.

And holding on.

Sam and me—star-crossed and still entangled up on a hill overlooking the city. On top of the world. I almost laugh at how ridiculous it is. How silly it is that we found each other, that we grounded each other, that we gave each other a sense of freedom and a home. Now I fear we're stuck in doubts and our heavy pasts and tenuous futures.

But we're here. Together.

"This shouldn't make sense," I say.

"What?"

"Us. You and me."

He presses his forehead to mine. "But we do. Maybe it's crazy, yeah, but it makes sense. *We* make sense."

I lace my hands into his silky hair, holding him so the moonlight spills across his face and I can see him. I kiss him. Softly, and just once. He pulls back far enough to look at me and he smiles. A sad but hopeful thing.

I smile back.

Acknowledgments

Any writer will tell you that writing a book is a strange process. While working on *Suffer Love*, I vacillated daily between self-confidence and complete self-loathing and every neurotic shade of gray in between. It's isolating and scary and exhilarating, and I would not have made it to this point without the support of so many lovely people.

To my agent, the amazing Rebecca Podos, who loved this book so much you helped me love it even more: From that first phone call, you made this story better and this entire process feel like an adventure. Thank you for supporting me at every phase and for fielding my panicked emails with finesse and humor. I could not ask for a better champion.

To my editor, Elizabeth Bewley, who understood my vision for Hadley and Sam, believed in it, and helped me communicate their story in the best way possible: Thank you for talking through that one pesky character with me until we got her right, for your wisdom and passion for this book, for knowing when to push and when to pull back, and for bringing me into such a wonderful family. Thanks to the whole team at Houghton Mifflin Harcourt.

To Destiny Cole, my first reader, first champion, first *everything* on this wild journey: You believed I could get here and you listened to me rant and rave during every peak and valley along the way. Thank you for helping to make *Suffer Love* presentable and for your infectious optimism.

Miranda Kenneally, thank you for the early read and the query rescue. Those three hundred words really would've been the end of me without your generosity.

Thanks to my wonderful writer community and everyone at SCBWI Midsouth, which is chock-full of the best people I've ever known: Courtney Stevens, for the early read, words of encouragement, and for inviting me into the fold. My critique group—Sarah Brown, Paige Crutcher, and Lauren Thoman—your constant faith inspires me every day. Thanks for the words, the wine, the laughter, occasional tears and terror-stricken emails, Zac Efron GIFs for all occasions, and, above all, the *queso*. Lauren, thanks for helping with the last-gasp round of edits and for falling so hard for Ajay. I'll write you that novella some day. Alisha Klapheke, for laughing at all the right moments while reading *Suffer Love* next to me at the coffeehouse. And to the rest of my coffeehouse girls—Paige, Lauren, Rae Ann Parker, and Erica Rogers—Friday is the best day of the week because of you ladies. Thank you for your kindness and for sharing your words and wisdom.

To my movie-witty-banter-and-just-all-around-amazing pals, Kathryn Ormsbee and Jennifer Gaska: You make the book world a better world. Thanks to the entire Twitter book community, for believing in stories, writers, positive change, and making me proud to be part of such a wonderful world.

Thanks to all the Sweet Sixteens for making this debut journey unforgettable. To my Sixteen to Read girls for all the love and support and general awesomeness. I'm honored to be among such talented, kind, and funny people. I've loved championing all of your debuts and can't wait to champion every book after that.

To Mom, for always believing this day would come, even when everything I wrote sucked. I know you would've loved Hadley and Sam, and I truly wouldn't be here today—in so many ways—without you. I miss you every day.

My family and all of their unending support. Brandon, Sara, Elliott, and Nicholas Herring, I love you guys. Brandon, you've always been my hero. Thanks for taking risks, for believing in your creativity and talents in a way that inspired me to believe in mine. Sara, I'm honored to call you sister. Pat and John David Strickland and the Todd family for unconditional kindness. All the Herrings, Blakes, and Cowns, who know all of my history and still like me.

Benjamin and William, I adore you a million trains and dinosaurs. Your love of life and the easy way you love me, even when my imperfections are glaringly bright, inspire me to be better every day.

Craig, thank you for loving me where I am. The way I am. Thank you for sticking with me on this wild ride.

And to all my readers, thank you for letting Hadley and Sam into your lives.